CONTENTS

COPYRIGHT

This publication contains the opinions and ideas of its author(s) and is designed to provide useful advice in regard to the subject matter covered.

All trademarks are of their respective owners. Rather than put a trademark symbol after every occurrence of a trademarked name, we use names in an editorial fashion only, and to the benefit of the trademark owner, with no intention of infringement of the trademark. Where such designations appear in this book, they have been printed with initial caps.

The purpose of this report is to educate. The author and publisher do not warrant that the information contained in this book is fully complete and shall not be responsible for any errors or omissions. The author and publisher shall have neither liability nor responsibility to any person or entity with respect to any loss or damage caused or alleged to be caused directly or indirectly by this book, nor do we make any claims or promises of your ability to generate

income by using any of this information.

ACKNOWLEDGEMENTS:

I wish to express my gratitude to all of the wonderful people who believed in me and that I was capable of telling stories to the world.

Especially to the editors/writers at Creative Book writers, you all rock.

DEDICATIONS:

"I love you as certain dark things are to be loved, in secret, between the shadow and the soul."

— Pablo Neruda, <u>100 Love Sonnets</u>

To my husband, without whom, my achievements would never have been possible.

I love you for being so patient with me when I am lost in my imaginary world, consumed by the words.

CHAPTER ONE:

It was the middle of December, with the first batch of snow kissing the ground. With the office Christmas party coming up, Jo asked me if I would go with her. The main reason was that she didn't want to go alone; but not only that, she had her eye on a fit guy in the accounts department and wanted to bed him that night, seeing that there was free accommodation on offer as the party was being held on the other side of the city.

She had been hounding me all week about it; eventually, I gave in and said yes. My reason was to get a break from the arguments that I had been having with Mick about starting a family who was getting a bit tedious. I informed him I was going out to the office Christmas party and wouldn't be back until the next day. I desperately needed some time from him, pecking at me about kids.

Mick and I were married for nearly a year and it was not like we were not happy but only that I had never thought about having children at all.

Friday had approached sooner than I would have thought with the weather bitterly cold, with heavy intervals of snow and blizzard-like conditions. For once, I wished I hadn't agreed to go with Jo to the party at all. I reminded myself that I had promised to go; therefore, I began forcing myself to get ready.

I wasn't in the mood to dress up too much, so I slipped on a pair of black trousers with a loose-fitting silver silky blouse and finished it off with an elasticated black and silver wide belt. The party was to start at 7 pm but I was meeting Jo for a drink first. The taxi was late due to the weather, so I texted Jo that I was running late. I had a couple of trains to take before I arrived and was over half an hour late.

As I reached, Jo was on her third glass of white wine with a glass waiting for me on the table. I sighed in relief and sat down, wheeling a small overnight bag and wearing a heavy winter coat.

"Late again," Jo muttered, gulping down the remaining wine in her glass.

"Ugh. What a night! The taxi was late, and the trains were slow because of the weather, but I'm here now." I said, sounding exhausted.

"Stop sounding so low. We are going to have a lot of fun." Jo smacked her lips together.

"YOU, Jo! You will have all the fun." I rolled my eyes at her.

We had another drink before setting off to the hotel where the party was being held. On entering the hall, the sound of 'The Pogues and Kirsty MacColl' hit us right left and center. The music was too loud; I already felt uneasy.

We went to the reception area to check-in. After signing in, the receptionist gave us keys to our room. We were next door to each other, so we went to dump our luggage and coats in our rooms before heading off to the party at the opposite end of the building.

"Free rooms." Jo waved her key in front of my face. She looked pleased. We slowly strolled towards the hall.

It was after 8.30 pm by the time we opened the door to the party; the room was buzzing with half the party-goers already drunk, thanks to the free bar.

Jo decided she was also going to make the most of the free bar so she went on asking for a couple of shots and a whiskey chaser; I just had an orange juice. I still wasn't in the party mood since having constant arguments with Mick had taken a toll on me. I stood there, sipping my juice and thinking what the hell was I doing there anyway.

Jo knocked back the shots and the whiskey chaser after which she asked for a glass of white wine. I could see she was starting to sway a little. With another four hours to go, I doubt that she would be able to stand on her feet. I was about to tell her to slow it down when she left me at the bar with her glass of wine in hand. She had spotted Dan the guy from accounts, so she went off heading towards him ignoring me completely. Why had I bothered coming? I cursed myself feeling like a spare part. Walking away from the bar, I tried to find some of my colleagues I knew and finally spotted Dawn from finance.

"Are you ok Holly? You look a bit pissed off," asked Dawn as I approached her.

"Yeah. Jo has been badgering me all week for me to come with her to the party because she didn't want to come on her own, and now she's buggered off after Dan in accounts," I replied, pissed off.

“Mm, I see what you mean,” she glanced across the room to look at Jo snogging Dan’s face off.

We chatted for a while before I went off the bar for another drink, I thought of having a gin and tonic for a change. It was after 10 pm, and I had had enough, so knocking back my drink, I walked back to my room in the hotel.

I changed and got into bed, once again thinking about what the fuck I was doing there. I was going to keep cursing myself for this for a while. I switched the TV on and sat back on the bed trying to relax but my mind was whirling around about Mick, and why the hell was he so hell-bent on me having kids, we hadn’t even discussed it before we got married. I was not ready; we hadn’t been married all that long.

Even around 11 pm, I couldn’t settle, so I decided to pack up and head off home before the trains stopped running. I checked out, managing to avoid seeing by anyone from work as I left the hotel. On opening the door, the cold wind hit me in the face, and my teeth started chattering. I tightened my scarf around my neck and face as I headed off wheeling my overnight bag down to the tube station.

It was midnight when I reached my destination. I couldn't find a taxi with only half a mile away from home, which made me think if it weren't for Christmas, it would have been different. I started walking, dragging the bag behind me, which was making weird noises; at least it had stopped snowing. It was freezing; after walking for about ten minutes, I saw a taxi coming up on the road. I hurriedly shuffled across the pavement towards the road to hail the cab down.

"Hey! Stop!" I waved my arms in the air, almost dancing.

Luck was on my side - the taxi stopped and the driver rolled down the window. He was picking a fare up, which was an obvious thing seeing the weather. I pleaded with him to just take me half a mile in the opposite direction. He must have taken pity on me because he gave in. Relieved, I thanked him and slid into the cab. He spun the taxi around heading towards my home. When we arrived, I jumped out and paid the fare plus a generous tip for stopping. The driver had a huge grin as he pulled away from my house.

There were no lights turned on in the house, Mick was either not at home or was in bed already. Opening the door as quietly as I could, I switched the dimers on and locked the door behind me. The house felt warm; I sighed in relief, appreciating my decision to come back. I headed upstairs for the spare bedroom in case Mick was in bed because I didn't want to disturb his sleep. Switching the dimers off, I closed the bedroom door and dumped my bag to the side of the room.

I took off my coat and scarf and threw them over the chair in the corner of the room. The lights on the street shone through into the bedroom, casting a shadow, which helped me see as I undressed and slipped in between the quilt. I laid there a while before I slowly drifted off to sleep. I was chasing the joker in my sleep when I was woken up by the sound of a car door banging shut outside the house.

I heard a woman giggling; I told myself it must be someone from next door and shifted in my bed. Suddenly, I heard a key turning in the door and after the door opened, the voices could be heard more clearly. I could not decipher what the voices were saying, but one of them I could identify. It was Mick.

I could hear Mick's voice and a woman I did not recognize; she had an accent. Was she a colleague or someone he worked with? But as the conversation went on, it didn't sound like it.

They went straight into the living room with the woman still giggling like a teenager. I still couldn't quite make out what they were saying, so I quietly slipped out of bed and found a robe hanging up at the back of the bedroom door; I slipped it on.

Creeping downstairs tiptoeing in the shadows of the street lights, I headed towards the living room. Mick's pleasure-filled groans hit me right in the face even before I entered the room. I pushed the living room door further back, and my heart sank. Mick was sat on the sofa with his trousers partially down; that was what I caught in the first look. I looked again, closer this time. He was lying back with his eyes shut, groaning in deep pleasure as a dark-haired woman with long hair sucked him hard. It was like he was savoring the moment enjoying every hard suck she made.

Fury filled my heart and soul, and I strode across the room, grabbing hold of the woman's long dark hair pulling her back harshly.

"You bitch!" I was shaking with anger.

I shoved her off his hard length, but as I did, she caught her teeth on his length making him open his eyes wincing with the pain. That was when Mick opened his eyes and colour drained off his face. I stood over him, and without thinking anything, I clenched my fist and punched him hard in the face causing him to lift slightly out of his position. I was ready to punch him again, but he managed to block me holding my wrist tight and pulling me down on the sofa.

"Let me go, you bastard." I gritted my teeth and wriggled in his arms.

"Holly, I... I thought you were at the party tonight and wouldn't be home tonight," said Mick sounding surprised.

"You fucking bastard! Get that slag out of this house before I do something stupid," I shouted at him.

Mick looked at the dark-haired woman and nodded his head as an acknowledgement for her to go, which she did without saying a word. As she was walking out, I realized how tanned and fit she was.

We heard the front door close, and I pounced on Mick again, catching him on the chin, this punch was harder than the last one.

"Holly calm down it's not what it looks like. She is from work," he begged.

"Fuck off, Mick! Sucking you off doesn't look like work to me," I shouted, going in for another punch to the face.

"I'm working on this case, and it's a bit sensitive, Holly you have to, believe me, it's just work." Pulling his trousers up, Mick sat up straight. His breathing was erratic, and his face almost purple.

"Do I look that stupid to you?" I tried to laugh sarcastically, but the sound came out like a whale's mating call. My robe had started to come loose after all that struggle which was now exposing my body. Mick tried to put his arm around the inside of my robe as the robe fell. I pulled away. "Don't fucking touch me, you bastard!" I pulled away from him, gathering up my loose robe and tying it up tight around my waist.

"Holly, I'm sorry. It's the first time, I swear. I got carried away. Please Holly - it won't happen again, don't tell anyone about this or I'll lose my promotion." Mick was on the verge of crying, but to me, it all looked like a drama.

"Mick, just fuck off! I need to think," I started crying. I couldn't believe that he would do something like this to me. With that, he got up knowing he wasn't getting anywhere with me; I heard the front door slam shut after a few seconds.

I curled on the sofa sobbing my heart out, blaming myself why did I go to that stupid party in the first place? Then I thought, why did we have to come here when we were happier living on the outskirts of Nottingham in a leafy village. I hated this place. Then my mind wandered to think why was he playing away if he wanted kids? Nothing made sense anymore. I loved him despite the fact of his job with the police force, even though I always felt I had married the force as well.

The day I had met Mick was the day that I had started with the Nottinghamshire Constabulary as a Special Constable. It felt like yesterday; everything was so fresh in my mind.

I was in the social club of the station, being served at the bar when he came up to me with those blue eyes and a thick set of curly blond hair, being 6ft tall he was a charmer. It later turned out that he was a good dancer and was generous. Making love to him was different from other guys I had been with. I was a little naïve in the lovemaking department, and as we dated, he showed me the ways of lovemaking and not just sex.

I found out that he had moved from Australia with his mother after his father had died of cancer. His mother settled down in Surrey in the house we now lived in until her death six months before we moved in. She died in a road traffic accident; she had been hit by a driver driving down the wrong side of the dual carriageway late at night. The incident had left Mick devastated.

Mick had taken it hard, with a couple of weeks mopping around but then eventually, throwing himself into his work. His mother had four hair salons in the city center and a beauty salon; she didn't work in the salons full time only if there were absences of sickness or holidays.

Mick had been the only child, so with his father's trust fund and his mother's house and businesses, he was well off financially.

I had been crying all night, and now there were no more tears to come out. My face had swelled with all the crying. I prized myself off the sofa, going upstairs to the spare bedroom, flopping on the bed where I eventually drifted off to sleep after some time.

I woke up by Mick calling me; I decided to ignore his calls. He finally came upstairs after hearing the bedroom door open; he stood there looking slightly bruised where I had hit him, with a boyish look as though he had been caught with his hands in the sweetie jar.

"Holly," he whispered. "I'm sorry darling I didn't want to hurt you, it was work. I know I shouldn't have done it. Holly, please talk to me, darling."

Lifting myself up, I sat on the side of the bed. My head throbbed from crying. I eventually got up and walked past Mick, ignoring him as though he wasn't there.

"Please." I saw his lips move a little, but I did not look at him.

I needed to use the bathroom. Splashes of cold water onto my face felt soothing on my red swollen and slightly burning face. I could hear Mick going on and on, saying he was sorry over and over again. I needed to get out of this house.

Mick followed me into our bedroom like a puppy, where I pulled out of the drawer a pair of jeans and a jumper, walking over to the wardrobe for my boots pulling them on. I then went towards the door where Mick was blocking my way.

"Fuck off Mick, let me pass or I'll fucking punch you again." I managed to speak with a raised and sturdy voice. He stood his ground then realized I was about to throw a punch he moved, letting me pass. I quickly ran downstairs, picking up my black long winter coat from the hanger in the hallway together with a scarf wrapping it around my neck and buttoned up, ready to set off out into the cold icy morning, not knowing where I was going.

As I stepped out of the house, the icy wind hit me taking my breath away. "God, it is so fucking cold," I muttered to myself.

Sliding my gloves on and tightening my scarf around my face, I headed off turning right outside the driveway heading towards the town. The roads had been gritted but the pavements were covered in a couple of inches of snow, walking wasn't too bad as it was still fresh. I did not know where I was headed, but I had to find a direction. There was no way I was going back to that bastard of my husband. Lost in my train of thought, I continued on the snowy pavement.

Mick watched Holly through the bedroom window, knowing which way she had gone. "Mia, it's me, Mick. Are you ok, baby?" He was phoning Mia now that Holly had gone.

"Oh, hello, my big boy. Are you ok?" asked Mia sounding sexy on the other end of the phone. "I was worried about you. Did she say anything?"

"No, No. Holly has walked out of the house, heading for the town. She won't listen to me. Can we meet? We need to talk." said Mick sounding slightly desperate.

"Mm, I'll meet you in our usual place in half an hour where I can finish you off and kiss that cock better before we get rudely interrupted again." Mia giggled, lusting for his cock.

"Yeah, I'm looking forward to that baby; I'll see you then, but I just need to call in at the station first." Mick replied, ending the call.

CHAPTER TWO:

I walked along the pavement heading towards the town center, with no particular destination in mind. My head spun and I felt faint- I could ruin Mick's career and promotion given his actions. I knew adultery is frowned upon in the police force and it could destroy Mick's reputation in the force. I badly needed a coffee, so I looked around until my eyes landed on an open café. I took off my gloves and dug deep into my pockets, searching for some loose change. I could feel some coins in the lining of my pocket. I hoped they would be enough for a coffee. I grappled in my coat pocket for the change as I made my way across the road.

Before I could feel the hit, I heard a loud thud; a car ploughed into me at full speed, throwing me into the air like a rag doll. My left-hand side suffered the impact, specifically my hip and leg. I was flung on top of the bonnet of the car before my body rolled off, and I hit my head on the tarmac as I landed on the surface of the road. It all happened so quickly that I never saw the car until I found myself sprawled across the road. I heard the car speeding off but did not hear it stop. The last thing I remembered before I slipped into oblivion was the sharp pain that shot through my entire body like a bolt of lightning, and then I finally blacked out.

The café owner heard the noise of screeching tyres and the banging of a body into the vehicle, so he made his way outside instantly to see if everything was alright. He quickly tried to note the details of the vehicle that ran me over. After he assessed the intensity of the accident, he ran to the café to phone for an ambulance, the police and a couple more people and stayed with me while the ambulance arrived. He gave his statement to the police once they arrived and told them he had just heard the thud but not seen the vehicle that had caused it. The police concluded that there would be damage to the vehicle due to the severity of my injuries.

I regained consciousness slightly, as the paramedics shined their lights into my eyes, tried to talk to me and asked my name. They asked me about what had happened. One of them asked me in a rather professional tone whether I had seen the vehicle, to which I could not muster a response; my body was in shock. I was excessively overwhelmed and I just wanted the pain to subside. I felt as if my body was floating. Was I dying? Was this the end? All I wanted was to sleep and ignore the paramedic staff's inquisition. I needed sleep, and my body continued to shut down until I could hear no more. I was unconscious once again.

As I regained consciousness, I could hear voices talking over me. The pain was substantially better, and I was practically numb. I was floating- where was I?

Darkness enveloped me- I couldn't see anyone, and I faded into nothingness until I couldn't hear anything.

I had been put under a medically induced coma due to the injury to my head; I also had a broken leg and a crushed pelvis, accompanied by numerous cuts and bruises. I was lucky that the owner of the café had come out on time. The severity of my head injury and the cold, harsh weather rendered it a touch and go if I would make it. I remained in a coma for just over a month, missing both Christmas and the New Year. When the doctors felt the swelling had decreased considerably and would not be a risk to my health, they brought me out of the coma.

Once I woke up, I heard voices; some I didn't recognize and some of them I did. I tried to move when I felt someone pulling the tube from my mouth. My mouth felt dry like a desert; I needed a drink. I tried to identify the voices talking to me; then, I felt my hand being enveloped into another soft, warm hand. I felt the hand squeeze mine gently.

I opened my eyes to find Mick hovering over me as he held my hand.

"Hello, my darling, you're back with us. I've been so worried about you, I thought I was going to lose you", said Mick, his voice laden with genuine concern. He sounded all wet and teary.

The last I could remember was Mick being sucked off by that dark-haired slag of a woman he had invited into our living room. He was enjoying himself and groaning in pleasure. I recalled having an argument with him and his incessant apologies as I stepped outside the house. The memory was fresh in my mind despite being knocked down for a month.

"Holly, it's me Debs, how are you feeling now? I am glad that you are back with us". Debs was a friend I had known since my teens. Debs had also married into the police; in fact, she served as an officer herself. She had eventually moved to Surrey because of her husband Pete, who had been promoted to the traffic department. Debs was also transferred to the same station but mainly worked on the front desk now due to her pregnancy.

It was only when I started at the station as a special constable when I had met her again after a couple of years as we seemed to have drifted apart. She was in town that night when I came in waiting to go out on the rural beat, but Paul couldn't make it back to the station due to a road traffic accident (RTA), so I was asked if I wanted to try the town where I had bumped into Debs.

"I feel shit, aching all over, and I've got a stinking headache, apart from that, Debs, I'm ok". I managed to reply to it with sarcasm.

"We're glad your back with us, Holly, but I'm afraid we have to go now as we have to be on shift in the next half hour", Debs said, smiling awkwardly.

"No problem, but thanks for coming", I replied with a croaky voice.

The nurse checked the machine I was wired up to and monitored my pulse and blood pressure. She asked me if I would like a cup of tea, but Mick had already answered in an affirmative, asking for two cups instead. Mick waited until the nurse had left the room.

Mick took my hand in both of his; he gently squeezed and kissed it. He went on saying how he thought he had lost me when he received the call about the accident. It was scary for him that I had been the victim of a hit-and-run driver and was in the hospital as a result.

"God, Holly! I couldn't imagine losing you. I love you so much." He added, kissing my hand and running his slightly stubbly cheek across my fingers. I could feel his stubble rub across my fingers and it was like sandpaper. All I could think was, for fuck sake, leave me alone you bastard! It's your fault that I am here in the first place, but I didn't say anything. I was tired and had no energy to speak, and with that, I closed my eyes and drifted off back to sleep.

I was in the hospital for nearly six months due to the crushed pelvis; I needed reconstruction surgery for my pelvis and leg, which was broken in four places. The doctors said it was terrible. I was well potted up, but I hated having to wear a catheter and colostomy bags due to the restrictions on mobility. It was quite embarrassing when I had my period, and I had to wear pads instead of tampons. They leaked often, and I was given frequent bed baths.

The nurses were wonderful and reassured me that it was normal and that they had seen it all before- they said nothing fazed anymore.

Over the six months being in the hospital, I had a stream of friends and family coming to see me every single day. I had to put a face on, for I knew it was Mick's fault, making me walk out in the first place. I wondered if he was still seeing that cock sucker of a woman. I needed at least a day with no one coming to visit; thoughts of her stressed me out and made me snappy.

The day had arrived for my restraints to be removed. I had been looking forward to regaining mobility and a proper shower with a thorough hair wash. The porter came into wheel my whole bed down to the room to have all of my restraints removed. My leg looked white and thin, as I had lost muscle strength in the impacted leg. I was told that I would need a physio. The doctor was pleased with my progress as I had healed quite nicely, but I would need a considerable amount of physio extending over six months.

I was wheeled back to my room by the porter, and after five minutes, a nurse came asking me if I wanted to be taken down for a shower. I didn't have to think twice about it; I was excited that I was finally going for a shower.

The bathroom was quite large, with different types of hoists for patients and an open wet room for easy access into the shower. The nurse hoisted me in position and seated me in the shower, as I couldn't stand being in bed all that time; I had my catheter and colostomy bags removed when I had finished, and I felt refreshed and free.

I had to spend another couple of weeks being taken to physio four times a day to try and get on my feet before they discharged me from the hospital. The hospital arranged me a referral to a hospital near my parents' home for recuperating purposes; it was a good excuse as I didn't want to go back to the house and needed help, so I was relieved when my mum suggested that I came home to them.

A young trainee nurse came into my room a couple of days before I was due to be discharged from the hospital to check my blood pressure and pulse. I hadn't seen her before while I had been in, all this time.

"Hello, Holly. My name is Anna, and I am a trainee nurse. I hope you don't mind", she continued in a slightly high squeaky pitched voice, "this is my last shift today, so I won't be seeing you, now that you are leaving us in a couple of days".

"Yeah, I can't wait to get out of here", I said, sounding excited. "You are loved by many friends and family. I only saw your cousin Liam the month you were in an induced coma; I haven't seen him ever since". She smiled.

"Oh, I don't have a cousin called Liam". I am sure I sounded puzzled.

"Well", Anna continued, "he was in every day, mostly coming out of visiting hours because his job was such that we let him through. He sat with you for a while, holding your hand, and prayed, hoping you would pull through. He was so upset I thought he was your husband at first."

"What did he look like"? I asked her in a casual tone, but I knew my voice was trembling.

"Well, I shouldn't say this, but he had long black curly hair and gorgeous eyes". The nurse slightly blushed. I thought, who the fuck was this guy? Did he have something to do with my accident?

"Oh, yes. I remember now,". I finally pretended that I knew him.

"Well, you will forget some things, as you have had a very bad head injury". she smiled kindly.

Once the young nurse had left, I focused my energy on figuring out who the hell that guy could that guy be. He had only come in to see me when I was in an induced coma. Obviously, no one had mentioned him over the six months I had been in the hospital, and I couldn't remember seeing anyone, especially someone that fit the description the young nurse had relayed to me. Again, had he something to do with the accident? But why would he be saying those things; Mm, did I have a stalker I didn't know about? It was boggling my mind.

My mum came down to pick me up and brought the more practical Range Rover to provide me comfort and room during the trip home. Mick was waiting with her and couldn't seem to do enough for me, clucking around me like a mother hen. Once I was seated, ready to go, Mick stood next to the open door of the vehicle, gave me a hug, and kissed me passionately on the lips. He said he would come up as soon as he could. I put on a brave face and said: “Yeah, whatever, Mick”.

My parents had been to the hospital a few times, but maintaining the farm with livestock was difficult as it needed 24/7 care, and it was not easy to find the staff to help out. Not only that, it was a long day travelling from Nottingham to Surrey and back; it wasn’t fair on them, but my mum kept in touch; she phoned the hospital every day to see how I was doing.

The end of June was fast approaching; the weather was dry and sunny with temperatures in the lower twenty degrees; the harvest was coming on well with only a few weeks to go before it had to be cut. All the livestock were out but still had to be checked, and the sheds had to be cleaned out to be readied for winter.

Coming back home was a major relief. I didn’t realize how much I had missed it; the quietness, the fresh air, open spaces and no neighbours. I finally had time to think now that I was home with my parents and did not have to see one person or the other all the time. God, how I hated that city. My mum hadn't noticed the tension in my marriage; I assumed she thought I had pain, which flared up now and again, and that I was fed up with being cooped up in the hospital for six months.

My mum had made me a bed up downstairs in one of the spare reception rooms which was near the downstairs bathroom. Climbing the stairs would have been a problem with my leg and the crutches. My mum had insisted when the renovations of the farmhouse had taken place that they should have a downstairs bathroom, especially for the harvest season with its long hours, the dust and the dirt. She beseeched my dad to leave his mess downstairs.

I hadn't brought my clothes since I had gone down a size. I brought only three pairs of joggers and tee-shirts, which hung off me, even my underwear. As soon as I was strong enough, I would have a go into town to purchase a small wardrobe of clothes and underwear, I had planned it in my head. I asked my mum during my stay at the hospital to get me some basic undies and some more joggers and tee shirts just so I could look presentable when I had my appointments for physio and swimming.

I sat out in the garden and took in the view from the farmhouse while I had some breakfast my mum had made me. I was thinking about how I had been here a few weeks now and I hadn't heard from Mick. I had tried a couple of times, leaving him messages and texts, but he hadn't returned my calls and texts. I needed to speak to someone in confidence regarding my predicament, but who could I trust?

My mum shouted at me, "Holly, there's someone to see you". I turned around thinking it was Mick, but no, it was Mags. Mags was one of my friends I had left behind when I moved to Surrey with Mick. We used to walk together to catch the school bus. Both of us were bullied during our school years, but we had managed to confront the bullies, and eventually, they stopped. After leaving school, we seemed to go our separate ways. I went to college while Mags hung out with her elder sister and took a year off from university; she headed to the South of France, and they worked their way up to pay for their keep. She had then joined the police force and was transferred to Nottingham after her two-year probationary.

I never saw her again until I had met her in the local village pub. I had already joined up with the police force when I saw her. We started going to the police social club where she had met Tony who had been there for five years, and that was where I had met Mick.

"Oh, Mags, it's been a while". I hugged her.

"Yeah, how are you doing now? Now you are out of the hospital"? She asked me while returning my hug with all her might.

"Mm not too bad, I go to physio a few times a week and I go swimming. I still get pain episodes, but I've got painkillers as and when I need them. I've got to get some strength in my leg muscle, but it's doing fine, thanks, Mags", I filled her in.

"God, you have lost a lot of weight, which I'm not surprised with what you've been through Holly", she said

"Yeah I know, I also need some cheap clothes as all my clothes are a dress size down. My mum brought these just to tie me over until I'm strong enough". I spread my arms for her to have a better look at my clothes.

"Well, I'll take you in when you're ready", she said with a huge smile.

"Oh, Mags, you are a godsent; please do". I grinned at her.

It was just over a week and a half before Mags turned up on Saturday early, so I had space to get out of the house with my crutches, as parking was a bit of a pain in the town center.

I noticed that there were even more shops since I had leftover a year ago. There was now a large departmental store offering furniture to clothing, everything under one roof. Luckily, there was an elevator as the clothing department was upstairs, and it would have been difficult for me to get the stairs. After a bit of maneuvering, Mags and I made it in the elevator to the top floor.

"Are you okay, Holly"? asked Mags. "We can go and have a coffee and sit down if you want", she said.

"No, I am ok, thanks; I've been sat down enough this year in the hospital", I said, ready to bolt out the elevator with my crutches. "Let's have a look around here first, and then we'll have one, Mags".

"Ok. you can lead the way then,", she replied, stepping aside.

The elevator had stopped, and a couple had gotten out, so we also slowly made our way to the clothing department.

"So what are you looking for"? Mags questioned me excitedly.

"Mainly trousers, jeans, a few tops and underwear", I said, looking around. Trying the clothes on was a trial in itself, but I managed with a little help from Mags; I wasn't going to be beaten by my temporary disability.

I was starting to tire after I had brought the majority of things that I needed, but we had set another day for shopping as well. The café was upstairs, and I found a seat as Mags went off to get two coffees and slices of chocolate cake.

"Are you trying to fatten me up, Mags"?

"You could do with some fat on you, girl", said Mags with a smile, passing me a plate with the slice of cake. We chatted for just over half an hour before heading back to the car.

Mags couldn't believe it when we turned to the car, both sides of the car had been nipped in by the cars parked on either side. Mags managed to squeeze in opening the driver's door, where there was just enough room to wriggle her body into the driver's seat. It was lucky she was fit. She reversed out of the jammed space and made me room for me to get into the front seat with my crutches. The car park was busy with limited space for parking, which was expected on a Saturday morning.

As we made our way home, Mags broke to me the news that she and Tony were getting married next year and that Tony was pushing to pass his sergeants exams, hoping to sail through the practical. Mags could not stop talking about him, how she loved him and how loving he was, and how he always made her feel special.

I broke down in tears; I couldn't hold it back any longer.

"Holly, what's wrong"? Mags asked as she quickly pulled into the nearest lay by and turned off the engine. She had a worried expression on her face. "Come on Holly; it's not like you. Talk to me, please,", she insisted.

"Oh, Mags, I've got to tell someone before I topple over with anxiety; it's been bottled up since the night of the accident, but you have to promise me not to tell anyone because I just don't know what to do". Mags promised not to say a word with furrowed brows.

"Not even Tony. I'm serious, Mags".

"Ok, Holly, spill".

I told her that Mick and I were always arguing since we had moved to Surrey. "Mick wants me to have a baby and to pack in work, but we had never discussed having kids before we got married. Then I went off to a Christmas party with Jo from work because she didn't want to go on her own. I had been arguing with Mick most of the week, I told him I had promised to go to a Christmas party with Jo and I would be staying over, and that work would be paying for the accommodation. But Jo had been knocking the drinks back all night, seeing it was an open bar and that she had her eye on a guy in the accounts department- she fucked off, leaving me like a spare part. So eventually, I came home before the trains stopped. I didn't know if Mick was in bed because I went into the spare bedroom just in case he was so as not to disturb him.

It went all wrong when I heard Mick come in later that night because he wasn't alone- he had a woman with him. I thought it was someone he was working with, but then I went downstairs and there he was on the sofa with his head back, groaning because she was sucking him off." I stammered at the last part.

"Fucking hell Holly, I'm so sorry", she said as she hugged me. Tears started streaming down my face. "So, when did you have the accident?" she asked. "Well.." I started sniffing. "Mick kept on saying it was a mistake and that it was to do with work and he got carried away. He kept on saying it was a mistake; then he came out saying stuff about his promotion and not to say anything, I couldn't cope so I left the house to get away from him pecking at my head. I walked down towards the town center, and later decided I needed a coffee, I saw an open café and started walking across the road, and that's when I got hit by the car". Mags couldn't believe what she was hearing.

"God Holly, you two were the perfect couple, you both looked so happy together". added Mags after a long pause, astonished by what she had just heard. "I don't know what to say, Holly".

"Mick hasn't even been in touch with me since I got here".

"You're kidding me, Holly". Mags was finding it hard to take in. "It's not like Mick". Everyone had always commented on us being the perfect couple.

"Do you think he may be on a delicate job?" asked Mags hopefully.

"Well, a phone call or a text wouldn't go amiss, would it, Mags"?

"Yeah, I see what you mean", she sighed. I asked her to make enquiries to see if he did get his promotion.

“I’ll see what I can find out for you, Holly”, she assured me. We sat for a few minutes more.

“Are you feeling ok to go home now as you have got it off your chest Holly?” Mags tried to force a smile on her face.

“Well, it’s a relief, but yes, thanks, Mags lets go home.” I felt relieved of the pressure of having spent over six months in hospital with bottled up tormenting thoughts of Mick and the unknown woman sucking him off. The accident had made everything so much worse. Confiding Mags felt like releasing a tight spring. I knew that I could trust her to help me find information relating to Mick and why he hadn’t been in touch with me. Was it just the pressure of work?

Once again, after I pulled myself together, I asked Mags to keep it between us as I didn’t want to deal with any repercussions. Mags hugged me and said that she would help me in any way she could.

It had been my first time out of the house, with the exception of physio, and that too a long day of shopping. It had worn me out. I thanked Mags for taking me into town and keeping my secret between us. Mags pulled up as close to the front door of the farmhouse as she could and helped me out with my crutches and the bags of clothing I had purchased. As she opened the door, I came across Mick. He started to come out with open arms and gave me a hug and a kiss on the lips. I was at a loss for words, especially after what I had told Mags only just half an hour ago while sobbing my heart out. Now here he was, making me look like a liar.

“Hello, Mick, it’s nice to see you; it’s been a long time.” greeted Mags casually.

“Yeah, we’ve got a big case on at the moment and it’s taking a lot of my time up, but I’ve managed to slip away for the weekend,” informed Mick justifying his absence. He looked like a perfect husband who showed up to see his wife the first chance that he had gotten. I stood there, lost in my own world, not sure what life would bring me next. I was on the verge of losing my sanity, but I had to stay strong and find out the truth about Mick and that woman. My life and my marriage depended on it.

CHAPTER THREE:

I was jolted out of my scattered thoughts when I heard Mags asking Mick what exactly the job at hand entailed. She knew quite well that he would respond ambiguously, yet she had gone straight for the jugular.

'I can't say at the moment, it's a delicate operation you see,' said Mick hesitantly.

'Oh well, at least you found time to check in on your wife, as always,' said Mags with a hint of sarcasm in her voice that was barely detectable.

'Yeah. It's been hectic since Holly came up here,' said Mick making excuses, his face slightly red with embarrassment.

'So, Mick, did you get your promotion you had been waiting for?' Mags asked casually during the flow of the conversation.

‘No, not yet. It’s being held back until September when the chief will be retiring. The office is undergoing quite a few changes,’ replied Mick. He sounded a bit miffed by the wait. Mick still had his arm around my waist, and he gave me a squeeze as he said it.

‘Oh, you mean, are they cutting back then?’ Mags kept pushing for more information in a subtle way.

‘No, they are recruiting for a couple of operation staff, so the chief decided he would stay a few more months till September,’ answered Mick with his eyes directed towards everything but Mags.

‘Well, I’ll leave you two love birds to catch up then. I’ll be going.’ Mags waved her hand. I wondered if she still believed the secret I had confided in her about amidst sobs. Mick had acted as though there wasn’t anything wrong between us.

'Mags, would you like to come in for a cuppa?' I asked her hoping she would, but Mick butted in and said that I looked tired, and I needed to rest. I rolled my eyes at his staged concern.

'No, but thanks, I'll be going. Tony's nearly done with his shift; I will see you soon, Holly,' said Mags. She sounded genuine as she gave me an awkward hug. Mags turned around and headed for her car. She drove down the farm road until she was out of sight.

I was alone with Mick now, who seemed like a stranger to me and I didn't know what to say to him. I felt vulnerable; Mags had always been my support and safety net. I was sure Mick would manipulate the situation in his favor. I shrugged to escape Mick's arm around me and started off on my crutches. I tried to pick up my bags when Mick intervened and took them from me; he tried to place his arm around me once more.

'Mick, just give me some space for fuck's sake!' I said, raising my voice. I moved away from his arm and made my way to the kitchen with the help of my crutches. He put my bags down near the welsh dresser in the large hallway before he followed me into the kitchen. A silence heavy with things unsaid ensued between us, and the distant noise of the combine harvester was all that punctuated it. I watched it through the kitchen window. Mick filled the kettle to make a pot of tea, then took two mugs from the rack and some milk from the fridge.

'Holly, we need to talk.' he finally said, breaking the silence. I couldn't believe after all this time; this was when he wanted to talk. I had been leaving him messages and texts, and now HE wanted to talk.

I pivoted on my crutches, hobbled off into the living room and gently slid into the recliner as I placed my crutches on either side of the chair. I pulled the lever that allowed the chair to recline and propel the footrest, and it lifted my legs up in a swift motion. It was nice to be home. My body had started to ache with the odd twinge in my hip. I needed to lay down.

Mick had made the tea and had brought two mugs into the living room, placing a mug next to me on the side table.

'Thanks,' I said in a low whisper. I was waiting for him to say something I was in no mood to listen to. Just as he was about to begin, my mum came into the room; thank God, saved by the bell.

Mick turned around to face my mum. 'Hello, Joan. Would you like a cuppa? I've just made one,' he said. I could sense that he was pissed off that she had arrived the same moment he wanted to talk privately with me.

'Oh yes, please, Mick.' With that, he walked back into the kitchen to make one for her. I sighed in relief.

'So, how was your first day out with Mags?' asked Mum.

'Ah, tiring, but a least it got me out of the house and gave me some exercise,' I added.

'Isn't it a nice surprise that Mick came up to see you? He's been telling me he's on a big case at the moment and that's why he hasn't been up,' mum filled me in with a smile. I didn't comment as Mick came back with a mug of tea, handed it to my mum, and chatted with her a while. I wasn't interested in listening, so I decided to get up from the recliner and commented in passing that I was going to my room to lay down for a nap.

Both Mick and my mum asked if I was alright, but I said I was tired, it being my first time out and all, and that I probably overdid it with the walking. Mick got up to help me and wrapped an arm around my waist to help me to rise from the chair.

Mick felt like a spare part, a little lost, and out of place. He was not in his own comfort zone or preferred surroundings. He left me to have a nap and went outside for a walk around the farm.

My mum had left the window open as the day had been warm and she thought the fresh air would do me good. As I lay on the bed and was about to dose off, deja vu returned to haunt me. I heard someone walking slowly, then stopping near my window. It was Mick, but who the hell he was talking to? Then I heard him utter a name- Mia. Was she the woman he had been with that night, the one who had been sucking him off?

I wondered if she was the same woman as I listened carefully. Tears started to roll down my face, and I felt a pit in my stomach. His conversation was very intimate; he kept on saying he would see her soon and couldn't wait for another blow job. The lying bastard was still at it while I had been up here, and he was trying to tell me it was a mistake.

I pulled myself off the bed and limped towards the window, but by the time I had reached there, Mick had left. I decided to go and find him since I was all wound up and ready to punch him. With the aid of my crutches, I dragged myself slowly towards the door only to find Mick coming back inside the house.

'Oh,' he said, not expecting me up and about. 'What's wrong? You look pale. Haven't you had a nap, Holly?'

I couldn't hear or see my mum around, so this was my window to ask him about his phone call.

'What the fucking hell are you doing, Mick? And who the fuck is Mia? Is she that slag I saw sucking you off? She must be a sucker being with you,' I spat out. 'You lying bastard, what are you trying to do to me, huh? Why did you bother coming up? You might as well have stayed with her so she could suck you off more. Trying to tell me it was only once Mick, who are you trying to kid?' Mick was visibly taken aback as the color left his face.

Then Mick's face turned a slight shade of pink. He ran his hands around the back of his neck; this was something he did when he felt uptight or found himself in a situation where he couldn't answer straight away.

'Holly, I love you, and I wouldn't do anything to hurt you intentionally. I swear, it has everything to do with the case I'm working on, but I can't tell you about the case. It's confidential and sensitive,' pleaded Mick.

'You would hide behind your job, wouldn't you Mick?' I said, spraying him with my spit, not believing him at all.

'Holly, I'm under pressure at work with this case,' begged Mick, still pleading his case.

'Well, you might as well leave then if it's getting to you that bad, Mick.' I spat back at him.

'Holly, if you're going to be in this mood, I might as well go.' Before I could say anything, he was gone. I heard his car skid off the stone drive in a rush. He could see it was not working, and that I wasn't listening to him or his lies.

I couldn't believe he was really gone, but that is what he always did when we argued about having kids- he would walk away. Although this was way different, a woman was involved here. He was messing with my mind, being lovey-dovey, saying he loved me, and when I was in the hospital, he had said all of those things sitting right next to my bedside. I just didn't know what to believe anymore.

My mum had taken sandwiches and a flask of tea out to the field where my dad and a couple of the farm hands were bringing in the harvest. Mick had left by the time my mum came back, so she asked me where he was. I made some excuse that he was called back to work; mum didn't question it, so life back at our little farm went back to normal. The only difference was that there was a storm inside me.

I had to do something, I couldn't live like this. I had enough pain to last me a lifetime from the accident, but this? What was it going to be like when I went home for good? I was dreading it. I had to talk to Mags, tell her about the phone call that I had overheard, the conversation Mick had engaged in and how easily he took off after our argument. I was physically disabled and mentally incapacitated, and it felt like I was dying.

I tossed and turned in bed each night, consumed by thoughts about Mick. Was there any truth to his words? I knew we had some heated arguments in the past, but those had mainly been about him wanting kids. If he wanted kids, why would he do such things? Unless he was telling me the truth- that didn't justify his sexual encounter while working a case. That was against police policy and could seriously damage his chances of a promotion.

Mick seemed like a stranger to me since that night and the accident. Living away from him, my feelings for him had started to fade. I no longer felt the tingles I did when we had met for the first time. I needed to find out about this woman called Mia he was talking to, but Mags was on shift for the next seven days.

I was determined to get better and pushed myself with the exercises I had been given, coupled with additional swimming. My mum drove me to the pool as I couldn't drive yet. My injuries were starting to fade as I reeled myself off of painkillers.

It was a Friday night before I saw Mags again. We had arranged a night out as I had been climbing and clawing at the walls and needed to get out. Mags came over to pick me up. I made an effort and put some makeup and wore the new blue jeans and a white tee shirt I had bought with Mags. It was decided we would stop by the police social club at the station for a drink. I hadn't seen many people, and it would be nice to meet some old faces since it had been over a year.

It was a warm evening as I walked out of the house with the aid of my crutches; the sun was starting to go down as Mags turned the car around in the driveway for my convenience. She parked at the front of the station. It was supposed to be for public use as there was a separate area for police and staff vehicles, but Mags took a gamble for my ease; this spot was closest to the reception desk.

The station still looked like it did a year ago when I had left. I made my way through the front doors into the reception area to find Gill on the desk. Her eyes sparkled with acknowledgement, but she couldn't talk on duty.

We turned right towards the stairs, and this was going to be my first attempt to climb them since the accident. I was surprised how comfortable I was with it; they were a gradual incline with a couple of stairwells in between. As I reached the top, I saw Jim coming out of the social room; he stopped for a quick chat while Mags went ahead to get the drinks; it was just like old times. He asked where Mick was and how he was doing. I mentioned he was due to get promoted and tried to lead the subject of conversation away Mick. We chatted further, after which I slowly walked off and headed for the bar.

As I opened the door, I heard loud cheers from three colleagues I knew before moving to Surrey with Mick. I expected questions about how Mick was doing, but they didn't ask as they were more interested in how I was doing since my accident. They enquired if the hit-and-run driver had been located. They offered to buy my drinks and left drinks that had been paid for behind the bar when I was ready for another.

After all the small talk, Mags and I went to sit down at the far end of the room. The middle of the room had a wooden floor to be used as a dance floor for the social events; it usually sported a DJ and a buffet. The bar was on the left-hand side and it occupied half the back wall of the room, which had a door leading into the storeroom that held kegs of beers, spirits, and beverages. The station had to apply for a license to sell liquor; it was exactly like a proper bar selling snacks with a wide range of beers and spirits.

Mags didn't want to start the conversation about Mick; I think she thought I was still fragile. I had drunk a couple of glasses of white wine before I brought the subject up, which helped me loosen up and feel numb enough to talk.

‘Mags, when you left me with Mick, we argued only because I overheard him on the phone talking to a woman called Mia; he was all lovey-dovey with her. I heard him outside my bedroom window; he keeps saying its work-related, and he went too far on the job, that bastard. He doesn’t want to lose his promotion, and that’s why he doesn’t want me to say anything. But I don’t know if there are any truths in this story he is feeding me about the case. What do you think, Mags?’ I asked her.

‘Mm, it’s hard to tell Holly; I’m not in your shoes,’ said Mags.

‘But would you do me a favor and check if you can find out anything about a woman called Mia?’ Mags was just about to say something, but she stopped herself as two guys approached us.

‘Hello, Mags, who’s your friend?’ Mags introduced me to Tom and John, two new recruits on two years’ probation. They were both of around the same age, had slim builds, short brown hair, and were about 5ft 9ins tall. There wasn't anything that stood out in their features.

Tom and John had been transferred from another station due to a shortfall in the workforce, and they had arrived sometime after Mick and I had moved to Surrey. Mags explained that I used to be special before moving to Surrey and that I was back up here to recuperate from a bad accident I had last December. She added that it had left me in a medically induced coma for a month.

'I hope you're recuperating well, and it's nice to see a new and pretty face here,' said Tom with a smile.

I was feeling a bit giddy and said, 'I bet you say that to all the girls.'

'No,' he laughed. 'Only the special ones.'

'Ahhh,' I said, getting the pun on special.

'Would you both like another drink?' he asked as he stood up.

'Oh, yes, please. I'll have white wine,' I smiled lazily at him.

'And what about you, Mags?' Tom glanced over at her.

'I'll just have an orange juice, thanks. I'm driving,' said Mags in a responsible manner. Tom went off to get the drinks; the room started to fill up with off-duty officers interested in pints and gossip. As they entered, their eyes glared around the room as though they were looking for someone. Mags noticed their eyes glaring at me; I hadn't noticed it because I was far too inebriated. I finally felt relaxed and did not want to pay attention to anything.

Tom sat down with the round of drinks as a couple more guys came over with their pints and sat with us. Mags noticed I was drawing in the guys like a babe magnet as I started talking about my time as a special. The guys talked about their past and where they were from and what they used to get up to. The evening was going well and was full to the brim with jokes and laughter.

Time passed in a blur, and we realized it was already 11 pm; the time was called for final orders. By this time, I was on a roll and honestly had not been so relaxed in months. I was happy having a few drinks blotted thoughts of Mick for a short while. I was also glad I had flirted with so many guys- two could play at that game. I still had it.

I suddenly remembered this was where I had been sitting when Mick had come over in his grey suit, charm and dashing blue eyes the first time we met. I had instantly fallen head over heels for him, and we had gotten married shortly after.

As we finished our drinks and headed downstairs, I was a bit unsteady, and the guys held me by my sides as they led me down the stairs. They all gave me a hug, and a kiss as Mags brought the car around for me to get in.

'You are pissed,' teased Mags.

'Yeah, I know. Fuck it.' With that, I wound the car window down and shouted, 'I'll see you, lads, again!' I slurred through the sentence as Mag drove us away from where they stood, shaking her head and smiling. She had only driven about four hundred yards down the road when I shouted, 'I'm going to be sick.' Quickly, Mags pulled over to the side of the road, where I opened the car door and leaned out to throw up violently. Mags managed to pull back my hair in time. I had closely missed throwing up inside her car and was glad she wouldn't have to clean my mess. Everything was spinning; Yep, I was definitely drunk, and I needed loads of coffee.

By the time Mags pulled up outside my parent's home, it was pitch black. Everyone had gone to bed as it was almost midnight. Mags helped me out of the car while I felt sick and sorry for myself. She guided me through the door into the kitchen and helped me get in the chair. Mags made strong coffee, one cup for me, and one for her. I leaned on the kitchen table while my head rested on my arms. I groaned- I was feeling sick again.

Mags dragged me to the bathroom downstairs just in time before I threw up on the kitchen floor. I knelt, bent over the toilet bowl while Mags held my hair so I wouldn't throw up on it. After another coffee, I stopped feeling sick at last. Mags washed my face before putting me to bed; it was 3 in the morning when she left.

Mags was exhausted as she has been up since 6 am the previous morning. Luckily, Tony was away on a course, and Mags had a few days off before she had to be back on shift; she was going to have an undisturbed lay in.

My parents were up at 6 am; it was still harvest season, and crops had to be brought in, two thousand chickens had to be let out and eggs needed to be ready for collection. Cows needed to be milked to have ample for distribution.

I was in a deep slumber, which was a good thing since I hadn't had a decent night's sleep in a while- I needed it.

'Holly, would you like a cup of tea?' asked Mum. When I didn't answer, she came into my bedroom. 'Holly love, would you like a cup of tea?' She touched my hair gently.

'Mm, yeah, please.' I groaned in a croaky voice.

'Are you alright, love?' mum asked, sounding worried.

'Yeah, I drank too much last night. That's all, mum.' I sounded half-asleep even to myself.

My mum went to pour me a cup of tea, brought it back, and put it on the bedside table. I strained myself to reach the mug and attempted to drink it. I felt an urge to throw up. Fumbling out of bed, I made it to the toilet, retched over the toilet bowl and only produced a watery liquid. After I retched a couple more minutes, I felt a little better. I wiped my mouth with a face cloth from the side of the hand basin and made my way back to bed; I just needed to sleep after months of unrest.

It was 3 pm before I surfed from my bed, had a shower, and felt more human again. There were no signs of anyone at home, but as I went into the kitchen, I noticed a large bouquet of red roses with a small sealed card placed on top.

'Uh, the bastard is feeling guilty.' I ignored the flowers and proceeded towards the kettle to make myself a strong coffee. The afternoon, or what was left of it, was dry with a few grey clouds that suggested it was going to rain.

Without the aid of my crutches, I took my coffee outside to get some fresh air; I found my mum gardening.

'So, you've managed to surface then?' smiled mum.

'Mm, I had a good night, though.'

'Oh, I take it you've seen the flowers on the side, aren't they nice?' Mum was now grinning.

'Yeah, aren't they?' I bet I sounded just as enthusiastic, although I said it out of pure sarcasm.

'Mick must really love you.'

'Yeah, I suppose he does,' I replied nonchalantly. I hurried to change the subject; I didn't want her to ask questions about what was up between us, and neither did I want her to know what had really happened before I had the accident. I was grappling with another secret of my own that no one knew about yet.

'Would you like a cup of tea?' I asked mum to lighten the mood.

'Yes, I'd love one, but I'm coming in now as I have gotten the tea ready for your dad. He's going out again.'

I made my way back to the house to make the tea while my mum cleared the tools from the garden to store them in the shed. I put the kettle on and washed my half-empty mug. I thought I'd have to do something with those flowers as I picked the card from the bouquet.

'I wonder what crap he's written this time,' I muttered to myself as I opened the card. I was shocked to find that the flowers weren't from Mick. The card said;

I am always thinking of you, no matter where you are. With all my love, 'L.'

I heard my mum coming in, and I quickly pushed the card inside my back trousers' pocket. I didn't want her to read it, else there would be questions. I needed time to process this- who it could be? They were red roses, flowers of love. I needed to get to the bottom of this case on an urgent basis. My heartbeat accelerated as I thought about the secret admirer I had. I wanted to know who this mystery man was as soon as possible.

CHAPTER FOUR:

I needed some time to process what I had just read. Who could it be from? Whoever it was, they had sent me red roses, the biggest token of affection in my eyes. I found a vase and arranged the roses. They smelt lovely, so I took them into my bedroom and set them on the side table next to my bed. I felt wild butterflies in my stomach at the idea that I had got an admirer. Then the smell hit me once again. Gosh! The roses smelt divine; they must have cost a bit.

I went back to the kitchen to finish making the tea, but my mum was pouring water into the pot.

'Oh, mum, I was just coming in to finish it off,' I said as I walked in. 'I'll give you a hand if you like.'

'Only if you're feeling up to it love, you can wash the vegetables. '

'Yeah, no problem,' I assured her, wiping my hands on a kitchen towel.

It was around 5 pm when my dad came in for his tea, and all three of us sat down around the table for the first time since I had arrived.

'This is such a lovely change, having all of us around the table together,' said dad taking his seat.

'Yeah, dad. It sure is.' I said, smiling at him. The conversation around the table revolved around the day on the farm until mum blurted out that Mick had gotten a large bouquet of red roses delivered to the house.

'That's nice of him, love,' said dad.

I hated lying to him and pretending all was good in my marriage, so I diverted the subject back to the day's work on the farm and asked him what he was doing after tea.

'I'm going to lead the bales in off the fields before the rain sets in, and before it gets dark,' he started explaining.

'Oh, can I come with you just to watch, if that's alright, dad? it's just that I need to get out more,' I shrugged.

'Well, if you feel up to it, but it will be a bit bumpy in the tractor,' he warned.

'I'll see how it goes. And I can always get out and walk,' I assured him.

Once we were done with the tea, I put on one of my mum's cardigans and went out into the farmyard where a couple of farmhands were coupling the tractors with the trailers. My dad climbed into the loader, and I followed him, pulling myself up into the cab of the vehicle where there was an extra seat. I felt an odd pull and twinge in my back but persevered as I would have to be doing more to get stronger.

The ride downhill towards the field wasn't all that unbearable, but when we turned into the field, the vehicle rocked and rolled over the uneven ground. I braced myself and suddenly wished that I hadn't come. I held my breath as I didn't want my dad to stop; I knew that time wasn't on his side to lead the bales as the weather was due to turn in the next few hours.

We were only half a mile from the farm, so when my dad was ready to start loading the bales onto the trailer, I told him that I would walk back home to the farm.

'Are you sure, love?'

'Yeah, I'll be ok, thanks, dad.' I was holding my breath as a sharp pain jabbed me in the side as I moved off the seat to climb down. I had caught one of the levers in the cab. I pulled off the lever and slowly descended down from the cab of the vehicle. Gosh, that was a close call. I managed to walk across the uneven field and tried my best to ensure dad did not see me struggling. Once I was on the farm track, I was feeling a lot better, but it made me hot and sweaty, and I thought to myself, *God, I must go swimming more. I need to speed up my fitness program.*

I had loved the water since I was a child. A few of us as kids used to hang around finding bits of wood and plastic drums on the farm, fastening them together and dropping them into the dykes to use them as rafts. We would spend most of our time squabbling about who would paddle with the makeshift paddles that we made out of a long piece of thin wood with a square bit of wood nailed to it. The dykes weren't very deep, about three feet, with the width five to six feet usually- it depended on the bank sides and the weed in the water. Falling in was a regular habit, and being kids, we had no fear of going home wet.

I took my time as I replayed my childhood days in my head when I heard a vehicle behind me; it was my dad. He had stopped to ask if I wanted a lift back to the yard. He had swapped over to the tractor and trailer that carried a full load and was taking them back to be stored in the barn for winter.

'Yeah, thanks.' I felt a bit shaken as my side still ached from the lever that my body had been flung against while getting out of the cab. As we set off, I thought I might have a nice hot soak in the jacuzzi, but that meant climbing up three flights of stairs. They weren't as steep as the stairs at the station, so if I could manage those, I could very well manage these.

It was after nine pm; I was enjoying the bubbles bouncing off my body. It felt like bliss lying there as the hot water eased my cramps. My thoughts drifted back to the arrival of the bouquet of red roses signed with the initials 'L'. I thought harder about who I knew whose name began with the initial 'L'? The only person I could recall was a guy called Leonard who worked in the account's office, but he was old enough to be my father- besides, he was happily married with three grown-up kids.

Then it occurred to me what the trainee nurse had said about a guy called Liam who had been by my side while I was in an induced coma. He couldn't have anything to do with the accident, so why would he say those things? Plus, he wouldn't know that I was back with my parents. I was totally baffled, and I thought if I should mention this to Mags. I felt giddy, once again, at the thought that I had an admirer.

I had a good buffing with the bubbles and felt refreshed- the aches and pains were gone. I dried myself with a soft towel and went downstairs into the kitchen to make a cup of tea. My mum had just made a pot of tea after she had heard my dad come in and take his boots off in the utility room. It was dark outside, and it had started to drizzle. Dad had managed to collect all the bales and had stacked them in the store shed.

'Aaaah, we couldn't have timed that any better.' said my dad looking pleased with myself.

'So, you have finished loading them?' confirmed mum.

'Yeah, now we need to start getting the winter barley in,' dad said yawning. He looked exhausted, so I decided to call it a night. I bid good night to my parents, took my mug from the kitchen, and went off to my bedroom. I was ready for bed despite the fact I had slept until 3 pm. The previous evening out with Mags was still getting to me; therefore, as soon as I hit the pillow, I was out for the count.

It was a month before I saw Mags again; she had been working a row of days and nights due to some of the officers being on holiday.

Mags arranged to pick me for a night out at the station that day. Les, the events officer, had organized a standup comedian and a buffet, with a disco, that Saturday night. Mags had got a couple of tickets as soon as they had been available as these events were very popular, especially those hosted by a comedian for entertainment. I was looking forward to it, not having stepped out since the Christmas party at work, which turned into a total disaster, having come home to see Mick enjoying himself with the cock sucker of that woman he was with. To top it all off, the event was briefly followed by the horrendous accident that I had.

I was feeling more human but still had the odd twinge, but going to the pool and swimming more had certainly helped with it. I had no intention of going back to work until January; the hospital said that it would take a good year to resume my normal activities; I was only dreading having to face Mick back home in Surrey.

With the changing weather, the evenings had now turned chilly; autumn was here. I couldn't decide what to wear and wasn't ready when Mags came to pick me up. Seeing Mags coming up the drive, I made it straight to the door still dressed in my dressing down. Mags pulled up, and her smile faded instantly as she asked, 'Holly aren't you well?'

'No, I'm ok thanks, but I can't decide what to wear Mags.'

'Thank God for that,' said Mags sounding relieved.

'I've been looking forward to this since you told me about the show,' I told her excitedly. As Mags walked in, we went into my bedroom. I had all the clothes I had bought on the shopping trip many weeks ago on sprawled across my bed. Mags was wearing a pair of black jeans and a blue round-necked jumper with trainers. That made my decision much easier. I slipped on my black jeans and a coloured blouse, which now reminded me that since autumn was here, I needed to get some jumpers. I asked Mags to apply my makeup; I hadn't worn any since the accident I was a little out of practice. It was just over half an hour before I was ready. I grabbed my jacket and bag, and we walked out to the car, ready for our fun night out.

As Mags set off down the driveway and headed towards the main road, I wasn't sure whether it was appropriate to mention the bouquet of red roses I had received many weeks ago. I hesitated and decided to say nothing at this moment in time.

It was around seven-thirty pm when we arrived at the station, but this time Mags parked around the back of the station, and we walked to the front and punched in the combination numbers to access the door. The station seemed busy, with officers having to drag in underdressed drunks shouting abuse, oblivious to what they were doing. The drunks would be spending a night in the cells to sober up until the next morning, which would keep them away from being involved in brawls for their safety. As we came in through the entrance and started to climb the stairs to the social evening, we were whistled at.

'Come on, girls, I'll show you two a good time,' yelled a guy as he turned around to flash us by trying to pull his trousers down. Thankfully, he was stopped by one of the officers on duty who had pushed him back to the desk. Another shouted, 'Come on, darling, let me give you one,' as he gestured towards his pants.

As we were climbing the stairs, we could still hear those guys shouting rude comments until we pushed through the door to the corridor heading towards the social bar. There were several officers; some dressed for the occasion, and some still on duty as we passed down the corridor. We were acknowledged by some who stopped to chat and asked me how I was getting on. Some inquired how soon it would be before I left for my home in Surrey.

Then it hit me. I had been enjoying the time with my parents despite spending much of it cooped up in their house.

I didn't realize how much I had missed being in the open air and freedom, but even less so that I would not enjoy going back to Surrey at all. The thought about having to face Mick and my marital problems always made me tense. I still didn't know what I was supposed to do. Mick hadn't been in contact since that day he came up to explain, and the phone call I had heard. I just didn't know what to believe anymore, but I held on to my secrets.

When we opened the door into the social room, loud music from the '80s greeted us. The room had been set out with tables and chairs at the far end towards the right. The buffet was next to the bar with, and a makeshift stage stood in the middle of the room against the wall. The seating area was nearly full; we turned as we heard someone shouting to us; it was Tom. He had saved us a couple of seats. It was a relief knowing that I would not have to spend the rest of the night standing.

'What would you girls like to drink?' asked Tom.

'Oh, thanks, I'll have white wine please,' I smiled at him.

'I'll have orange juice with lemonade, please. Seeing that I'm driving,' said Mags. While Tom got a round of drinks in, we went over to the table where Tom's party had saved our seats. They were the same guys I had met the night I got drunk.

'I bet you had a bad head in the morning that night we saw you with Mags.' grinned John, who was sitting directly across me.

'Yeah, just a bit, but it was a good night seeing that I hadn't been out for months,' I replied, sounding I little embarrassed.

'Well, you certainly made up for it that night,' continued John. Tom came back with the tray of drinks. I took my jacket off, hung it on my chair, and I sat down next to Tom as he put the drinks on the table. The playlist ranged from the '60s to the '90s, but it was mainly the '80s unless someone put in a request. The buffet was to start at eight-thirty pm with the comedian going on around nine pm for an hour. Les's wife and daughter had put arranged the buffet as they ran a small catering business and helped Les out with the social events at cost price so he could find a good turnout for the entertainment.

The drinks started to flow, the spread was superb, and the comedian was hilarious as he picked on people in the audience. Luckily, we were near the back; if someone got up to go to the toilet, the comedian would point them out and make them as part of his act.

Once the comedian had finished his act, the disco ensued with beats from the '80s.

‘Come on you lot, let’s dance, Holly show us how it’s done,’ said Mags as she pulled me by my arm and dragged me to the dance floor. We were all on the dance floor dancing to the rhythm when the music changed to ‘The Latest Flame’ by Elvis. I felt relaxed as the wine loosened me up. I felt supple, and then I started a shuffle dance routine Mags and I used to do. Mags picked up on this and joined in, causing the other dancers to scatter as we moved to the beat. I assume we had taken the watchers by surprise, and the guys with us started to shout and whistle.

I felt terrific; the wine must have numbed any pain as I gave my dance my all and kicked and twisted my legs. Mags couldn’t keep up with me, and I finished the steps myself. I noticed Tom had been staring at me in astonishment and then heard him commenting to John about how fit I was. Once the music changed tempo, everyone applauded me for the additional entertainment.

The music then changed to a mellow song, and couples flooded the dance floor.

'Come on, Holly, let's share a smooch,' said Tom.

'Let me just have a drink first,' I said as I gulped down more wine. Tom had his arm around me, which reminded me that Mick was the last man to have his arms around me. I felt a sense of closeness which I had missed all this time, it was comforting, but it felt different. Tom's arms felt tight around me as I rested my head on his chest and heard his heartbeat. His chin rested on my head, and our feet were synced in time to the slow music despite the drinks we had consumed. I felt safe as were no spark there like there was with Mick. The music stopped, but Tom still held me as if he did not want to let me go.

The music changed to 'Lets Twist' by Bill Halley and the Comets. Mags was twisting with John as I went to sit down. I saw another drink that had been bought for me.

God, how many had I had? I couldn't remember. I didn't want to be as wasted as I was the last time I was out. I needed to sober up and get some water.

I walked up to go to the bar for a glass of water; the bar was heaving with people. I had to squeeze between officers standing with drinks already in hand. As I pushed through, comments came out saying I had put on a good show with the dancing and that I was looking well since the accident. I seemed to be getting the impression that I was the gossip at the station, whether this was a good thing or not. I would have to have a word with Mag to see if she had heard anything.

It was almost one am, and people had been leaving since around midnight. The music had slowed to a smooch with a few couples on the dance floor. Tom tried to get me on the dance floor for another smooch, but I had sobered up a little and thought it would be better to stop before things got out of hand. I was already the talk of the town, it seemed.

Mags was driving me home, and on the way, I asked her if there was any gossip about me at the station.

'What makes you think there is gossip about you, Holly?' she asked in a surprised voice.

'Well, I went to the bar for some water, and a few people were asking me about the accident and the physio.'

'Well, you know what it was like the first night here. Questions were being asked, and that's all. There's nothing to worry about Holly, but I do think Tom has a bit of a crush on you,' said Mags.

'Mmm yeah, I think you're right there; he was quite persistent about smooching.'

'Yes, and I noticed that as well, and he doesn't know that you're married,' added Mags smirking.

'No, I'll have to be careful,' I felt a bit paranoid with everything going on at the moment.

I thanked Mags for the night out; it had been another excellent night, and I had enjoyed every minute I could because, at some point, I would be going back home to Surrey, not knowing what I was going to do.

It was a little after nine am when I woke up and looked at the clock on the side of the bed. I turned over to lay flat on my back, and God I ached all over, I must have put too much effort in the dance routine last night, but it was worth it; I hadn't done it for a while.

Sunday was a regular working day at the farm; it was a 24/7 routine because there was livestock to feed and check on, cows to milk, and eggs to collect. I decided to have a hot soak in the jacuzzi to allow my body a massage with the bubbles to soothe the aches from last night's dance. I started to think about Mick; I still hadn't heard from since that day he showed up, and I confronted him about the conversation he had on the phone. I didn't know whether it would be fruitful to confront him face to face and if I should catch a train to Surrey to talk to him undisturbed. I would first phone him to arrange a meeting.

The house was empty; my mum was out helping my dad with the livestock, so I decided to call Mick. It was nearly ten-thirty am; after a few rings, I heard him say, 'DCI Inspector Sheppard speaking,' I knew then he had gotten the promotion he had been waiting for. I didn't speak for a few seconds, taken back by his formal work voice.

'Hello, hello, hello? Who is this?' Mick raised his voice over the phone.

'It's me, Holly,' I said, and there was a pause on the other end of the line. Mick wasn't expecting me to contact him, it seemed. I had rung him on the landline as I knew my mobile number would come up on his phone.

'Hello, my darling! What a nice surprise to hear from you. How are you?' replied Mick, a little surprised and lost for words.

'We need to talk but not over the phone. I thought I would come down on the train so that we can talk without any interruptions, Mick.' I said bluntly, yet calmly.

'Ok, if that is what you want, but I could come up and pick you up if you like,' said Mick offering me the option.

'No, I'll come on the train, and you can pick me up at the train station.' I insisted.

'Alright, my love,' he finally said. 'When are you planning to come?'

'I've got physio on Friday morning, so I'll come down after that.'

'Just let me know the time, and I'll be there,' Mick said.

'Ok. I'll text you the time when I'm on my way.' I bit my lip. I kind of missed him a little.

'Love you, Holly,' I heard him say before ending the call.

My appointment at the physio was at 10 am, and my mum dropped me off with my overnight bag. It was a short walk to the train station, where I would catch the eleven-thirty am train to Kings Cross and switch a few trains until I ended at the Surrey Quayside station.

It was evening by the time I arrived; Mick was waiting with the bustle of people going about their business, not interested in anyone, focused entirely on their goal to get home. God, what had I come back to? Mick stepped out of the car; he was wearing jeans, a shirt, and a bomber jacket that looked rather flattering on him. His blonde curly hair was longer, and he had not shaved his stubble. Man, he looked sexy, but could I forgive him? Maybe this woman was a one-off in the line of duty. I didn't know. Mick looked up as I approached him and opened his arms out wide to give me a hug and a peck on the cheek.

'God, I've missed you, darling! You're looking well Northern air must be doing you some good.' Mick kissed me again with a hug. I wanted to snog his face off as I missed the intimacy we had together, but I still remembered that woman sucking his cock. I kissed him lightly on the lips, but Mick took hold of me and pressed his lips harder against mine. I started to melt into his embrace. It had been nearly ten months.

We drove back to the house, the place where it had all started. The house was still the same outside; the trees nearby held leaves the shades of yellows and browns which they dropped now and then. It seemed winter was well on its way. At least it wasn't snowing and freezing cold as it had been the last time I was here,

Mick went in first, carrying my overnight bag. I hesitated at the door before I took a step in and looked around to observe if there had been any changes. I was most interested in the signs of a woman 's presence in the house since I had been away, but it seemed exactly the same as when I had left.

'Would you like a drink Holly? Mick turned towards me and smiled.

'Yes, please,' as I walked into the living room, I could smell perfume- or was it air freshener? I was starting to get paranoid again. I walked around the living room while Mick made the drinks in the kitchen. I started poking and lifting things up, as though I was on a case doing a forensic examination on a crime scene. Mick came through with two mugs of coffee and handed one to me; he asked if

I wanted to go out for a meal or have a takeaway meal. I had enough for one day, so take away it was. I hadn't had one for over a year, so I thought it would be nice for a change.

'I'll order it now then if you like,' said Mick.

'Yes, that's fine.'

It was after nine pm by the time we had eaten the meal. Mick cleared up the table and then brought back an opened bottle of wine from the chiller.

'You are still drinking wine on your own, then?' I blurted out to test him.

'Yeah, it helps me to wind down after a difficult day,' was all he said. Mick poured me a large glass of wine; I took a couple of deep gulps from the glass. I was starting to relax, and Mick switched on some soft music as he gulped some down as well. He was acting as though we were meeting again for the first time, and he struggled with what to say. As we drank the wine, however, both of us started to loosen up.

I started to talk about my night out with Mags at the station where we listened to a comedian, had a buffet and danced at the disco. I told him the event had been completely sold out. Mick brought another bottle of wine and filled my glass again; I was starting to get sexually aroused. It must have been the wine and Mick's presence. I inched in closer to him; his hand stroked the back of my neck, leaving me more aroused. God, it had been a long time. I put my hand on his leg and faced him, so our eyes met.

'Holly, I love you so much. I've missed you,' whispered Mick as he kissed me. Mick moved his hand around my waist and drew me towards him. I moved over to straddle him and took hold of his belt, releasing it to get the button on his jeans. Mick moved quickly, kissing my neck while he unbuttoned my blouse to reveal my black lacy bra. He was kissing me across my breast while he unhooked my bra; my breasts were bare in no time, revealing my hard nipples. He leaned onto them and sucked them, then pressed my breasts together to squeeze them. God, I had missed this. We'd have to talk in the morning.

Mick picked me up and took me upstairs to the bedroom, not forgetting to grab the bottle of wine before we climbed the stairs. We were half undressed by the time we were in the bedroom; it was exactly like when we had first met and had passionate sex. I had missed this intimacy.

It was late before we stirred the following morning, Mick had his arm over me, and his left leg was over mine, tightly snuggled around me. I started to stir and turned on my back; Mick was already wide awake and had been watching me, it seemed. He started kissing me, then straddled over me to kiss my neck, massage my breasts, and run his lips down to my hard nipples waiting to be sucked. The flicking of his tongue aroused me yet again; I could feel him hard, his length pressing on my thigh. I parted my legs to receive him.

He slid almost effortlessly; I was wet with lust, and I wanted more and more of him. I lifted my legs to receive more of him inside of me as he squeezed harder on my breasts. He moaned with pleasure and pushed harder and harder; he had never pushed this hard before, and he moved me upright as he did. He was done soon, and he rolled off me and headed towards the bathroom. He closed the door behind him; I could hear the shower running.

I rolled over to see what time it was; it was after ten am; I decided I would get up while Mick was in the shower and make some toast and coffee. I slipped on a long tee shirt and made my way downstairs into the kitchen. Mick had left his phone on the side in the kitchen, and I heard it ping to announce that a text had come through. I glanced down at the phone out of curiosity; the name Mia popped up.

What the actual fuck?! Why had he got her name on his phone? I felt like a complete mess; we had sex last night despite the fact we had a bit to drink, and I wanted it to rekindle our intimacy and the pleasures. But had he also been waiting all this time, or was I a means to an end? I just didn't know.

I finished preparing breakfast and took it upstairs. Mick had finished showering and was now dressed in a pair of jeans and a black jumper.

'Oh, I was just coming downstairs,' he said. He took a mug of coffee off the tray along with a toast and kissed me on the lips.

'Mick, why don't you come back to bed? We've got all day.' I asked, sounding disappointed.

'I wish I could, but I have to pop down to the station and check on a couple of things with what's going on at the moment.' replied Mick sounding as though he had something on his mind.

'Oh, how long will you be? We need to talk. I haven't come all this way for nothing.' I said, sounding a little pissed off at this point.

'I know. It's work, and I have more responsibilities now that I have my new promotion.' Mick was already heading for the door. 'I should not be too long. We can talk once I am back.' And with that, he was gone.

I dumped the tray on the bedside table with a thud, which caused a piece of toast to fall off the plate and bounce under the bed. I crouched down to pick it up and was shocked to find a red lacy bra under the bed. I dragged it out; it was definitely not mine, and it wasn't my size. My heart started sinking again, the same way it had when I had seen him with the woman. Did he have her stay over while I had been recuperating? No wonder he hasn't been up to visit me. Mick had been making a fool of me. Was I that naïve? Regardless, I now had evidence to confront him, the lying bastard. I wasn't going to be made a fool of, and I packed my bags. I would go back home, see a solicitor, and file for a divorce. I had had enough. I needed to get away from this unfaithful man and this toxic relationship.

CHAPTER FIVE:

I had a quick shower before leaving the house. While I was drying myself, I noticed long black strands of hair in the hairbrush on the shelf next to the washbasin. No, this couldn't be real; with the bra and now the strands of hair in the brush, Mick had tipped me over the edge. There was no way they could be mine; the color was so different, and I had been away for a long time.

I suddenly felt that I had been used last night by my own husband. I had missed the intimacy and thought that Mick had too. But with the newly-found evidence of a woman having been in my home while I was recuperating at my parents' home, I was beyond angry. I left a note on the bed with the bra and hairbrush for my lying bastard of a husband to see, and then I left the house for the train station. I was just in time to catch the one pm train back home. Mick just didn't know when to stop lying to me-why was he doing this? Well, that woman could happily have him. I could not stand that lying piece of shit anymore anyway.

It was a long journey home, and I needed to talk to Mags, but I knew that she and Tony were on holiday for two weeks in Spain. I couldn't confide in Debs with her and Pete working at the same station as Mick. I would have to wait until Mags got back from her holidays. I rang my mum to pick me up from the train station; she was surprised to hear from me as she wasn't expecting me to come back for another day.

As the train headed into the station, I could see my mum waiting for me in the car parking; it was just after eight pm. I dragged my small suitcase on wheels across the station platform, and as soon as I saw mum walking towards me, tears started streaming down my face. I couldn't hold it all back any longer and needed to talk to someone about it. Watching me burst into tears, mum put her arm around me and hugged me, but said nothing. Obviously, she knew it must be about Mick, seeing I had come back earlier than I had planned. We walked back to the car, and I threw my suitcase in the back seat of the car as I got into the front seat. I waited for my mum to start the engine, but she didn't.

'It's Mick. He's married to his job, isn't he, Holly?' asked my mum sympathetically.

'Well, yes, but there's more to it than his job; he's been caught on the job, so to speak,' I said, sobbing some more. Mum went quiet as she stared at me in disbelief.

'Hm. Do you know her?' she finally asked.

'No, he said it was a case that he was on, and it just happened. First, he said it had just happened that one time and it was a mistake, but last night I found a bra under the bed and long black strands of hair in the hairbrush.' I buried my face in my hands. 'When I first walked into the house, I thought I could smell perfume, but dismissed it as it could be just the air freshener in the room but no, mum.' I sniffed and wiped my face with hands.

'Have you spoken to him about it?' mum questioned, lost in thought.

'No, he had to go to the station this morning to sort something out and would be back later. Oh, and also, while he was in the shower, I went downstairs to make some breakfast. He had left his phone on the kitchen table, and a text came through from someone named Mia. I wished I had read it now; oh mum, I don't know what to do, mum.' I bet I sounded frustrated.

'Well, love, you'll have to speak to him at some stage, or you will never get to the bottom of it. Not only that, you will soon be going back to work, won't you, dear?' My mum slowly ran her fingers through my hair.

‘I’m dreading it, mum. I know work has been very good to me, still paying me my full salary, but I don’t know.’

‘Well, you’re lucky in that sense, but you need to sort it, or you will get suffer from recurrent nervous breakdowns, Holly.’ Mum sighed and started the car, then reversed and backed out from the space. We set off for home.

As soon as we got home, I went straight to my room. I closed the door behind me, leaving my bag aside, and lay on the bed, weeping my heart out. It was after ten pm, and I still had no texts from Mick ever since I had left that day.

I realized that I needed a shower. My long curly hair took ages to dry if I didn’t use the hairdryer. I had no more tears to shed, and the shower had freshened me up, making me feel human again. I had to start planning which way to go, and I needed to pull myself together to do so.

After drying my hair, I slipped on a dressing gown and began plodding off into the kitchen to make myself a drink. Mum and dad were in the living room watching TV. I didn't know if mum had told dad about the problems I was having with Mick, but mum wasn't one to say a lot. She usually, more or less, let me get on with it, which suited me as I didn't really like discussing things in detail. I had to wait nearly two weeks for Mags to come back from her holiday.

'Mick. I am going to start pushing your buttons, and we'll see what you have to say about this.' I texted him the word *DIVORCE* in capital letters; that was sure to stir him up. I then switched the phone off and went to bed; *I bet he'll respond to that*, I thought.

The next morning, I asked mum if I could use the car because I wanted to go into the town. She said she didn't need it. I picked up my bag but left my phone behind as I jumped into the car. It was my first time behind the wheel since my accident less than a year ago. I was feeling a bit strange since it had been a while I had driven a 4x4; I'd only been driving my Ford Fiesta.

Parking in London was scarce, so having a small car was more practical to maneuver the tightest parking spots. I was used to driving my dad's Land Rover and farm vehicles before I met Mick, though. I had also done a bit of grass track racing with my cousin, winning many races as I had the knack of speeding around a bumpy track and making the car slide around the corners at speed.

I was like an adrenalin junky, always getting a thrill from speeding and letting all my aggression out. I supposed it still had a bit of that spark left in me, which came out from time to time. Racing off from the traffic signals when

I had someone in a flash sport number pull up alongside me waiting to go, straining at the light to change, was a delight. I was always the one to set off first, but they would catch up soon with their four litre engines.

I rested my back against the seat comfortably, making my way down the farm drive. It almost felt like riding a bike, bringing back good memories of my tracking days. It was Sunday, and some of the big shops were open, but I had to drive twenty-five miles to the main city. Parking was easy, with the shopping center being on the outskirts of the city.

I parked and sighed to myself; I needed some retail therapy. I hit the shops, just browsing, trying to decide what to buy. I had put on a little more weight since I had moved in with my parents and was looking healthier. I was not looking forward to rejoining work from January, as people would ask me questions about Mick, and how had he been coping without me while I had been recuperating at my parents'. Well - what they didn't know was that he was coping quite alright with that woman, who was probably sucking him every night, the slag.

I had flexed the credit card that Mick had given me when we first got married, and he paid all the dues with no questions asked. However, I used it wisely, not spending unnecessarily. I had always been like that since I started my first job straight out of college. I never bought expensive clothes and always looked for a bargain. Why pay a hundred pounds for one item when you could buy three different items for the same amount of money?

It was after five pm before I got back from my shopping spree. As I drove up the farm driveway, I noticed Mick's car parked outside the house. The bastard had obviously read my text, and that must have given him a wakeup call.

Parking the vehicle, I took out my shopping from the boot and took the bags into the house. Mick rushed to greet me, helping me with my bags of spoils, but I pushed him away.

'So, you got my text then?' I said bluntly.

'Holly, you have got it all wrong, nothing is going on,' Mick said in a persuasive tone.

'We'll have this conversation in my room,' I announced, and we both walked into my bedroom, where I dumped my shopping on the floor.

I sat on the bed, waiting for Mick to explain, he started to rub the back of his neck with his hand, which was quite normal given the situation he was in. He paced up and down the room, not knowing where to start.

'I'll tell you what? I'll give you enough time to think about what you're going to say while I go and make some coffee.' I stood up to walk off towards the door, leaving an agitated Mick behind.

Mum was in the kitchen; she had already made the coffee and was just about to ask if we would like some. She didn't say anything as she didn't want to interfere, which I was pleased about as I was uptight as it was; it was my problem to sort out.

I took the mugs into my room, handing one over to Mick, who was still pacing up and down, rubbing his hand on the back of his neck. 'Well, I'm waiting for answers,' I said in anger.

Mick started. 'I've had a couple of friends round, Dave and Jo, to stop over for a while, they were waiting to buy a house- they had already sold theirs and didn't want to pay rent, so I offered them to stay in our house until they were sorted. They only moved out a couple of days before you came up, and they used our bedroom because it was the largest of the three. I didn't have time to tidy up before you came because of work.' He continued. 'One of Jo's bras must have fallen under the bed, and she must have been using the hairbrush in the bathroom,' said Mick sounding convincing.

'Oh, how come I don't know this couple you are talking about? I asked.

'Dave and Jo came to the station soon after you had your accident, so I helped them out thinking that I wouldn't have an empty house to come home to,' added Mick seeing I was buying it.

'Alright. so, what is Dave and Jo's surname?' I asked Mick.

'Err *Jones,'* said Mick.

'Wow, how original.' my voice was laced with sarcasm.

'No, really,' said Mick sounding desperate.

'I don't believe you, Mick; it's not working between us. You are married to your job; you've only been up twice, which includes this visit. The first time around, I caught you talking to your slag on the phone while I was recuperating and still in pain. How can this work? I don't know what to think anymore.'

'Listen, Holly, we can work this out, you know I want to start a family with you,' said Mick. I went quiet for a moment. I was hiding a secret; *Do I tell him now or leave it until I go back home*? No, I was going to ask Mags to find out about this couple who Mick said had been living with him.

'I will be coming home after the New Year, and I would feel better if you find somewhere else to live until we sort this out for good.' I sighed.

'I'll do anything you want, Holly.' Mick said earnestly.

'Ok, are you staying the night in the spare room, or are you going home tonight? I asked him.

'I'll go,' replied Mick feeling a bit deflated at my suggestion of the spare room.

'Would you like another coffee before you go?' I asked in a robotic tone.

'No, thanks. I'll start now so I can reach home before it gets too late,' he said.

I walked him to the door and kissed him on the cheek, but Mick grabbed hold of me around the waist and kissed me on the lips softly. He whispered to me that he loved me. While releasing me and walking towards his car, he said, 'I'll see you in New Year; this is sensitive and complicated, but this is us, Holly.' said Mick. He started his car and waved to me before driving off down the drive to who knows where.

I was feeling stronger physically and mentally for the first time since nearly a year ago. I still did not know where to turn, though. I needed Mags help to find the truth out about the couple in question. Mags had to work a couple of shifts when she came back from her holiday with Tony. I was desperate to talk to her and give her an update on Mick.

Mags also had some news to tell me. She arranged to pick me up on Saturday evening. We decided that we would go to the pub instead of the social club at the station for a change. We used to go to the Dog & Duck on the outskirts of the town, and as we began heading that way, Mags started to tell me that she and Tony had set a date to get married; they weren't even engaged. It was going to be on the twelfth of April next year. I was pleased for her and just hoped she wouldn't experience what I was going through after marrying into the police force. There wasn't much time left as coming up was the end of October.

'You're not preggers, are you, Mag?' I asked.

'No, don't be draft; I need my career first, then the kids,' said Mags with her eyes fixed on the road, suppressing her smile.

The pub was heaving, so we had to wait until someone left their seat to go. It was an hour before we were seated; luckily, it was in the corner with a bit of privacy. I had an orange juice; I wanted a clear head. Approaching the subject of kids, I asked Mags if she had planned on having any.

'Well, we both haven't really thought about it, but we'll see how it goes.' she shrugged.

'Mm well, there's something I need to tell you, Mags, and you're the first to know, not even my mum knows.' I played with my fingers as I tried to choose my words carefully.

'Gosh, this sounds serious,' said Mags alarmed.

'It depends on how you feel about it, I suppose. You know Mick and I have had arguments about starting a family, and I told him that I wasn't ready. Well, I don't have a choice now. When I was in the hospital in that mess, they ran some tests, which show that I will not be able to have children. Having that reality check and being told that I can't bear any children,' I continued slowly, 'I'm just gutted that I don't have that option.'

'Holly, I'm so sorry,' said Mags rubbing my hand. 'Does Mick know about this?'

'No. I requested the doctors and nurses not to say anything to anyone, so you're the only one who knows.'

'I don't know what to say,' was all that Mags could say, as she looked at me empathetically.

'Don't feel pity for me, Mags. I'll get over it.' I struggled to smile.

I went to the bar for another round of drinks before approaching the subject of Mick. Mags chatted about their holiday, how Tony had proposed to her and decided that they should get married as soon as possible. I finally brought up the subject of Mick, my findings during my trip to Surrey, and the excuses he had come up with.

'Mags, could you do me a big favor and find out about this so-called couple he was supposed to have staying with him? I was still undecided despite the sex I had with him that night. I wasn't sure until I find some information on this couple, whether to stay or divorce him.' Mags nodded and promised she would make some discreet inquiries to find out if there is a Dave Jones based at Mick's station.

It was just after eleven pm when we left the pub; some of the drinkers were heading to the night club further into the town center, but I wasn't in the mood for clubbing and was ready to go home.

Halloween had come around, but Les wasn't organizing a Halloween party since he was away with his wife on holiday for two weeks. Mags wasn't working either, so we wondered where to find a party. The Dog and Duck was having a Halloween Party open to the public, with no tickets to buy. We agreed that we would go there, but would stop at the station first for a quick drink.

'What are you dressing up as, Mags?'

'Mm not sure. I thought both of us could dress like a couple of sexy devils, in black short dresses and suspenders with the full makeup. What do you think? Or is that too much for you with what's going on?' asked Mags.

'No sod it, I need to let my hair down and have some fun.' I grinned.

'Right then, that's settled. We'll have to get to the fancy-dress shop in town to look for the dresses. If not, I know other places too.' Mags looked excited.

Mags came up trumps with the costumes; she had found a fancy-dress shop with a good selection to choose from; both of us ended up choosing short black dresses with slight adjustments in places and room to show a bit of cleavage. I needed to get a push-up bra for the maximum effect; Mags was good in that department, having D cups.

Halloween eve came around soon, and it was time for the party. Mags wasn't on shift for the next four days, and she had offered that I stay over at her place for the night so we wouldn't have to drive and could get wasted. Mum drove me over to Mags flat, where we both got ready to go out. I brought a bottle of wine with me so we could start out with a bit of Dutch courage.

Mags had booked the taxi to pick us at eight pm; the driver honked right on time.

'Well, here goes nothing,' I muttered, stepping out of Mags's flat feeling rather intoxicated, with an 'I don't care attitude;' I was going to have some fun. We heard a few whistles from down the road as we opened the car door.

'You ladies won't have to use your magic on me-I'm under your spell already,' someone said from behind the wheel; we were giggling as we got in and instructed the driver to drive us to the police station.

'Oh, I didn't mean anything by the naughty comment girls; I'm sorry,' said the driver.

'We'll let you off this time,' said Mags.

'Alright, ladies where to?'

'The police station that's where we are going, honestly,' I said seriously now.

'Mm, they will probably lock you two in the cells, looking like that. No guy will be safe with you two roaming like that,' said the driver.

‘I hope so,’ I said, grinning at him through the mirror from the back seat of the taxi.

We paid the driver after he had dropped us off at the police station, we were whistled at as we went through the front door. Luckily there weren’t any unsavory guys waiting to be processed, only the desk sergeant with his eyes popping out of his head. He gave us a whistle of an acknowledgement as we turned to go upstairs to the bar. Pushing through the door to the bar, not having a care in the world, I was feeling good; the wine we had drunk before coming out had started the night. Whooping appreciation and whistles came from the bar area as we walked in. Tom and John were standing at the bar, wearing jeans and white shirts. They bought us each a drink, and we all headed across to a table to sit down.

‘Hey, sexy ladies, where are you heading tonight? asked Tom with his tongue hanging out.

'Oh, just a Halloween Party at the Dog & Duck pub, you don't need tickets to get in,' Mags shrugged and sipped her drink.

'What do you think, John? I think these sexy ladies need escorting for the night,' said Tom.

'They sure do,' sniggered John.

We phoned for a taxi from the station. Mags and I had the guys escorting us to the Dog & Duck. The cab drew up outside the door of the pub, and Tom quickly jumped out of the car to open my door. Upon reaching, Mags slid across and climbed out unaided, but John was there in case she needed him to lean on. Tom wriggled his arm around my waist, holding me close as he pushed the pub door open, with Mags and John following behind. The pub was heaving with colours from different Halloween costumes, heavy makeup, and people disguised to the point of no recognition.

Mags couldn't recognize anyone in their costumes. As we tried to approach the bar, random guys were touching our backsides, making rude comments. Tom started showing his horns by being protective towards me; he was getting too close for my liking, so I tried to escape his side by making my way to the ladies' toilets. Mags stayed with the guys at the bar, waiting for the drinks. I kept pushing through while I was being touched and slapped until I reached the toilets. I was hot with the number of people in the pub; luckily, I wasn't wearing anything that covered me totally. I sat on the loo for a few moments after peeing as my feet were aching a bit.

Once I was through, I washed my hands and readjusted my hair, wiping the eyeliner around my eyes that was beginning to smudge in the heat. As I stepped out of the door, a hand took hold of mine, ushering me towards the back door of the pub; it was a tall guy dressed in a Count Dracula costume. I started to giggle, thinking, *what the hell? I'm going to have some fun.* He opened the back door, a low light casting a shadow over us as we stood close to the wall. He put his finger to my lips, lowering his head closer as though he was going to kiss me.

'Holly, you are the love of my life,' he whispered, and then he kissed me softly on the lips. Then he slowly kissed me down my neck. I felt like a bolt of lightning had just gone through me. God, this guy had some touch, making me come alive. He looked in my eyes, and I could make out his eyes behind the makeup- they were beautiful, brown with long eyelashes. He kissed me again with the same passion. With my eyes closed, I was savored this moment with him.

I put my arms around his neck, but he stopped me, pulling away, muttering he had to go. I opened my eyes, and he was gone already. Gosh, who was that guy? He made me tingle; his touch was so soft, his kiss, and those eyes? I needed to meet him again. But who was he? He knew my name. I was going nuts.

'Where the hell have you been? We've been looking for you,' said Tom coming down the corridor heading for the ladies toilets.

'Oh, I had to queue for the loo.' I lied. I was still besotted with Count Dracula.

The music was excellent, and with the right music, Mags and I started dancing to our routine, parting the dance floor. We heard wolf whistles and rude, sexist comments, while Tom and John looked on feeling a bit lost. I knew Tom was waiting for a smooch; he was like a moth drawn to a candle. After the dance, we needed a drink, but this time it had to be a glass of ice-cold water. We gulped it down, ready for another.

It was getting late, well after midnight and the pub was starting to thin out. The music changed to a slow tempo, and on cue, Tom grabbed me around the waist, taking me onto the dance floor, he embraced me. His grip tightened as Mags and John looked on from the side. Tom kissed the top of my head while we were dancing, holding me close as he didn't want to let me go. I looked up to him to say something but was stopped when he kissed me. It was hard, wet, and felt forced, and I pushed him away, telling him I was married.

'I'm sorry, Holly, I fancy you,' said Tom looking abashed.

'It can't happen. Don't ruin your career, you know the force frowns on adultery, and it will stop your prospects for promotion. I will be going back to Surrey in the New Year, so we'll forget this ever happened,' I said, and Tom agreed reluctantly. With that, we both walked off the dance floor to join Mags and John.

We all left the pub, where a taxi was waiting for us; we were dropped off first at Mags's flat, leaving the guys to pay.

'I noticed you and Tom were getting a bit close,' smirked Mags as she opened the door to her flat.

'Mm, I had to nip that in the bud. I told him I was married, that he shouldn't ruin his career in the force, and that we should forget that this ever happened,' I filled her in.

'Then what did he say?' Mags asked.

'He was a bit reluctant, but he agreed.' I didn't mention the mystery man to Mags, the one who had been kissing me outside, sending a bolt of lightning through me. I could not shake off his touch and deep-set eyes.

The following morning, I felt a bit sick from the previous evening. Mags was still asleep. It was seven, and the air was damp. It must have started raining soon after we had got in. I got up to make coffee, trying not to disturb Mags. She only had one bedroom, and neither of us was fussy about sharing a bed; we used to do it when we were kids, so what was the difference now? I made a mug of coffee for Mags, took it into the bedroom, and left it next to her side of the bed on the table. Whether she would be awake to drink it or not was another question. As I was getting back into the bed, Mag stirred, asking me what the time was.

'It's just after 7 am,' I said, sipping on the coffee.

'Bloody hell. Holly, don't you ever have a lay in after a night out?' Mags commented as she turned over, snuggling under the quilt.

I was feeling a bit sick, that's why I am up, not because I want to.' I frowned.

'Well, don't be sick in the bed then,' said Mags.

'Yeah, thanks for the vote of confidence, Mags.'

She smiled and dozed off again, and I sat there, sipping my coffee, thinking about the mysterious stranger who I had met last night. Each time I thought about him, it sent a shiver down my spine. I couldn't wait to meet him again. What if he was my secret admirer? The thought stirred something inside me. I had to find him, and soon.

CHAPTER SIX:

It was after one pm when Tony arrived at Mags's flat; he had been working night shifts, as he didn't need as much sleep as Mags did.

'I'll give my mum a ring to come and pick me up, Mags,' I said.

'No, I'll take you home, Holly. I've got my car outside,' Tony offered.

'Oh no, I don't want to put you out,' I said, slightly embarrassed.

'No problem,' said Tony shrugging. Uttering goodbye to Mags, I headed down to the car. Tony seemed happy, despite a 12-hour shift. I asked him about the wedding plans and where they were going for their honeymoon. Tony was really chuffed about getting married to Mags, as he was talking about her nonstop, and I couldn't get a word in. I felt a little jealous as I was thinking of getting a divorce. But at least it showed he was deeply in love with her and I was happy for them.

Within half an hour, I was home. My mum and dad were in and have just had their Sunday roast. Both were in the living room with dad in the recliner, taking a nap and mum knitting. The TV was on, but no one was paying any attention to it.

'Hi mum,' I said as I entered the room. 'I'm going to make a drink, would you like one?'

'No, thank you, dear. Your dad and I have just had our dinner; we didn't know if you would be back, so I've plated dinner up for you if you want it,' she looked at me as she spoke.

'Yeah, thanks, mum, I'll probably have it later.'

'Did you have a good night, sweetie?' she asked. I shouted from the kitchen, 'Yes, thanks, mum, it was great.'

After that, I didn't see Mags until Christmas. She was working extra shifts to cover up for sick leaves, but luckily, she was off, though Tony wasn't home for Christmas. We arranged to meet on Christmas Eve, and mum drove me to the station where we met up; I would be getting a taxi home so Mags could have a drink. It had been snowing, but the roads were clear, although they were due to freeze later.

The station was decorated with Christmas decorations and loads of tinsel everywhere. A huge artificial Christmas tree had been put up at the entrance of the reception area of the station, and Tinsel was lining the bannisters of the stairs going up to the social club room. We could hear muffled sounds of Christmas songs from the social room. Les and his wife had put on a small buffet and a disco, which had been financed from the proceeds from previous events throughout the year.

The room was heaving, people laughing, frolicking with Christmas kisses under the mistletoe. I couldn't see Tom and Jon, so I asked Mags if they were coming. She said that they were asked to cover for over the Christmas period. Just as well with what had happened on the Halloween night at the Dog and Duck. I was relieved as I hadn't seen Tom since that night, and it would be a little embarrassing meeting up again.

'What are you drinking, Mags?' I asked her before heading to the bar.

'Err, I think I'll have red wine seeing its Christmas,' replied Mags.

I thought I would have the same; I had always gone with white, possibly because Mick did, and I just went with the flow. Yes, I definitely needed a change of drink. After a few hello's and Christmas kisses, we settled down at a table right at the back of the room, away from the disco speakers.

I asked Mags if she had found anything out about Mick's fictitious lodgers Dave and Jo.

'Well,' said Mags thoughtfully, 'It doesn't make any sense; there is someone called Dave Jones, and his wife is called Jo, but when they came to the station, they moved straight into police accommodation before they bought their own place.'

'The lying bastard, I just knew it. You didn't find anything out about the woman called Mia?' I clenched my teeth; I knew he was lying.

'No,' Mags shook her head. 'but you did mention that you thought she could be an Italian with the accent.'

'Yes, why?'

'Well, by what I did find out is that the drugs squad are after several Italians organizations, dealing in drugs coming into the country- it's strange she is Italian.'

'Mm, do you think Mick was telling the truth that it was work-related and he'd overstepped the mark, Mags?'

'I don't know what to say, Holly,' replied Mags.

I knocked back the red wine, 'Mm not bad, would you like another, Mags?'

'I'll get these,' said Mags taking the glasses.

'No, you won't. You have done enough for me, Mags. You are a true friend.' I grabbed her glass as she took her last mouthful and put the glass on the table. The bar was full of people holding their drinks. It sometimes annoyed me when they stood there in the way when you needed to get to the bar. Eventually, I got served by Les, who eyes me up and down.

'Hello, Holly, we're seeing a bit more of you these days, are you totally recovered now?' asked Les.

'Yes, thanks, Les. I'll be going back home to Surrey after the New Year.' I smiled back at him.

‘So, how’s Mick been coping all this time without you?’ he mused.

I had to sound upbeat in how I answered him not to show that there were cracks in our marriage. ‘Er ok, he’s surviving since he got his promotion. He’s on a sensitive case, so he tells me, but I haven’t got long to go before I see him again.’ Paying for the drinks, I picked them up and quickly made to across to the table before Les asked me any more questions.

‘Phew that was close,’ I said to Mags as I reached the table.

‘Why? What was he saying?’ asked Mags.

‘He was asking about me if I am totally recovered, and if Mick was missing me, I told him I was going back after the New Year and quickly wrapped it up before he could ask me any more questions.’

'Good, you need to watch what you say to him. He likes a good gossip,' warned Mags, and after a brief pause, she continued, 'Do you think you are going to go through with it then, Holly?'

'I still don't know, but I can't live like this Mags.' After that, I changed to the subject of her wedding and where she was up to with it.

'Well..' she said, 'I was going to ask you about that. We're thinking of going to Las Vegas to get married and about asking a few family and friends to come- how would you feel coming with us, Holly?' she asked me.

'Wow that's different, will it still be legal then?' I asked her, surprised.

'Of course, it is. A lot of couples do it now,' she explained.

‘Mm, well, why not? I’ve always wanted to go to Las Vegas.’ I started nodding as she filled me in with the details.

It was just after eleven-thirty pm before I got home and was still sober for a change. It must be the red wine; I was starting over in a number of ways, it seemed. The roads were slippery with a light covering of snow; the forecast predicted heavy snow for the next couple of days, and I was glad to be home as memories of that evening were coming back.

It was Christmas Day; I turned over in my bed, opening one eye to see what time it was. It was eight am and was still dark, the heating was on, and I could hear my mum in the kitchen. I got up to have a quick shower. After getting dressed in a pair of jeans and a jumper, I made my way into the kitchen.

'Happy Christmas, my dear,' said mum as she saw me coming down.

'Yeah, happy Christmas, mum,' I said, hugging her from behind. 'I'm going to make coffee would you like a cup?'

'No, thanks, love. I'm going out in a minute to help your dad; the water pipes are frozen outside, and the livestock needs water,' mum said.

'Oh, do you need a hand with anything then?'

'No, it's ok love, but you could give up a hand with the livestock if you feel up to it.'

'Yeah ok, I'll be with you in a few minutes, mum.' I started preparing the coffee.

Mum had still left my wellington boots in the utility room, along with my Barbour coat and scarf set. Pulling on all my gear, I headed out into the cold weather. I looked outside to see how the weather was; it seemed a snow blizzard had struck, and my dad had all the livestock inside, so defrosting the pipes wouldn't take too long. Opening the door, I instantly felt the cold wind gushing against my cheeks. As snow flurries blew into the house, I quickly shut the door, heading towards the cattle sheds where mum and dad were trying to defrost the water pipes.

They had already sorted the other sheds out, leaving only this one to do. This one was on a ball cock, and my dad was carefully running a gas burner over the pipe. The cattle were pushing each other, almost desperate for a drink; mum was keeping guard in case they decided to push dad over and trample on him over the water trough. The water began to drip, slowly and then faster until it was coming through at a normal pace. Mum and dad then had to let a few in to get to the water trough because if they didn't, they would all rush at it pushing each other and pushing the water trough over, breaking the pipe. It was about half an hour until all the cattle had a drink and were back to normal.

I went back to the house to make some tea in the meantime. As I got to the door, I noticed some footprints that seemed to be heading from the driveway, and hanging on the handle of the door was a bag containing a small box wrapped in glittery paper with a red bow. I picked it up as I walked in, shutting the door behind. I stood there and opened the box; there sat an expensive chain and a gold solid heart shape with rubies set in the middle. An inscription on the back said, 'With all my love,' but mentioned no name. This left me confused again.

I couldn't see Mick coming all this way up to drop it off without stopping; could it be Tom after the incident that happened at Halloween party? No, I couldn't see that either, but then something caught my attention in the box; there was a small card. It said, 'Happy Christmas darling, I will always love you- keep this next to your heart,' signed with the initial 'L.'

Oh, my God, who could this guy be? I wondered as my heart started to flutter with excitement, albeit slightly apprehensive at the same time. Taking my gear off and putting it back where I had found it, I picked up the box and took it to my room, placing it in a drawer in case my mum came in and saw it. She would be asking questions.

I was in the kitchen when mum and dad came in from defrosting the water pipes out in the sheds; all the livestock had been sorted now that they had running water. Tea was ready, as they took off their coats and boots, I poured it for them.

'Cor, I'm ready for this,' said dad, rubbing his hands that looked red with the cold. I handed him a mug of steaming tea; he cupped his hand around the mug to warm his hands up. We all walked into the living room where the wood burner was burning brightly, emanating heat into the room. My dad stood next to it, trying to warm himself up.

'When are you starting to prepare dinner, mum? I'll give you a hand with it,' I said, sipping my tea.

'Oh, thanks, love, in about an hour,' replied mum. In the meantime, presents were exchanged, and a bottle of red wine was opened.

Christmas soon passed, and so did the snow. New Year's Eve fell on a Thursday, and as usual, Les had organized a New Year's Eve party, which was fancy dress. Mags was working until six pm that evening, finishing up for the next five days, so that a celebration was on the cards to bring in the New Years'.

'What are we going to dress up as, this time, Mags?' I asked her.

'Err, I don't know; what about dressing as a St Trinian?' Mag rolled a lock of hair around her finger.

'We'll have to go to that fancy dress shop I found where we got the costumes for the Halloween party. The only problem is that I'm working until six pm, so you'll have to get me sorted with something, Holly,' said Mags.

'Mm ok, I'll do my best, see what they've got,' I said, feeling slightly nervous now.

'Well, that's sorted then,' said Mags.

'No pressure then, Mags.'

'You'll be ok. You know my size,' Mags said at last.

I borrowed my mum's car to go to the shop where we had rented our Halloween costumes from, thinking that I should have gone on a Wednesday so that Mags could try the costume on. Well, at least I could take it back and find something else if it didn't fit her right, but it fit her like a treat. I got her a goddess costume and an Indian Squaw costume for myself. I left the costumes with Mags; it was arranged that my mum would drop me off at Mags's flat just after six pm with an overnight bag as I was staying over. Mags was going to celebrate the New Year coming in. I was going to make the best of it as in a couple of days, I would be back in Surrey.

It was New Year's Eve, with the weather still cold, but at least there was no more snow with most of it had melted. We even had the freezing temperatures at night. At least it wasn't that cold to freeze the water pipes inside the cattle shed as temperatures had been below -5C.

I had been looking forward to this, as it was going to be my last evening at the station and being a party animal with Mags before going back home to Surrey. Mags was already at home when I turned up at her doorstep. I had brought a bottle of red wine to get the party started while we got ready just like the last time; we both helped each other applying our make up before putting our costumes on so as not to smudge it.

Mags had booked a taxi for seven-thirty pm; the driver turned up fifteen minutes late, pipping his horn. We both checked each other to see if anything was out of place and finishing the last mouthful of wine from our glasses, we headed out to the taxi. Opening the taxi door, we recognized the driver as the guy who had picked us up for the Halloween party. The driver turned around and grinned at us.

'Hello ladies, we meet again. I take it, you are going to the station,' said the taxi driver.

'Oh, you remember us then?' said Mags with a smile.

'How could I forget you two sexy ladies?' he exclaimed. The station was busy when we arrived, officers were bringing in drunks who were abusive and aggressive, the usual drill, and there must have been ten or so shouting obscenities- the officers on duty had their hands full.

'Tony will have a busy night tonight,' Mags sighed as we started to climb the stairs up to the social club room.

'Couldn't he get the time off?' I asked Mags.

'No, they were short-staffed.'

'He'll have to make sure that he books it off next year then, Mags.'

'Well, that depends as he's applied for a move and promotion upon the Scottish Borders, and there is a position for me as well,' Mags added with a smirk.

'Bloody hell, Mags, I'm not going to see you?' My heart sank.

'Oh no, we'll keep in touch. Holly.' Mags wrapped her arm around my shoulder.

We entered the function room where, in front of us was a huge table laid with a buffet spread, Les and his wife had done it justice again. It was just a disco night and buffet, Les couldn't find anyone to do a turn as they were all booked up. Even so, it still will be a good night, I thought. There were a few people who were not in fancy dress, they had just come off the same shift as Mags, but had to finish some paperwork off before coming up to the function room. We pushed through to the bar asking for a couple of glasses of red wine.

'Giving Mags some money, I told her, 'Here pay for the drinks while I just nip to the loo.' Mags took the note while I walked off to the loo. Partygoers were still coming in as I went down the corridor to the ladies. There were four cubicles, two of which were occupied, so taking the empty one and locking the door behind me, I sat down. A woman in the next cubicle to me started talking to the other women in the next cubicle.

'So how long have you been up here then?' said the woman in the far end cubicle.

'Oh, this is my first week up here,' replied the woman next to me.

'Where you were stationed at before you came here?' asked the woman in the cubicle on the far end again.

'Surrey.' continued the woman in the cubicle next to me. My ears soon picked up, hearing the name, Surrey.

'Ahan, what made you leave and come up here?' then asked the woman in the far end cubicle slightly interested.

'Er, it was a bit complicated. I was seeing a married guy who was in the CID. We were getting a bit too close. He stopped it, so I asked for a transfer,' said the woman in the next cubicle. The two women finished what they were doing and left their cubicles to wash their hands. I wondered if she had got long dark hair.

I asked myself if this could be a coincidence; was I thinking too much into this? I stayed in my cubicle until they both had gone. God, I needed a drink after hearing that. I quickly left as I heard the door close to see if I could see them down the corridor. All I could see were two women in their uniforms, one of whom had dark hair, but it was tied up, and I couldn't guess what length it was.

Fuck, once they had gone through into the door leading to the stairs, I came out from the ladies and headed through to the function room. I was desperate to talk to Mags; I stood near the door, adjusting my eyes into the darkness of the room. All of a sudden, Mags thrust a glass of red wine into my hand and went on. 'Where the hell have you been?

'I need to tell you something but not in here, Mags.' I looked at her with a serious expression. 'Where can we go and talk?'

'Come on; let's go into one of the offices down the corridor.' Mags pointed to the door at the end of the corridor. With that, we walked through into one of the offices.

'What's up, Holly? It's New Year's Eve, and it's party time,' said Mags slightly drunk.

'Mags, you won't believe what I've just heard in the lady's toilets. Have you got a woman officer just started last week or so?'

'Um yeah, but there are two of them, I think, why?' asked Mags.

'Did one of them come from Surrey?'

'I don't know.' Mags frowned. I filled her in on the conversation I had heard in the toilets and the description of her from the back view.

'Well, that sounds suspicious, Holly,' said Mags.

'Will you do some digging for me, Mags?'

'You know I'll help you if I can, Holly. Always.' Mags' voice was earnest.

'Thanks, you are a true friend.' I rubbed the back of her hand.

Knocking back the wine, I went back to the bar for another couple more glasses of red wine. I needed to know, to drawn-out what I had just heard, and to block it out for tonight at least. It was now getting crowded, we both danced, drank, and shared a plate full of food from the buffet to soak up the drinks. Mags told me that Tom and Jon were working like Tony because they were short-staffed.

I was relieved in one way because of Halloween; not only that, I wouldn't see him again, now that I was going back home in a few days to Surrey. It was nearly midnight to celebrate the new year in, so I nipped to the loo again; there wasn't anyone in the corridor or in the toilet. I felt as though I hadn't drunk enough to drown out the thoughts of the conversation I had heard.

I was coming out from the ladies toilets when someone took hold of my hand, pushing me towards one of the offices. The room was in complete darkness apart from the light, casting a shadow into the room. I got a glimpse that it was someone dressed as Zorro but did not have a clue who it was as there were could a few dressed in the same costumes. He took me around the waist with one arm and stroked my face with a finger as he whispered, 'I love you, Holly,' and then he kissed me softly on the lips, I could just see his eyes through his mask, long eyelashes and his brown eyes looking at me. It then hit me hard, who that could be.

I murmured to him, 'You have beautiful eyes.' He then lowered his head and gave me one of the same passionate kisses, I recalled back to the guy dressed as

Count Dracula at the Halloween party at the Dog and Duck. He had melted my heart again.

'You're going back soon, aren't you?' asked Zorro with an edge to his voice.

'Yes,' I said, my breathing getting shallower.

'Be careful. Mick isn't what he seems and says he is,' he warned me.

'What do you mean by that?' I widen my eyes.

'I can't say much, I've said too much now, but please be careful,' said Zorro placing a kiss on my forehead. There was shouting and cheering in the function room; it was midnight.

'Happy New Year, Holly,' he said, kissing me passionately, and I closed my eyes to savor the moment once again. He released me and left before I could realize that he had gone. I came back to my senses and tried to run after him, but I didn't know where he had gone, as the doors to the stairs and function room were moving. Which way had he gone? God, he must be the same guy from the Halloween party who had kissed me. It was the same guy. Obviously, he had a connection with the police because he wouldn't be allowed in the building otherwise, and he knew Mick, but why was he warning me to be careful. And why did he keep saying that he loved me? Ugh, I hated mysteries.

Going back into the function room, I thought I would keep what had happened to me to myself. Mags shouted from across the room and coming over to drag me into singing Auld Lang Syne. With everyone giving New Year kisses, the party soon dispersed. Mags had arranged for the taxi to pick us up at twelve-thirty am to take us back to Mags flat. Mags was more drunk than I was, and I didn't know if it had to do with drinking red wine instead of white, or the disturbing conversation I had heard in the ladies' toilets.

When we got back to her flat, I made coffee while Mags was too sozzled and went straight to bed. I had so much on my mind, with so much to process- first what I had heard in the toilet, and then there was the Zorro guy. I could never forget his kisses and his beautiful eyes. I knew that I had to find this beautiful man.

The New Year was cold; snow was in the forecast, with negative temperatures at night. This was all that I needed, as I was going back to Surrey. Mick had never been in touch with me, apart from coming up once which didn't go down well, not even a text since he came up after I'd sent him a text saying DIVORCE, and he had shown up the next day, which didn't really resolve anything apart from me telling him I was coming home after the New Year and that I didn't want him living there.

I had said my goodbyes to Mags while she was still in bed; she had a bad hangover and was feeling rough, and I knew that feeling well.

I was packing the few extra things I had bought over the period I had been up here when I came across the solid gold necklace which someone had left in a bag hanging on the outside of the house door. I opened the box before I packed it in my bags, to take a closer look. I turned it over and rubbed my thumb over the words. Who had sent me such an expensive gift? Then a thought crept in my head- the two times a mystery man had kissed me had sent me to eternity and back- it had to be the same person. Besides, I could tell by his beautiful eyes- just everything about him was gorgeous. I wished to know more about him, but the question was, would I ever find out?

My mum and dad took me to the train station to see me off. Now I was on my own to face the facts head-on, I wasn't looking forward to the journey home, the last I spoke with Mick didn't end well, so I was hoping he wasn't going to be there when I had told him to move out. By the time I arrived home, it was after 6 pm, and it was dark with the weather being cold and sleety rain.

The house was in the darkness, my car was in the driveway, and I noticed that it had been moved to one side since I saw it last. Mick's car wasn't there; he'd either moved out or was still at work. Putting the key in the hole, I unlocked it and switched the light on. I stepped in the house, dragging my bags into the hallway, the house was warm as the central heating had kicked in. I wondered if anything had changed ever since I was here the last time, three months ago. On the first inspection, I could smell the same smell as last time. Was it the air freshener, or had Mick had his tart over while I was away?

Switching the lights on as I walked through the rooms, inspecting as though I was going through a crime scene collecting the evidence. It looked as though he had given it a thorough clean; it didn't even seem like the same house. Every room was spotlessly clean, too clean even for Mick's standards.

I found myself in the kitchen and opened the fridge as if that would give me some idea if he were here, but the fridge was empty, not even milk. I then went upstairs to our bedroom to see if he had taken his clothes with him. His clothes were still there, so was he still here or living somewhere else? I was confused. I had tried phoning him while I was going down on the train, but it went straight to voice mail. Was he busy or just avoiding me? This was the problem since we had moved down here, he had changed, he wasn't the Mick who I had first met. I just didn't trust him anymore; his excuses always revolved around the job, so he said, but was it true?

I'd taken a stroll over the house and had realized that we now needed some basic groceries. I would have to find a late-night shop open. The car keys were in the usual place, hung up in the kitchen. Leaving some lights on before I left, to warn Mick that I was home if he was to return home unexpectedly, I got inside my car, checking it out to see if there were any evidence of it being used. No, the seat was still in the same position as I'd left it in.

By the time I'd got back, it was after eight pm. Mick's car still wasn't there, but that didn't mean anything; he didn't get in until after ten pm at times. I made myself some scrambled eggs on toast and a cup of tea, taking it into the living room and switching the TV on. After I had finished my meal and washed my dishes, I decided to go for a soak in the bath. While the water was running, I sorted my bags out of clothes that needed washing and put away those that didn't, at least that was done.

I stepped into the bath, slowly sinking into the hot water for my body to get used to the temperature. I lifted my foot up to turn the hot tap on to fill it a little more, plus I wanted it hotter. Once I'd got it to the temperature I wanted, I slid down the bath, covering my shoulders with my knees slightly bent above the waterline; this felt good. I started to think of my mystery man, the kiss, and his beautiful eyes, the gold necklace and the red roses, could he be the same guy? I needed to find him.

My train of thoughts was broken by the front door opening and closing, oh Mick was still there. I could hear footsteps walking around, downstairs, and then eventually heading upstairs.

'Holly, are you there?' shouted Mick.

Oh, fuck! I didn't want to see him. I shouted back, 'Yeah, I'm in the bath.' With that, he entered the bathroom, dressed in his suit as though he had just come home from work; he didn't look like himself. I felt as though he was now a stranger and started feeling vulnerable being in the bath, naked. I knew that he would start being Mr. Nice Guy trying to win me over like he did last time, but I would not allow it this time. I was prepared.

'Hello, my darling! Have you been home long?' asked Mick coming over and kissing me on top of my head.

'Hmm, just after six pm. I think I'd asked you to move out, Mick,' I said in a flat tone.

'Yeah, I know, but I thought we would have a proper chat now that you are home for good,' he said sounding hopeful. God, did I want this conversation again? Nothing was going to change, but this was going to be my only chance to sort this mess out.

'Mick, can we talk tomorrow? I've had a long day, and I'm tired,' I said, trying to avoid making eye contact with him.

'Yeah, sure. I can wait, my dear,' said Mick trying to sound like a caring husband. Mick went downstairs into the kitchen, and I could hear him filling the kettle. I got out of the bath, dried myself, and quickly headed for the bedroom. The bed felt as though it had been stripped, and clean sheets had been put on. Feeling clean and fresh, I sank into the bed.

I heard Mick coming back upstairs, and then he walked into the bedroom with two mugs of tea. He put mine on the bedside cabinet while he walked around to the other side, putting his on his side.

'Mick, can you go and sleep in the spare bedroom, please?' I said in the same flat tone.

'Holy, I haven't seen you nearly three months, I just need to be with you darling,' Mick said, almost pleading.

'No, Mick,' I said a bit sternly.

'Oh, come on, darling. I'll keep to my side of the bed. I promise,' said Mick.

'Oh God,' I couldn't be bothered to argue after the journey. 'Fine! Do whatever you want, but behave.' After drinking my tea, I settled down into the fresh, clean sheets and drifted off to sleep.

I fell into a deep sleep and began dreaming of my mystery man; his beautiful eyes, his kiss, his touch, his smell- yes, I would like for him to make love to me, to take me to the limits of ecstasy. I was feeling wet; my nipples were getting hard with him near me. I felt his hands on me, cupping my breasts and using his tongue to suck on my nipple. Next, I was on my back, ready to receive him as he straddled over me, and as he entered me, I realized it was Mick on top of me; I was out of the dream in an instant.

It was too late; he had already shot his lot and was rolling off me with his arm across my waist. The bastard, he couldn't help it. I turned over his arm and slid it off me, but he snuggled up to my back and put his arm back on top of the waist.

It was Saturday morning, and I could feel Mick lying next to me with his arm still over my waist. My biggest mistake was letting him sleep with me, and secondly, we both were naked in bed; it had always been like that from the first time we slept together. It was eight when I started to get out of the bed, but Mick took hold of my wrist, stopping me. Bugger, I thought he was still asleep.

'Stay in bed with me, darling,' said Mick in a sleepy voice. Still trying to get up, I pulled away, releasing his grip; I grabbed my dressing gown and went to the bathroom for a pee. Mick rolled over, spreading himself over the bed. Once I had finished, I made my way downstairs into the kitchen to make some breakfast.

While making breakfast, I considered telling him the secret I had been holding since the accident. I wondered how he would take it, but I still wasn't sure I could live like this, not knowing if he was telling me the truth regarding his infidelity.

Then my mind wandered back to the New Year's Eve party and Zorro telling me not to trust Mick, and that kiss, what did he mean by that? I had to find this guy.

I took the tea and toasts upstairs, where Mick was spread out like a starfish in the bed. I put the tray on the side and tried to push him to one side, then all of a sudden, he grabbed hold of me, rolling me onto the bed. It reminded me of when we first started sleeping together, and how we would always play fight and finish up by making love.

'Stop it, Mick. I've made breakfast. It'll get cold.' I broke free as he took hold of my dressing gown, leaving me naked; Mick leaped, grabbing me by the wrist. I lost my balance and fell back onto the bed. Mick jumped on top of me, smothering me with kisses and sucking my nipples, which started to turn me on; he cupped both of my breasts, squeezing them together, sucking and licking them. I was aroused, wet, and ready for him to come inside me; my body was betraying me.

He took hold of both my wrists and held them together in one hand above my head, using his leg to part both of mine further apart; he put his fingers inside me, finding my spot to make me come, but his lovemaking seemed different to what it used to be- he was rough and in a hurry. He brought his hand back out to my wrist, and spreading them both apart as though I was tied to the bed; he entered me with force. He continued pushing hard, and within a few seconds, he had shot his lot. He then let go of me and rolled over off me.

I lay there, stunned. What was wrong with him? He had certainly changed. I got up from the bed and went to the bathroom and switched the shower on. I stood there under the shower, water washing over me after the sex we had- yes, it was just sex, not lovemaking like it used to be. I had been in the shower for about fifteen minutes when I heard the bathroom door open. It was Mick; he opened the shower door and stepped in, grabbing hold of me around the waist, kissing me again. I felt a fury floating in my system.

'Mick, what are you doing in the shower now?' I said in a surprised yet angry voice.

'I want to fuck you as many times as I can since I've missed you so much. I've got some catching up to do,' said Mick in a wicked voice. I was taken back by this statement. He had me in the shower and fucked the hell out of me, Christ! Had he really got all this testosterone in him waiting to be released over these few months? When he had finished, he said he would go and make a fresh cup of tea.

He left me in the shower, again letting the water run over me, cleaning the sex off. By the time I had dried myself and walked back into the bedroom, Mick was there with the tea waiting in bed for me.

'Come on, my darling, get back into bed and have your tea before it gets cold.' I was flabbergasted as I had never seen Mick like this before. I must admit I had missed the sex and was up for it even though he had been rough, but he wasn't going to like what I was going to tell him later. But I was still unsure regarding Mick's infidelity; I might as well make the most of it- I hadn't had sex since I was here the last time.

We sat in the bed, drinking our tea in silence; it was nine-thirty am by now, and there hadn't been a phone call, which was almost a miracle. I put my cup on the side as Mick was waiting for me to finish. He slid me down the bed and started kissing me down my body to my clitoris, playing with it with his tongue, parting my lips with his fingers moving them in and out then sticking his tongue inside.

He pressed his face into my vagina as though he was going to eat me. He moved his tongue quickly around and then came up, licking me and sucking me hard. My nipples were hard and pointed, ready to be received by his mouth, sucking hard and cupping my breast hard, he entered me again, harder this time, I felt him pushing me hard and again, and within a few seconds, he had shot his lot.

It was four pm before we got up, after making up for a year of missed sex. Mick had done well- his sex drive was strong, making up for all the time he had missed while working in the force. We both took a shower together and had hard sex again before we both got dressed at last. Mick went downstairs to make a drink while I changed the bedsheets, as with that much sex, they needed freshening up.

Mick had booked us a table for seven pm at a nearby Italian restaurant; I caught myself thinking about the Zorro- was he Italian or Spanish, with that fancy accent? I must listen tonight in the restaurant if they spoke it. I was upstairs deciding what to wear. My choice was limited as I had lost weight, and only the ones I had bought when I was at home with my parents fit. I was standing with just my underwear on; when Mick came upstairs, he took me from behind, stripping my underwear off and throwing me into bed. He then released his manhood, which stood to attention, waiting to enter me. He thrust it hard inside me without warning, I groaned, and he pushed harder and harder like he was possessed until he finally shot his lot. We were both breathless for several moments, and I was thinking to myself, where was all of this taking us? I had to get out of it if I seriously wanted to sort my life, and I had to find my Zorro.

CHAPTER SEVEN:

We walked down to the restaurant, arriving just before seven pm. The restaurant was packed, almost all fifty tables occupied. We were shown to a table at the back of the restaurant, which was dimly lit and romantic. The restaurant was busy with the waiters and hostesses rushing around serving and taking orders as quickly as possible. We had a male waiter serving us, and he had a heavy accent, so I asked him if he was Italian. 'Yes, signora,' he replied, 'but we moved when I was ten years old.'

'So, you are part of the family business then?' I asked again while Mick just stared.

'Yes, we all are apart from two of us signora,' he said while nodding.

I figured that Zorro must be Italian too, but why did he have the authorization to access the police station? It was strange.

After a delicious meal and red wine, we walked back to the house. I was slightly tipsy flirting with Mick all night; it was like we were on our first date. He asked if I was still taking the pill, and I told him I wasn't as I had no need to. I wondered if he was testing me.

As soon as we walked into the house, Mick dragged me upstairs and started undressing me in the bedroom. He took over stripping me until I was completely naked, then he pushed me onto the bed, after which he finished removing his clothes. He dived in straight away, hard. Mick entered me and started pushing hard, pumping me and pushing me up the bed with the pressure, and finally, he shot his lot within a minute. He lay there for a few seconds before moving, then rolling off the bed, exposing my naked body. I rolled off the bed to the bathroom to clean myself up before getting into the bed for the night.

Mick had gone downstairs. I lay there wondering what he was doing downstairs; I could hear him talking to someone but couldn't make out who it was. Was he up to something, or was it work? He had no one to phone him since I'd come home last night. It must have been an hour before he came up, and I had just started drifting off to sleep. I could hear him stripping off and slipping into bed. He reached for my waist and worked his hand up my body to my breast, squeezing hard, but it was hurting; he was now getting rough, and I didn't like it. I took his hand and tried to move it, but he wouldn't move. I turned over and said, 'Mick you're hurting me,'

'Sorry, my love, I just can't get enough of you,' he was on top of me by then. I felt his hardness on my body as he was ready to enter me.

'Mick, haven't you had enough for one day? I want to sleep,' I said as I rolled to my side.

'No, but you're going to have it whether you like it or not,' said Mick with an abrupt voice, and with that, he was on top of me. He pushed my legs apart quickly and entered me. It hurt a lot and didn't feel right.

'Mick, stop it, you are hurting me,' but it fell on deaf ears. He kept on pushing harder and harder, and I was in tears shouting for him to stop, but he wouldn't and kept going until he had shot his lot. He rolled off me after a few seconds. I struggled to get out of the bed as he was holding on to me, but I managed to free myself, heading to the bathroom. I was in tears, and as I looked down, I saw blood. He had made me bleed, fuck what'd got into him? I must have been in the bathroom about ten minutes cleaning myself, before tiptoeing into the bedroom to get my dressing gown and locking myself into the spare bedroom.

Mick was waiting for me to come out, and when I did, he grabbed hold of my wrist.

'Mick, just stop it, will you? You've made me bleed, what's got into you? Have you had a personality change?' I yelled at him, tears rolling down my cheeks.

'Holly, I'm sorry darling, I didn't mean to hurt you. I'm so sorry. Come on back to bed.' Mick pleaded.

'You were too rough. Didn't you hear me telling you to stop Mick?' I raised my voice.

'I got carried away darling I couldn't stop,' said Mick with zero remorse in his voice.

'Well, you've had your lot, Mick. I'm sleeping in the spare bedroom.' I repeated in a flat tone.

'Oh no, you're not, you are my wife you are staying here with me in this bed,' said Mick in an authoritative voice. I tried to undo his grip, but he dragged me across to the bed and pushed me backward, rolling me over onto my front face down where he forced himself onto me again. He was hard again in a moment, so he started thrusting it straight in, missing and going straight into my back passage.

'Mick stop, stop, stop, it's hurting,' I screamed, feeling sick with pain; he wasn't listening. 'You're hurting me, Mick! Mick, are you listening to me? Mick.' I was shouting at him. He then stopped and turned me over onto my back then pushed hard entering me from the front, I was trying to wriggle free, but it wasn't any good. He was holding my upper arms tight I could feel his fingers digging into my flesh. I couldn't move; he was solid like a dead heavyweight. He stopped after he had shot his lot.

'I want you pregnant, Holly and you're going to be fucked as many times as it takes tonight,' said Mick with venom-filled voice. I was sobbing in pain; there was blood on the sheets.

‘Fuck off, Mick, you’ve changed. This isn’t you, what’s got into you? Are you on drugs?’ Then I came out with what I was holding back from telling him. ‘Well, Mick, you’re wasting your time, I can’t have kids,’ I shouted back at him.

‘What? Why?’ I’d got his attention.

‘Because when I was in the hospital, they did some tests and they told me I'd got a million to one chance of having any. Happy now?’ I said with caution, lowering my voice.

‘You’re lying; you’re just saying it to bluff me,’ said Mick.

‘Well, ring the hospital then,’ I shouted and got up from the blood-stained bed. Grabbing my dressing gown, I ran into the bathroom, locking the door behind me. Blood had been running down my legs, but it had stopped and had now dried. God, the pain was unbearable. How some people enjoy having sex in the back passage beats me. I shouted from behind the bathroom door, 'Mick, I'm filing for a divorce.'

There was silence. I waited- was he still there, or had he gone downstairs? I couldn't hear him or where he was in the house.

I must have sat slumped next to the bathroom door for nearly an hour before I thought he must have gone or was asleep. Carefully I unlocked the bathroom door opening it slightly, trying to catch a glimpse of him. He was knocked out cold, face down with his arm hanging down the side of the bed. I quickly tiptoed across to the spare bedroom and locked the door behind me. I decided that he was not going to touch me ever again; he had just raped me- repeatedly.

It was Monday morning. I was due to go back to work; I felt sore and bruised from the previous night with

Mick. Mick had already left when I got up; I did not know the state of mind he was in after what he had done to me. I needed a hot bath to wash away the hurt and forced sex Mick had put me through. I needed to phone work to let them know I wouldn't be in the rest of the week telling them a little white lie that I had to go back home, as my mum was ill and my dad needed help.

They bought the story and told me to stay as long as it took. I went into the bedroom and seeing the dry blood-stained sheets on the bed all crumpled up; I gathered them up. I took them downstairs and bundled them into a bin bag to throw them away. I didn't want to use them knowing what he had done to me. I had to find a locksmith and get the locks changed today just in case he came home. He had lost his right to step in this house anymore. I managed to find a local locksmith that could come within the hour. Good- the sooner, the better. Now I had to find a good solicitor, and I began flicking through the phone directory.

I found one specializing in divorce settlements. That would have to do, so I rang to make an appointment.

The locksmith turned up just after eleven-thirty am. There were a total of three locks to be changed- the back and front doors, and the patio door. It took him about an hour; I was now relieved knowing that Mick couldn't get back into the house. My appointment with the solicitor was later in the afternoon at three, so I had time to gather all of Mick's clothes and stuff them into the back bin liners. He wasn't going to like it; he liked his clothes hung and neatly pressed. Tough- on this occasion, he deserved it. Dragging them downstairs, I put them next to the door, ready to be put outside for him to pick them up.

I made myself a quick coffee and left the house to go to the solicitor at three pm. I checked all the windows and doors before leaving just to make sure Mick couldn't gain access to the house. What ground was I going for, and the best way to go about it? While waiting for my appointment, I flicked through a magazine not really taking anything in, when ten minutes later, I heard the receptionist call me.

'Mrs. Sheppard Joanne's ready to see you if you would like to follow me,' she said. The receptionist was an older woman in her mid-fifties smartly dressed in a grey trouser suit with a white plain blouse. Joanne was sat at her desk when I was shown in; it was like going in to see the headmistress when you had done something wrong. Standing up, she held her hand out to shake mine, asking me to take a seat. I thought grey suits must be the firm's uniform.

I explained the basics about having arguments regarding having a baby, Mick being always at work and hardly getting to see him, catching Mick with the other woman, and me having my accident. I also filled her with Mick only coming to see me only twice while I was with my parents recuperating, but I didn't say anything about my homecoming and what had taken place in the bedroom.

'Well,' she said 'you have three main reasons, first is adultery; second is unreasonable behavior and thirdly separation for two years. Have you discussed the divorce with your husband?' She asked.

'No, not yet. I just wanted to know my options to put forward to him.' We had a brief chat expanding these options before I left.

It was just after four pm when I left the solicitor's office; I headed back home feeling a bit relieved that I got to offload some of my problems with options of how to deal with them. When I arrived home, the house was in darkness.

'Damn, I should have left a light on.' I had not realized it was going to be dark when I got back. Mick's car wasn't in the drive, so I parked the car in a position that if he came back, he wouldn't be able to park his car, and that would only leave him an option to park it out on the roadside. Locking my car, I quickly nipped inside, locking the door behind to feel secure and relieved. Mick's bagged clothes still were lined up next to the door; they still reminded me of him, the sooner he took them, the better.

I hadn't eaten anything all day, so I went into the kitchen to make some toast and put the kettle on. I buttered my toast and sliced some cheese to make a toasted cheese sandwich and a mug of tea. I went through into the living room, switching the TV on. I sat down on the sofa, putting my feet up and started to relax despite feeling sore and bruised.

It must have been after midnight when I woke up to a banging on the door, I was sleepy and just wanted to turn over and ignore it, but it needed sorting. I slipped out of my bed in the spare room to put on my dressing gown. Walking to the window, I opened it to find Mick in a light being cast across the driveway from his car in the distance.

'What do you want?' I hissed at him.

'Holly darling, I can't get in. Can you let me in?'

'No, I've changed the locks, and you're not coming in,' I hissed at him some more. 'Communication will be through my solicitors or the phone Mick. I don't want you near me - you know what you've done. I can't live with you anymore, Mick.' I closed the window and went back to the spare bedroom.

Lying in bed, I started thinking I should go to the hospital to get checked. As going for a pee was hurting and stinging, something didn't feel right. The next day I went to the hospital where the doctor and nurse were concerned about what had happened to me to get these injuries. I had bruising on both of my upper arms where Mick had held them while me pinning me down, but the reason for the bleeding was that Mick had split me both ways, which why it was hurting and sore. I needed a couple of stitches. I burst out crying while telling the nurse who was really sympathetic. She did advise me even if I didn't want to press charges, that I should have photos taken for evidence in case I wanted to press charges in the future. After I had calmed down and thought about it, it made sense, so the nurse organized it.

I left the hospital; it had taken six hours to process me just in case I needed it in the future. I was relieved that I did it, and had filed my case with the hospital. Driving home like this at this moment in time didn't feel like right after everything that had happened over the last year. I needed to move on and start a new life somewhere else in the country.

The next morning, I phoned Mags and asked her if I could come up for a couple of days? I didn't say much over the phone but would fill her in when I got there. Packing a few bits, I left my car parked in the driveway and took the train as the weather wasn't too good. I hadn't heard from Mick since the night shouting at the window when he wanted to come in as though he hadn't done anything wrong.

Mags met me at the train station; I started crying as soon as I saw her.

'Holly, what's wrong? You've only been gone four days,' said Mags genuinely concerned.

'It's Mick; he's changed. He's become someone else, a monster.' I said sobbing while I took out a tissue from my coat pocket.

'Let's get back to my place, and you can tell me all about it,' said Mags putting an arm around me. As soon as we got back in her flat, Mags went to put the kettle on to make two mugs of coffee. I was ready for a drink after the long journey due to a number of stops on the way up.

Bringing in the coffees and placing them on the side table next to the sofa, Mags sat down next to me, waiting for me to begin.

'Mags what I'm telling you, please don't tell anyone, not even Tony. Do you promise Mags?' I pleaded with her.

'Holly, you know me better than that,' said Mags giving me a hug. With the reassurance, I told her everything that had happened. Mags was silent for a few moments before she spoke. She gave me another long hug;

'Gosh, I didn't think Mick could be like that; he looks so easy going.' sighed Mags. 'So, are you going to press charges?' asked Mags.

'No, I don't feel like I should. I'm going for a divorce, though, so I'll see what he has to say on that first.

We've been married for two years, one of which I was up here, it all changed when he got his promotion and moved to Surrey. That's where he is from originally, started in the force down there making his way up the ranks, moved up here as a detective sergeant for a couple of years until he got his promotion and went back to Surrey. He knows Surrey like the back of his hand and knows a lot of people there. To be quite honest, Mags I didn't really want to go, living in the city, it was a bit of a culture shock, but I married him with the job, and now I regret it.' I explained.

'Holly, you have to do what's right for you, you are the only one who can make that decision,' said Mags with a calming tone. 'I'm sorry that you can't have kids; I bet it was a bit of a shock when they told you,' Mags went on.

'Yes, I know we were arguing over starting a family, but I wasn't ready. I wanted to still go places and do things we used to do, but then he said he had this sensitive case he was one which could take a while, and before my accident, he was in for another promotion. I understood everything, but since I caught him with that woman, I'm not so sure anymore.'

'I don't know what to say, Holly,' said Mags.

'Yeah, I suppose time will bring clarity.' I shrugged.

I felt a lot better now that I had offloaded my ordeal with Mick. It was late, and Mags was covering half a shift the next day. I woke up after ten am. I must have needed the rest as I didn't hear Mags get up for work. As I rolled over and spread out feeling comfy with the bed covers snuggled around me, I could hear the rain beating on the window, thinking about poor old Mags being out in this weather.

I once again drifted off and then woke up to my phone ringing; it was noon. I let it ring, thinking it would be Mick. Once it had stopped ringing, there was a ping announcing a text. I rolled over, picking the phone up and flipping the lid; it was Mick asking me where I was as he needed to talk; yes, I bet he did. I got up and made my way to the bathroom. I looked in the mirror and could see the bruises on my arms; they weren't as vivid now, and we're slowly starting to fade. It was good that I went to the hospital to have this whole incident on record. Having a pee wasn't too bad now, but the other was painful, they told me at the hospital it would be a couple of weeks before the pain and soreness would wear off. I had a quick wash and got dressed.

I was just about to make a bit of breakfast when my phone rang again. Oh fuck, it was Mick; I was ready for him now.

'Hello?' I said in a dull tone.

'Holly, my darling, where are you? I'm at the house. Aren't you in?' he asked as though nothing had happened.

'No,' I said bluntly.

'Holly, I am so sorry I don't know what came over me, please forgive me Holly darling,' he begged.

'Mick, I want a divorce.'

'Holly,' he began, but I cut him short and gave him the full rundown of our marriage.

'We haven't been getting on since you got your promotion and when we moved to Surrey. You come home late and I hardly ever see you. We used to go out on the weekend, you demanded you wanted to start a family, and then I caught you with that woman sucking you off in our home, I was hit by a car, while I was recuperating for a year with my parents and needed my husband, you only came up twice to see me. I come home, and you fucking raped me, you bastard! Plus, it's all on the record with the hospital if I need to press charges. So, what have you to say to that, Mick?' I yelled with tears in my eyes. There was silence at the other end of the phone as I waited for him to respond, and I could imagine him pacing up and down, running his hand around the back of his neck as he was in a corner trying to dig himself out of a hole.

'Yes, you're right, Holly,' he said in exasperation.

'Oh.' I was taken back, thinking he was going to come up with another lie; he was admitting to what he had done. 'I've got all your clothes bagged up ready for you to pick up, so I'll arrange a date and time and let you know, but I'm not there at the moment.' I finished it bluntly.

'So where are you then?' asked Mick.

'It's irrelevant where I am; I'll ring you when I'm ready, Mick, so we'll leave it at that then, and anyway I've got to go so I'll speak to you later. Goodbye, Mick,' I cut him off before he said anything else.

I stayed there for a couple of days before going back to Surrey, feeling a bit better with having Mags to talk to and the healing process. I knew what I was going to do when I got back. I rang work to let them know that I would be off for another week, another white lie; Mick must be rubbing off me.

It was the weekend I was ready for Mick to take his clothes. I phoned him, he answered it straight away, and I was taken aback as I was expecting it going to voice mail.

'Holly, where are you?

'I'm at home, and I need to talk to you about the divorce.' I gave him all the options that the solicitors had advised. 'You raped me, causing bruising to my arms and splitting me down below; this has been reported with the hospital as I needed stitches, just in case I needed the report for future reference.' Mick was silent, I had walloped him, as this could change everything he had worked for and his career. I had the control now and was the one to call the shots.

'Holly, I'll give you everything I have, but please don't take my career I've worked for,' Mick begged for his career to be saved.

'Mm well it will have to be unreasonable behavior, we can say that a year has already gone because of the accident, so you're not living here will make it two years apart and agreeing on a settlement, so if you mess me about, I will bring up the other business, and I will finish you.'

'Yes, Holly anything you say,' said Mick, panicked.

'You will have to let me know your solicitors and get this started- the sooner, the better,' I said with no emotion. 'Oh, and I'll leave your clothes outside the door tomorrow afternoon at one, and I expect them gone by three. Ok, Mick?' and then cut him off.

I got the ball rolling with the solicitors; I was going for the reason regarding two years of unreasonable behavior, seeing that over a year had gone by, and another would soon pass. Mick had agreed for me to have the house and to do what I wanted with it, and also to pay all the bills. All I had to pay for was my food and the running costs of my car.

I went back to work the following week, but my heart wasn't in it. People asked how I was and kept asking me about the accident. I didn't say much about it, I wasn't in a chatty mood, especially with what was happening with my life. Could I stand it until the divorce came through? So I could sell the house and move out of the city. I hated the place; city life wasn't for me. The house belonged to his mother; she had left it to him together with a substantial amount of money due to her death six months before we moved here. She had died in a head-on car crash where another driver was driving down the dual carriageway late at night. She died instantly on the scene.

Mags was getting married in Las Vegas with me due to fly out with her to have a hen night before the wedding. Tony and his brother took a flight scheduled for later, so we didn't clash and see each other. It was nearly an eleven-hour flight; despite the long flight, I wasn't feeling too bad as I had managed to get some sleep and the change from not being in Surrey having a change of scenery.

We arrived mid-day, and as soon as we left the plane, the heat hit us. It was in the mid-twenties.

'Wow,' I said to Mags. 'I wasn't expecting these temperatures.' I continued taking off another layer of clothing. Mags had already stripped off stuffing her clothes in her hand luggage. The taxi was waiting to take us to the hotel, bundling our luggage into the boot of the cab we set off to the hotel. It suddenly hit me that it was going to be a life-changing experience for me.

CHAPTER EIGHT:

I had never been to Vegas. The only time I had travelled to the east coast was a sixteen-day package tour I had opted for with my mum when I was eighteen years old. My dad had been busy with the harvest on the farm he wasn't able to go for two weeks. It was an eye-opening sort of a trip which started from New York; we saw as many sightings as possible and later on took a trip down the River Hudson, seeing the apartments of famous people such as Jonny Rotten of the Sex Pistols.

Some people from our party were robbed, two couples had their luggage taken from the hotel bedroom, and one guy going up in a lift with another guy got robbed, as a guy took his watch and wallet at knife point. There was another time when we were travelling back by coach from the Statue of Liberty and stopped at the traffic lights; across the road, there was an area where you could see a shootout going on. But this was a normal day in New York. I remembered when we were in Miami, a group of us went for a night out. We were friendly with another couple; Lynne had treated her niece Karen to a holiday. My mum and Lynne went back to the hotel while Karen and I went on clubbing; it was a good night until we needed to get back to the hotel, and there weren't any taxis about, the road being completely deserted.

The club we had come out of was a large boat moored on the mariner. We were also slightly tipsy, and after waiting for about ten minutes, we saw some car headlights coming down the road. It freaked us out when the car stopped in front of us, with four guys sitting inside started trying to entice us to go with them. We were shit scared and desperately hoped someone would turn up as the guys were getting rather persistent. Then all of a sudden, out of the blue, a security guard came out from the mariner, and that's when the guys escaped. The security guard phoned a taxi for us and, more or less, saved our bacon. We finally finished our tour in Orlando and visited Disney land, which I enjoyed a lot.

We soon arrived at the Mirage Hotel. It was nice to be inside with the air conditioner cooling you down from the dry heat. After checking in, we made are the way to our room, which had a view of the swimming pool that looked utterly inviting in this heat. We both flopped on the bed after the eleven-hour journey. Mags had soon drifted off to sleep while I was wide awake. My feet ached badly- they usually did when I had shoes on in this heat, and they had swollen a little.

While Mags was asleep, I decided that I would go for a swim, and hence I dug out my bikini and made my way down to the pool. The heat hit me as soon as I walked through the hotel door heading towards the pool. Taking a sun lounger next to the pool, I lay my towel over the lounger. I was so absorbed in myself that it took me a while to notice a guy in black trousers standing next to me.

'Hi, there! Would the young lady like a drink from the bar?' I glanced up to see that it was the waiter from the hotel talking.

'Oh yes, please, I'll have red wine, thank you.'

'One coming up,' said the waiter pacing back to the bar. The pool area was fairly empty, so I waited for my drink to arrive before heading off to the pool. I was surprised at how cold the water was, but it was refreshing once you started swimming the lengths. I finished twenty laps before I knew it. I noticed the barman watching me as I got out of the pool and walked towards my lounger; he probably watched everyone; only there was hardly anyone around the pool at that time. Gulping down my wine like it was water, I picked up my towel, wrapped it around me, and went back upstairs to my room to see if Mags was still asleep. I think jet lag had caught up with her. I was hoping that she felt better to go out in the evening, though. With that thought, I decided to have a nap as well. I peeled off my bikini and dried myself before putting my long tee-shirt on.

It was after nine before we both came back to the land of the living; I was surprised how long I had slept as I had slept on the plane as well. We had both recharged our batteries and were ready for the night to celebrate Mags's last night as a single woman.

'Mags, where are we going tonight?' I asked her, excited now.

'Let's see what the clubs here are like,' Mags sounded equally excited.

I got dressed in a pair of pale blue cotton trousers and a white vest top; Mags was wearing a pair of black cotton trousers and a white tee shirt with a logo saying

'Only single tonight; getting hitched in the morning.' We left the hotel and walked down the main street; it was heaving with people, and you could easily tell who the tourists were with their heads looking everywhere and pointing at things. I could understand why they were easy pickings for the pickpockets. There was loud music coming from all sides of the street, mainly rock music, with the exception of music from the sixties booming from one club.

'So, is it rock or the sixties?' asked Mags with a huge grin.

'Let's do the sixties for a change. I fancy a bit of Elvis, what do you think Mags?' I said, and we headed towards one of the places that were playing Elvis. Funnily enough, there was an Elvis outside enticing people into the club by handing out a flyer for a free drink. *Why not?* We thought as we took a flyer and headed into the club. The decor inside was in line with the sixties, with the majority of people dressed in sixties costumes. There were guys dressed up as the Mods and the Rockers with the women in mini-skirts and white knee-length boots wearing their hair beehive style.

The atmosphere was electric; we moved over to the bar with our flyers in our hands. The track playing was 'Twist and Shout' by the Isley Bros. I had a large glass of red wine while Mags was drinking a shot of tequila.

'Mags, I've never seen you drink tequila,' I said in a surprised tone.

'No, but it's going to last longer,' she said with a smirk.

'Mm, fair point.' I sipped my drink. The next song was 'Shout' by Lulu. We started to move our bodies to the rhythm tapping our feet, and then the beat got to us and started to spill our drinks. We could not resist any longer and asked the barman if we could leave our drinks behind the bar just in case someone spiked them. He was accommodating, so he took the drinks. We went off to the dance floor with the sound of 'The Latest Flame' by Elvis Presley in our ears. We gradually started moving our bodies; it was our song, and we did the routine of the shuffle dance. We were joined by two other girls, and we all started dancing as we had performed as a group. The dance floor opened up, giving us more space. Then nearly halfway through, we all were joined by another couple of girls, and amazingly enough, we were keeping in perfect synchro. The song was about to finish, and 'Spirit in the Sky' by Norman Greenbaum put an end to the dance routine. We all hugged each other and congratulated ourselves as a group, as the people started applauding and cheering for us. We then headed back to the bar where the barman saw us and handed over our drinks.

'There's another drink for you when you're ready,' said the barman before turning to serve another customer. I wondered who'd bought us a drink, but the barman was too busy serving, for us to ask. We knocked our drinks back with the thirst of going back to 'Lets Twist Again' by Chubby Checker, 'Surfin USA by The Beach Boys, 'The Loco-motion' by Little Eve, 'Pretty Woman' by Roy Orbison,' Good Vibrations' by The Beach Boys and finally 'Daydreamers' by The Monkeys. We were sweating buckets with our faces red, beads of sweat dripping from our foreheads as we headed to the bar for our freebie drink. The same barman served us our drinks, but by the time we had got our breath back to ask him who had bought them, he was gone again serving customers.

We had been in the club for nearly four hours, and it was after midnight, the club was heaving and was starting to get too full to dance, so we decided to move on. The air outside was refreshing, as we stepped out despite it still being warm. We realized the club was starting to get a bit stifling with the number of people inside, causing enormous amounts of suffocation. Walking back to the hotel, we could hear punters on the slot machines as we walked by.

I asked Mags, 'Do you fancy a flutter on the machines and anything we win we split it in half?'

'Yeah, go on then,' said Mags. First, we got a drink and started to watch a number of punters playing the machines; you could see who the tourists were and who weren't as the tourists floated from machine to machine. We noticed a guy playing a machine; he had been there when we had arrived and was still playing after we had gotten a drink and had stood to watch for about 15 minutes. He was winning the odd a few dollars - nothing big, but in the end, he gave in after running out cash tokens. We jumped on the machine just before we could see a woman eyeing the same machine. Having a hundred dollars to play between us, we started feeding the machine. We had been there for twenty minutes and had only won a few times.

'Mm, what you think, Mags? Do you still want to stay on this machine, seeing we are down by thirty dollars already?' I asked.

'Well we said we would gamble the lot whether we win or lose, but have you noticed there is a guy over near that water fountain opposite from the bar watching us?' said Mags a little disappointed.

'God, he must know something was going to happen with this machine.' I sounded disappointed too and wished the machine would just drop what we had put in; we wanted our money back. We were on our last dollar as the wheels spun round. We faced each looking disappointed now we that we had to put the last dollar of the hundred dollars we originally had. We were about to go when we heard the machine making a chime, and then there was a ringing noise on the machine. We turned to face the machine and saw that the wheels were all saying WIN with the machine ejecting tokens.

We could not believe it; we had won the jackpot of five-hundred thousand dollars. We started dancing and jumping around whooping with happiness; many other people came to have a look followed by a tall slim woman smartly dressed wearing a light grey skirt, white blouse, and medium-high heels.

'Hello ladies, my name is Sophia, and I work as a concierge for the casino. Congratulations on winning the jackpot. Would you like to follow me while the tokens are collected and have a celebratory drink in the VIP room?' Our heads were buzzing with excitement; we could hardly believe what had just happened.

'Mags, what are we going to do with all this money? We can't keep it on us, or we'll probably get robbed.' I remembered our last time here.

'I'll ask the casino if they would escort us back to our hotel with the cash and then ask the hotel if we can put it into their safe until the banks open then we can sort an account out and bank it,' said Mags with her forward-thinking.

'Yes, good idea, Mags.' The casino obliged, taking us back to our hotel with our winnings after we had to prove of ID to obtain our winning cash.

The banks opened at nine am, we were both up and ready to go to open an account to deposit our winnings from the casino. After taking a taxi for security, we travelled to the bank with our spoils of the night desperate to load it off and taking the pressure off us having hold of it. The taxi pulled up to the door of the bank; we paid the driver and gave him a good tip. We stepped out of the taxi, while I was clutching the bag, Mags looked around for any unwanted persons near us, and we hurriedly walked through the doors of the bank. The bank was expecting us as the hotel had rung the bank to say that we were coming over with the money and wanted to deposit the money as quickly as possible, due to a wedding taking place in a two hours' time. Mags was going to let Tony know about the money after they were married, wanting the wedding to go smoothly with no questions asked.

It was a simple wedding with only Tony's brother and myself as the witnesses. I was due to fly home that evening, while Tony's brother Al was staying on to travel for a month. Tony was moving into the room with Mags as soon as I left to go. There was so much excitement when Mags told him about the winnings from the casino, but I had to go up to my room to pack as there wasn't much time left to catch the flight back. I met up with them in the reception of the hotel later where they were a little worse for wear after celebrating at the wedding and the winnings. I said my goodbyes before leaving for the airport.

The flight back took half an hour less than going due to the weather conditions. Docking at one of the ports at the airport, I didn't notice the temperature until I walked out of the airport, it felt cold being in the temperature of 6c. I dug out my jumper and a lightweight coat to put on and then looked around for the taxi that I had pre-booked, a taxi pulled up, and the driver shouted across, 'Are you, Holly Shepperd?'

'Yes,' I shouted back and started to walk to the taxi dragging my small overnight case and bag behind me.

I was home; that's if you called it home, I hated it, once this divorce was over, I was going to sell it. I thought about the money that I and Mags had won. The money being in a USA bank account, I had no need of it presently but may need it at some stage once the divorce was complete.

The divorce was going through with no hiccups, seeing that I had Mick over a barrel. I found out that he was living in a flat in a bit of noisy area, but thinking that it was all he could afford with paying my bills, but there again he hadn't had a mortgage to pay only rent. I was curious to see it, so while I was in the area shopping, I walked to the area, trying not to make as though I was spying on him. I found a café that was opposite his flat. It was a late Saturday afternoon, and the café was busy, but I managed a window seat. I must have gone through four cups of coffee and a sandwich before I saw him. He looked tired and withdrawn; his clothes didn't seem to fit snug; he had lost weight; I must have hit him hard. Then from the other direction came a woman walking up to him, kissing him on the lips and he put his arm around her. They then both headed towards the entrance of the flat. The fucking bastard, it was that same woman he was with that night I caught him. I felt sick, my heart pumping fast with the shock of his lies, telling me it was a mistake and that it was to do with the case he was working on. I was breaking out into a sweat, I needed some air and had to get out of the café.

I hurried home now, wishing I hadn't done what I had by spying on him, but then again, what did I expect with his lies? I had to tell Mags what I'd seen. I couldn't tell Debs despite that we were friends but not the sort that could keep things to herself as she would tell her husband Pete, and seeing that he was stationed at the same place as Mick, the cat would be out the bag and my divorce wouldn't go smoothly. Mags was the only one, not even her husband Tony knew. It was a couple of days before I could speak to her; she had been on a cruise and had just come back. I filled her in with what I had seen.

'Hmm, but something doesn't add up,' said Mags. 'Why what makes you think that?'

'Well, think about it, Holly. So, ok, he has lost weight, and he is with this woman. Yes, it could be because of what he has done to you, and you have one over him. But what if this woman has something to do with a drug-related gang? Maybe he is investigating, or maybe he is taking drugs. I don't know, Holly, but time will tell,' Mags explained in detail.

'I suppose so.' I bet I sounded a bit downbeat. 'Anyway, now that you're a married woman, how is married life-changing the mood?' I tried to smile.

'Just the same,' shrugged Mags, 'but that money we won has given us a boost for sure,' she said, sounding excited.

'So, what are you going to do with it?' I asked.

'Well we're waiting to hear about the transfers and promotion to the Scottish Borders, if we get it, we're going to buy a cottage with a bit of land,' said Mags.

'Oh, that will be nice for you, Mags,' I replied, sounding envious, 'I know as soon as this divorce is over, I'm selling up and moving back up north to find a cottage.'

'Why don't you come up our way if we get the job?' Mags said, sounding sincere.

'I will bear that in mind, Mags, but I need to get through this divorce first before I can make plans about what I want to do.'

As the months went by, I finally received my decree nisi from the solicitors, which meant I only had to wait for another six weeks before receiving the decree absolute. It couldn't come quick enough, I needed my life back and to get out of this hell hole.

Work was becoming a drag; maybe it was the thought of leaving pastures as soon as the divorce and the house was sold, I had no interest in the job, and as soon as it was five pm, I was out of the door heading home. Through the solicitors, it was agreed that all the furniture and fittings came with the house, meaning that I could do as I wished with them, but I had to wait for my decree absolute and to change back to maiden name of Benson.

The day had arrived for the decree absolute at last, and I was jumping with joy- finally, the stress and the pressure of it all was going to fade away. I took a week off work to organize the sale of the house. The board was going up the following day despite the fact it was December, and nothing was moving due to Christmas, but the estate agent had said that from January, things would start picking up depending on the weather. I crossed my fingers, hoping for a quick sale but wanted the most I could get out from the sale as I had agreed with Mick that the house was only my divorce settlement. I would have to sit tight, hoping for the right buyer.

I woke up with the sun just peeping through the slits in the blind. I had slept well and woke up feeling revitalized; it must be a good sign. It was the best sleep I had gotten after I had caught Mick with Mia sucking him off hard as he sat with his head back moaning in pleasure. I had not slept well for months going through the heartache of what he had done to me, the divorce, and the accident. I was glad to get out of the rat hole of a city that I had never wanted to come to in the first place, but Mick had insisted because of his promotion, so we had to move. He had not even considered my career or what I wanted from life, but I loved him.

I had managed to secure a job with the council in the area doing the same position in the planning department, so that made me feel needed. Mick didn't show much enthusiasm when I told him, saying things like 'why don't you give up work and stay at home? you don't have to work.' Only because there was a reason, he wanted to start a family, but I wasn't keen, I wasn't ready. We were always arguing over starting a family; we had only just been married a year. Mick would walk out to cool down, and then when he came back, things would go back to normal. I needed my independence and my own money, I had always been independent, and I wasn't ready to have a baby yet.

Mick always paid all the bills, leaving me with a credit card to use for shopping and anything that I needed. One reason I had always wanted to be independent was if anything happened to Mick while he was on duty, what would I do? I would have to try to get back onto the employment market, which was changing all the time with new technology coming on the scene. I found it hard enough when I first started looking for employment after leaving school and finished going to college to learn a career, then being lucky to get employment while in my two years in college. All the money I earned was put into savings for what if the unthinkable happened. My instincts were right but for the wrong reasons.

The divorce was straightforward; Mick signed over the house as agreed to save his job and guilt. Once the shock of it all had gone, I had time to process what had happened. It was agreed that I was given all the proceeds from the sale of the house, which made Mick squirm like a child who was being denied a sugar rush. But he had to as I was calling the shots and he hated it. This gave me a substantial amount with house prices skyrocketing, I had a nice nest egg to play with and the wining from the casino in Las Vegas. Mick never liked talking about money; I had sometimes questioned him on the odd time. I knew he would be on a good salary, but some of the things we used to do like expensive holidays, eating out at posh restaurants, weekends away in expensive hotels though I thought no more of it after a while because they soon stopped. Mick started coming home later in the evenings. I never questioned it with his first promotion; I took it at face value that was his job and crime was happening 24/7, so his hours were anytime night/day. Not only that, I was also starting to get involved in my projects at work with a number of large developments being summited into the planning office.

It was the last day in the house as the new owners were moving in, and I had to be out by noon. The sale had gone through quickly as the buyers were due back into the country from Dubai and needed a property with no chain attached. They had viewed the house in February, and April was the latest they were leaving Dubai. Paying extra for a quick sale with no chain, I ensured that this was followed through; ringing the agent and solicitors checking every other day to make sure the sale went through smoothly. I had already sorted the cottage out in Derbyshire and was ready to go.

After a quick shower, I popped on my jeans and a blue jumper and an old pair of trainers for comfort as it was going to be a long day. I thought I'd walk down to the café seeing that it was a nice day, to have breakfast before packing the last of things I was taking with me. I double-checked the road I was crossing ever since the accident had happened, which I had always thought had been deliberate, but nothing was found due to lack of evidence.

All I needed was a bottle of water to take with me for the journey. The furniture I didn't want, because of what had happened, but not only that I didn't need any reminders of Mick, so all of the furniture and beds were sold or given to charity. I definitely didn't want the bed as it reminded me of him having intimate times and the night, he had raped me. I had decided that I would buy a new one, as I wiped traces of Mick clean from all the furniture and fittings. All the white goods were to stay; I just had a few clothes and a few bits and basic utensils from the kitchen. I had sent most of my clothes to the charity shop with most of them being bought from Mick and a few work clothes, but the majority of them didn't fit since the accident, so it was an excellent excuse to get rid of. Just as well, as it was all I could get into my car. There was nothing else to take up in a removal van; I was starting fresh and looking to the future by moving to Derbyshire.

Having no job to go to, I was going to spend a year out doing my cottage up, doing what I could myself, and getting tradesmen in as and when needed. When I had handed my notice in, it worked out very well, all but a couple of days before my last day. It hit me I was leaving the house that had been home for nearly three years, but now, I had to move on without looking back.

CHAPTER NINE:

After arriving at Derbyshire town, Buxton, I had to navigate my way to the cottage. I stopped to read the directions the agent had given me over the phone. I was looking for a road called Brown Edge Road according to the instructions, which suggested that I had to make my way through the town before making a left turn just before the Horse and Jockey pub. 'Bingo!' I found it straight away as I began turning left off the main road; the road started to get narrow, and the houses sparse. I must have travelled about two miles without seeing any buildings further down, but just as I was about to give up, I finally noticed a cottage.

Approaching the cottage, I saw that it was in excellent condition with a manicured garden and orchard. *This can't be it*, I thought in surprise, as the agent had said it was in need of a renovation. I was considering turning my car around from the spot right outside the cottage when a petite, a well-groomed, middle-aged woman came out from nowhere to greet me, almost making me jump. I got out of the car and looked at her closely.

"Hi my name is Janet, are you looking for Keeper's Cottage?" She smiled brightly.

"Yes," I said. "How did you know?" I must have been frowning as her expression changed to a more serious one after she saw the look on my face.

"I was asked to keep a lookout for you by James, the farmer, the man who's selling it. He lives right at the end of this road after about another mile." Janet informed me in detail.

"Oh, I thought I'd taken the wrong turn for a moment there, and I was just about to turn around. My name is Holly Benson by the way, nice to meet you," I said as I shook hands with her with a little smile.

"I can show you around if you want," she offered.

"Oh, that would be great," I said, sounding genuinely grateful.

"Well, just a minute then while I go and lock the door. I'll be back in two ticks." Janet smiled again.

"Yeah, thanks, Janet," I mumbled.

The weather had started to change, and it started to snow as Janet got into the car. Setting off slowly further up the road, as we approached the bend, I could see the cottage in front of me. I pulled up, and we both got out of the car.

"I think it's starting to freeze; it has been so for the last couple of weeks now," said Janet as she shivered lightly.

"Winters started early this year?" I asked.

“Well, if you decided to purchase this cottage, you will notice that the weather is way more severe up here than down south,” she said with a shrug.

The agent had informed me he had left the key under a stone next to the back door of the cottage.

My very first impressions on opening the door were, “Hmmm, this is going to need some work, isn’t it Janet?

“Well, yeah, but look at the big picture when it’s done, this will look incredible, like home,” said Janet.

“I suppose so.” I pictured myself reading a book on my couch with a cup of tea lying next to me, as it snowed outside. It did feel great. The garden was large, almost the same size as Janet’s, and there was an orchard with a lot of fruit trees. The grass had been cut some time ago. The brown and mushy dispersal of grass and weeds on the ground had begun turning white and crispy in the frost as the temperature had started to drop. The good news was that at least the picket fencing surrounding the cottage and garden was in reasonably good condition apart from the peeling paint, which could do with a coat of fresh paint.

The cottage had running water, but there wasn't any central heating, only an open fire with a back boiler for hot water; This was going to be interesting as I was so used to having instant hot water from the tap and central heating, especially ever since the day I had stopped living on the farm with my parents. The farmhouse didn't have that luxury at first until I left home; that was when my father had it totally renovated. It would be like going back in time. Yes, I could put up with this temporarily; winter was coming, so heating would have to be one of the first priorities.

The cottage itself was fairly straightforward, which made it easy to arrange furniture upstairs and downstairs.

The only problem was that the bathroom only had a toilet and a sink with no bath or shower.

"Ugh," I thought out loud, "What did the previous resident do for a hot bath?"

"Oh yes, Jim had a tin bath in the shed at the back which he used," Janet told me.

The wallpaper was peeling off in all of the rooms, and the cottage smelled of damp, which was understandable because it had been empty for over two years and had no heating. At least it had a good roof but needed new windows and doors for sure.

"Well, Holly," said Janet, "this is in fairly good nice shape in comparison to ours, and ours had most of the ceilings down due to the roof leaking. We had to have a new roof, and we had to completely gut the place down to the bare stone. But I must say, Holly, it was well worth it." I nodded as she continued. "At least your roof is good as

James had to replace it just before his gatekeeper, Jim died. Not in the cottage, by the way, it was a road traffic accident," said Janet.

"Oh, that is sad," I muttered.

"Yeah, they said he wouldn't have known about it, because of the speed the other guy was going at as the car had been nicked. The guy was being chased by police, and Jim had just turned onto the main road and had to swerve when out of the blue this guy ran straight into him, it killed him instantly, so they say." Janet looked genuinely upset. "Incidents like these don't happen here often. This place is pretty peaceful."

We must have spent about an hour looking around. I was trying to see the cottage beyond the work that needed to be done, trying to picture the end result in my head. *Yes*, I thought, *I'll try and get the price down, and I'll give it a go.* I really liked the place. While we walked back to the car, I realized that it had started snowing again. We climbed in, and I started the car, reversing into the driveway of the cottage to turn around- I had no problem with it. Janet was a little surprised at how well I maneuvered the turn but didn't comment.

Later on, she told me that most people who came down the narrow road after getting lost had problems turning around due to a lack of experience driving in such terrains. There had been times when Janet had helped them out by getting into the vehicle herself and had turned it around for them, and especially if it was a guy, she secretly felt good.

"Thanks for your help, Janet. For showing me the way to the cottage, I would have given up if I hadn't gotten to your cottage." I earnestly thanked her.

"No problem at all, I'm pleased I could help and got someone to talk to for a while," said Janet. "It does sometimes get a bit lonely being down here, but I wouldn't change it for anything. Would you like a cuppa before you go, Holly?" Her smiled had returned to her face.

"I would have loved to, but I'll have to decline as I have to look somewhere to stay for the night. Thanks for the offer, though." I smiled back at her. I had started to like her already.

"That's no problem. You can stay here with me in the cottage if you like," she offered. "You are very welcome."

"Oh, I wouldn't like to impose." I blushed. "I'll find someplace to stay."

"No, I would love the company; my husband is away for another two weeks on the rigs," said Janet.

"Well, if you are sure, then yes, I'd love to stay." I was too tired to drive anymore, so it felt like a blessing to me.

While the water in the kettle was waiting to boil, Janet was eager to show me around her cottage, showing me what she and her husband Bill had done to it. I was taking this all in as I was going to need some ideas and inspiration for my cottage. I had decided that I was going to purchase it. The cottage had two bedrooms decorated with flora textiles, the exposed stonework, and wooden floors.

The bathroom had an old-fashioned toilet with a pull chain, a basin next to the window, and a white bath with an electric shower and screen; they were behind the door as you went in. The kitchen was as good as any country kitchen with a light oak effect on the wooden cupboards and an agar stove running the central heating around the cottage. There was just one living room which was a decent size and looked very cozy with not too much furniture, and an open fire which was already glowing; the warmth from it made it very comfortable.

The other cottage was nearly the same apart from the kitchen being slightly smaller, Janet and Bill had knocked the coal house in the cottage to make the kitchen larger. Janet kept her cottage very homely looking with manicured garden and orchard, even though it was winter. Both the cottages overlooked an opened grass field that backed into a forest. I was determined to purchase this cottage now that I had a friendly neighbor, albeit the cottage I was going to purchase was further down the lane. But I felt I had a new friend I could rely on, and it was going to be a fresh start.

I sat in the living room while Janet was in the kitchen, making the tea. I was relaxed and comfortable getting that feeling that this could be what felt like moving into a cottage. Janet came through into the living room with a tray containing a large pot of tea, milk, sugar, two mugs, and a section of cakes and pastries.

"Well, get stuck in Holly," said Janet offering me the section of cakes and pastries.

"Thank you," I said gratefully, "these look lovely, did you make them yourself?"

"No," said Janet, "I sometimes work at the bakery in the town and any spares from the shop, we all can take home. It gives me something to do when they ring me. I used to work there full time before I met Bill, my husband." I nodded my head up and down while I savored a cupcake, which was delicious.

"So," asked Janet, "what brings you up to this neck of the woods then?" I felt I couldn't tell her the full truth of what I was running away from, so I just said that I had to get away from the rat race of city life, and I had been given some inheritance money. Janet glanced down at my hands, which I had noticed. Luckily enough, there weren't any signs of a ring being on my wedding finger. Janet left it at that, though I could tell that she knew something wasn't right, but, thankfully, she didn't push it any further. She would eventually find out everything at some stage when I moved up.

Quickly changing the subject, I asked Janet how long she had lived there.

"Oh, it will be ten years this year. Bill and I just fell in love with it, both of us used to live in the village and had always wanted to be a bit more secluded. James, the farmer, had mentioned who owned the other cottage and the one down the road and said he had this cottage he was selling but needed a lot of work. We lived in a large house in the village which was really too big for us, so we jumped at the chance and bought it. Just as well, we lived close by with the work that needed doing on it. We do have a couple more properties we rented out in the town, as well as the one we had lived in. Bill wanted to invest his money from the rigs, so the property was the answer as a pension pot."

She gave me a very detailed answer as we two enjoyed the tea.

“So how long has Bill been on the rigs then?”

“Since the year we got married, we couldn’t afford to rent or buy a place and had to live with his parents, so he decided to make up for it, making sure that we were never skint again. He left for the rigs, and he’s never looked back ever since,” said Janet. “Not only that, he gives me a bit of breathing space, but he comes back home every six weeks for two weeks, so it’s not too bad. It does get a bit lonely, especially in winter, with the dark nights. But the summers make up for it.” I felt bad for her a little, but as long as she was happy.

The following morning, I was up early as I wanted to get an early start. After a bit of breakfast and thanking Janet for her hospitality, I set off heading for home, well not for long I hoped as this would be home soon.

After a good breakfast, I walked back to the house, the sun was bright, and the leaves on the trees seemed to be ready to burst out taking in the rays of the sun after the long winter. Winter was slowly moving on after being a cold one for some time. It didn't seem like April; the weather was forecast to change soon, getting warmer with a possible heatwave for the summer.

There had been no goodbyes as I had shut the door to my house for the last time, handing in the keys to the estate agent before leaving for my new life in Derbyshire. I had seen Debs the night before, and it had been emotionally challenging. I would have to start over, making new friends, but at least I had Janet to rely on waiting for me. I had serval conversations over the phone since the purchase of the cottage, which had made me more relaxed, and there was finally something that I was looking forward to.

As I set off, hitting the traffic at the wrong time of the day- it was bumper to bumper- I wished I had either left early or later in the day. But it really didn't matter as I had all the time in the world to get up there. Once I was on the M1, I was sailing up, stopping a couple of times for tea, and finally something to eat as I didn't want to put Janet out as I was to arrive late in the evening. I had been held up by accident on the motorway and had to wait for four hours before being directed around. I phoned Janet and told her about the delay. I also told her not to bother with a meal as I had eaten due to the accident on the motorway. All I was waiting for was a bed to dive into and a week's sleep.

It was nearly evening by the time I had pulled up outside Janet's cottage. At least there was still daylight left to see and appreciate Janet's garden waking up from the cold winter months. There was an abundance of daffodils with many coloured tulips just starting to open up, which was a breath of fresh air to see. Janet had been waiting for me as she sat next to the window in the living room. She came out after seeing me from the window and came down the narrow lane. She jumped up and walked straight outside, greeting me as soon as I had pulled up.

"You have had a long day driving up, Holly," said Janet with concern.

"Yeah, it's been one thing after another, heavy traffic getting out of London then the accident on the motorway, but at least I'm finished with that now." I sounded relieved even to myself.

"Come on in, and I'll put the kettle on, I bet you're ready for a cuppa," said Janet.

"Yes, please, I would love one. Thanks, Janet." I inhaled the fresh air; I was already feeling home.

Your garden looks lovely, Janet; it was the first thing that I noticed. What beautiful colours, breath-taking."

"Thank you, Holly, I try and put as much colour in for the spring as winter is so dull," said Janet from the kitchen.

"Well, you certainly have done that."

"When you're ready to do your garden, I'll give you a hand." She had said, and I smiled.

"That would be great, thanks, Janet."

While Janet was making the tea, I started to empty my car - not that I had brought much, but I made at least four trips to my car before I had finished. Janet had told me that I could put my things in the spare bedroom where there was enough room for me to sleep in the bed. The bedroom was square with a wardrobe and a chest of drawers on one side of the wall opposite the double bed. I had a few loose clothes on hangers, which I put straight into the wardrobe that Janet had left empty for me to use. The boxes were stacked next to the chest of drawers with the remaining bits and pieces that I had. Once I had finished, I walked through to the living room where Janet had placed two mugs of tea and a selection of cakes and pastries again. We chatted for a while, and then I suddenly started to yawn, not realizing the time. It had gone midnight, no wonder I was so tired. With that, I told Janet that I was hitting the pillow, and so did she.

I slept well; I must have been tired after the long journey with the hold-ups along the motorway. It was another sunny day with no clouds in the sky. Janet was already up, as I made my way through to the kitchen.

"Good morning, Holly. Did you sleep well?"

"Yeah, that bed is so comfy." I grinned.

"The mattress is made of duck down; you just sink into it, we have one on our bed, too." Janet grinned too.

You must tell me where you get them from."

"Well you'll have to ask Bill when he comes home, he got them from someone he knows, and Bill seems to know a lot a people in the town."

"When will he be back? I'll ask him."

"He's just gone back a couple of days ago," said Janet. "Anyway, it'll be a while before you need a bed." She reminded me.

"Yes, well, that's one thing to add to my list to buy," I said.

Once we both had breakfast, and Janet had brought the key to my cottage, we decided to see what needed to be done first. I picked up a writing pad and pencil to take with me to the cottage to make a list of jobs that needed to be attended to and to priorities them in order.

I pulled up outside my cottage with Janet by my side. As we got out of the car, I grabbed my bag with my pad and pencil, and we walked to the front of the cottage. Janet gave me the key to my cottage, and I opened the door with excitement, I was home. Everything was the same as when I had come down to see it a few months ago. I turned around to say something to Janet, but she had disappeared somewhere, so I took my bag and pulled out my pad and pencil ready to make a list. Just after a minute, I heard Janet coming back and turned to see her holding a bag.

"You need to celebrate Holly; I've brought a bottle of champagne to toast the cottage" She waved the bag in front of me.

"Aw Janet, you're so thoughtful and a dear friend." I gave her an awkward hug.

"I'm glad you see me as a friend," said Janet beaming.

"Of course I do, you don't realize what you are to me."

"You're a breath of fresh air since the first day you came out to see the cottage, and I was secretly hoping that you buy it," said Janet.

"Oh, thanks." I giggled.

Janet took the champagne out of the bag, followed by two fluted champagne glasses. She opened the bottle, which she seemed to be a dab hand at, and poured the fizzy liquid into the glasses without spilling a drop.

"You must have had a lot of practice opening champagne bottles without spilling any." I commended with surprise.

"I've done a lot of outside catering, which involves opening champagne," said Janet.

Sipping the champagne, I started to make notes as Janet pointed out in each room, her thoughts and ideas about what needed to be changed or tended to. Further inspection on the roof needed to be sorted first, this would ensure that the cottage would be watertight. There was no damp course in the cottage; hence the smell of damp was there, and it had no heating apart from an open fire in the living room. The doors and windows needed to be changed, but I wasn't sure if I should change them for double glazing. Janet's cottage was wooden which needed painting every few years; I didn't fancy doing that, I wanted to put things in place that didn't need maintenance, I did not want to be a slave to my property.

Once we had enjoyed the champagne with the list of priorities to start to work on the cottage, it was after mid-day. I thought that I could start in the garden while I waited for tradesmen needed on my list. Janet knew a few trades' people from the town who had done work in her cottage, which she was delighted with.

"Come on, Holly, let's get a bit of lunch." Janet insisted.

"Good idea, I'm hungry too." I didn't lock up the place as I was coming back after lunch. Janet had to go into town to help out at the bakery due to the hotel in the town having a function later that evening. With such a large order, they needed all the help.

Janet made some sandwiches while I put the kettle on to make tea. "I'll get those telephone numbers out for you to ring and get some quotes for the jobs that you need help for," Janet said.

"Ahan, that would be great."

"You probably better ring them in the evening as they will be working, and they don't normally answer their mobile phones." Janet filled me in further.

We both sat down to eat our sandwiches and drink our tea. Janet said that I could take some gardening tools from the shed to help with the tidying up of my garden, which was a bit of wilderness in places. I had only seen it the day I came up in the freezing weather; everything was brown with white crispy bits of frost on the ground. I thought I would start with the boundary fence by cutting the rough grass and brambles that had built up over the months, clinging to it as a foothold to escape out of the boundary.

It was the beginning of me trying to shape up the cottage as my home—the place where I not only would find solace but will start a new life. I was ready to move on and forget what had passed; I was prepared to leave the bitter memories behind me. I had a new life, a new home only that someone to lean on. I had stopped myself right there at the thought. I had no place for anyone, a relationship at the moment. I needed to be on my own and explore the world.

CHAPTER TEN:

Janet waved me from around the corner as she went off into the town while I made my way to the shed, deciding what I needed to tend my garden. 'Mm, a cutter of some sort?' I thought as I looked around to see what we had got. I found some shears, and a hand scythe that I hoped had been sharpened. I tested it with the slide of my index finger, the blade felt smooth, and it had no rust, so it had to work fine.

'Yep, that's sharp,' I muttered and walked back to my cottage, kitted out with the tools from Janet's shed to attack the weeds climbing the fence. The weather was still sunny, but grey clouds had started to form, showing some signs of rain.

'Where the hell do I begin?' I said out loud with my hands on hips. I surveyed the fence line thinking of ways to tackle it.

'Do you want some help with that?' a voice piped out of nowhere. I spun around to find a tall blonde guy, probably in his early thirties. For a few seconds, I thought it was Mick standing there, and it made me flinch; his features and build looked quite similar to Mick's. A slight panic came over me, but I gathered my bearings when I realized it was not him.

'Hi, I'm Mark. I'm sorry if I startled you,' he said while waving his hand in front of my face, which pretty much brought me back into the moment.

'Oh, no. I thought you were someone else,' I said, and instantly regretted it; I didn't want my past popping up again.

'Oh, I hope not someone scary,' joked Mark. I quickly changed the subject, so he didn't ask any more questions.

'What are you doing down in this neck of the woods then, Mark?' I asked casually.

'I've just come up from the farm at the end of the track,' he pointed his finger in the direction. 'It's a wonder you didn't see me passing by this morning. I saw your car at the cottage, I was going to stop, but James had a bit of an emergency on with a burst pipe,' said Mark.

'Oh, so you're a plumber? I asked, relieved as I would need one soon.

'Well, a little bit of everything, really. I'm a carpenter by trade, but I am involved in other trades as well; you have to be these days. But I don't do electrics.' replied Mark in detail now.

'Do you know anyone who could give me a price on checking if the roof is okay or if it needs any maintenance?' I asked him.

'That roof is sound. I did it just over three years back,' he shrugged.

'Phew, that's good; one less cost for me.' I sighed in relief. 'You don't do windows, do you?' I asked him again.

'It depends on what sort you want, wooden or double glazing,' said Mark turning his head to look at the windows.

'Well, I was thinking of double glazing, so I don't have to paint them.' I had decided double glazing would be better as Janet had told me that it got a bit nippy up there in winter, and I told this to Mark also.

'Yes, it does a bit nippy indeed. It's a bit different from living in the city,' Mark nodded. I thought to myself, *how did he know I had come from the city? Has Janet been talking about me to the folk here?* I would have to be a bit subtle in and around about the way I mentioned it, so I brushed over Mark's comment.

'Do you know anyone who can do the damp course for me?'

'I do. I can give him a call if you like,' he offered.

'Yes, thank you. That'll be great if you would,' I said, sounding grateful.

We chatted for nearly ten minutes. The sky was coming over cloudy, and a curtain of grey clouds entirely engulfed the sun. It looked like it was going to rain. As Mark got into his pickup truck to go, the gates of the heavens opened, which made it look like someone had turned a shower on. I dropped my tools which I was holding and ran into the cottage as fast as I could, but I was still drenched as I got inside. I sighed, thinking that the rest of the day was lost with the rain, not only that, time was getting on. I was wet and needed a hot soak in the bath. The rain didn't hold up, so I locked up and gathered my tools quickly to throw them in the boot of the car and set off down the lane back to Janet's cottage.

Janet was helping out at the bakery with the hotel order for an event that was taking place that evening; hence, she would be home around seven pm. I was going to prepare tea for the two of us; there were a couple of steaks in the fridge, so I thought I would make something simple with it like chips and peas, followed by a sponge pudding with custard. I let the water run in the bath while I quickly made the sponge mix ready for the microwave, as this only needed four minutes of cooking time.

After clearing up everything, I went to check the water in the bath. I had worked the temperature and the amount of water needed for a deeply relaxing soak to a tee. Peeling off my clothes and dropping them in the laundry basket, I eased myself into the bath, feeling the heat of the water as my body tried to adapt to the same temperature.

'God, this feels good!' I just laid there not moving at all as the heat started to soak through my body. It was about 6.30

pm when I emerged fully dressed into the kitchen to start making the tea for when Janet came home. Janet liked her steak well done, which made it easier for me as I preferred it that way as well. I partially cooked them ready for when Janet came in to finish off, the same with the chips, peeling them ready to put into the fryer. It was past seven-thirty pm when Janet got home; she had a bit of a stressful evening due to one of the staff dropping a couple of trays of cakes onto the floor in the kitchen of the hotel. New supplies had to be brought back from the bakery, which luckily had been enough for the days baking.

The bakery supplied to several hotels and businesses in the area, and it was swamped. The staff always called on Janet in busy times when hotels were putting on events needing extra supplies of cakes and pastries. She helped in organizing the staff for the deliveries and setting them up in the hotel dining room for the event to take place that evening.

Janet was glad to get home after that had happened at the hotel. She told me the details as she sank on the sofa, with her head in her hands. Her feet were aching as she had been on her feet the entire time.

'Oh, you are a darling for starting the tea; I wasn't looking forward to it,' said Janet with gratitude.

'Well, it's the least I could do; you have been so good to me and helpful. I thought I'd start pulling my weight around here now that I'd be with you for a few months until I get my bathroom and heating sorted.'

'Aah, you don't have to do that,' said Janet. 'It's nice to have company while Bill's on the rigs.'

'Well, you've been a god sent as I would have had to work around the dust and dirt in my cottage with a temporary bed and no bath to soak in.' I was genuinely thankful.

After we had eaten, Janet went for a soak in the bath to ease her aching feet and to relax, while I cleared the pots and washed up. I'd just made the tea as Janet came through into the living room where I had switched the TV on, not as though there wasn't anything to watch. Janet sat in her recliner while I sat on the sofa with my feet folded under me to one side.

'So how was your day, Holly?' asked Janet.

'Well, I'd manage to find what I needed in the shed and was weighing up where to start when someone called Mark turned up. Do you know him, Janet?' I said.

'Oh, so you met Mr. Charmer, have you, Holly?' she asked.

'Why? what do you mean?' I said it with caution.

'He is okay, really, but he's a bit of a Casanova with the ladies around here, so watch yourself. He'll be making a beeline for you,' warned Janet.

'Is he a builder because he said that he did the roof on the cottage before the keeper died? He also said that he could help with some of the work that wants doing in the cottage,' I filled her in with the details.

'Yes, he is very good and knows what he's doing despite his reputation,' said Janet.

'Don't worry about that; I can handle him. Though I don't like guys who are so sure of themselves thinking they are a babe magnet, I'll soon burst his bubble,' I said and then sipped my tea.

'So, you have had experience in that department then?' Janet smiled and raised her eyebrows.

'Well, I have worked a couple of years with the police. You meet all sorts,' I shrugged and quickly changed the subject back to Mark.

'So, what's the story with Mark then? I might as well be ready for him if he is going to do some work for me, Janet,' I inquired.

'Yeah, I suppose you are right,' said Janet.

'It started when his parents split up. He was about eighteen and was working for his father in the building trade. That is how he started learning different trades. As the years went by, his father re-married to a woman younger than him. Later on, his father caught them together in a comprising position, when they were not expecting him to come home, obviously you can guess the rest,' said Janet.

'Hmm,' I said, thinking to myself; *I know exactly how that feels*. 'How awful! What did his dad do?'

'He dragged his wife off his son, punched them both before leaving, and nobody has ever seen him since that day,' Janet shook her head.

'What happened to the business, did Mark carry on with it?'

'Oh no, his wife sold everything and buggered off with some guy she used to go out with a few years before meeting Mark's dad, so Mark set up on his own. Since then, he's been seen out with a different woman every night,' she informed me.

'Well, as long as he does a good job, I can manage the rest. I've asked him to quote me on some jobs that I want to get done so that I can keep in control of my costs.' I went on.

'Yes, you need to do that as they so get out of control. We learned from experience with the properties we have, and with doing this cottage as well. I had to have everything written down,' said Janet.

'I'm going to write everything down on this cottage. I don't want to spend all my savings on it as I haven't got a job to go to. I was hoping to take a year out before looking for work.'

'What sort of work would you be looking for Holly?' she asked.

'I used to work in the planning office for Surrey council, so something in that line of work, I suppose,' I gave her the details of my last job.

'You've worked for the council? Well, you'll soon be sorted with your cottage with the extension, knowing how they work.'

'I guess so since I've done a bit of building work when I was living with my parents, they had some farm cottages for the farmworkers, so when something needed doing, I used to go with him and give him a hand,' I filled her in.

'Well, between you and Mark, you'll be able to get that cottage in some sort of order then,' Janet said as she rubbed her hands together and put them on her cheeks, and I smiled.

'Yeah, I suppose you could say that.'

The following morning was bright, with the sun rising up into the cloudless sky, with no rain on the horizon as the forecast was dry weather with sunshine all week. I was ready to get going with so much to do. It was 7 am, and I wanted an early start. Janet was still in bed, so I thought I'd treat her to breakfast in the bed, but she heard me walking about in the kitchen.

'You're up early, Holly?' said Janet entering the kitchen.

'Yeah, I need to get on with the outside until the inside is sorted, if I don't the garden will soon get out of hands, so I need to get it tamed. I was looking at the fence, which seemed to be in good condition, but it needs a coat of fence paint to brighten it up.'

'Well, if you hang on a few minutes until I've had my breakfast, I'll give you a hand.' Janet offered.

'No, that's okay, thanks. I don't expect you to help me; you must have work to do, Janet.'

'Holly, I want to help, it'll give me something to do, and there is nothing to do in my garden at the moment,' said Janet earnestly.

'Well, thank you. It will be much appreciated,' I smiled at her brightly.

It was just after 7.30 am when we arrived at Keepers Cottage. Janet had brought her spare kettle which she had in the back of the cupboard, a couple of mugs and a small jar of coffee and milk, at least we had running drinking water on tap, which was the only thing that was working apart from one socket switch for the electricity. The whole cottage needed re-wiring and plumbing at some stage over the months ahead. I needed to be in by autumn as I didn't want to impose too much on Janet's hospitality.

I had brought some tools from Janet's shed with us, and I was ready to attack the garden.

'Well, Janet, where do we start?' I looked at her as we both got into the garden.

'You start on this side, and I'll start the opposite side. What do you think?' Janet had experience with tending to the gardens, and it showed.

'Works for me,' I replied. Janet took the shears while I had the scythe. We both cracked on with the task in front of us. We had been working over an hour hacking at the brambles and weeds when I heard a vehicle pull up next to the cottage. The vehicle door banged shut, and then we heard footsteps of someone approaching us. Next, I heard a wolf whistle and a sarcastic comment when I bent down and revealed my cleavage. I'd taken off a lightweight jacket and was in my tee-shirt, not realizing I was showing any skin. I was about to say something, but Janet butted in, causing Mark to stop in his tracks, not realizing that I wasn't on my own.

'Mark, we'll have none of that around here, or I'll have to wash your mouth out with soap and water,' warned Janet. It looked like they were used to this banter.

'I thought I'd bring you the prices for the jobs you asked me to give to you,' Mark said. I stood still where I was hacking at the brambles. He walked towards me, holding an envelope and handed it to me. As he placed it in my palm, he subtly pressed his finger and stroked the back of my hand. I quickly retracted the envelope, I was hoping Janet hadn't noticed, but she had by the look in her eye.

'Thanks, I'll have a look at it later and let you know then, Mark,' I mumbled.

'Just give us a ring when you're ready, and I'll be there,' answered Mark with a twinkle in his eye. God, he did look a bit like Mick, especially with the build the same haircut and blonde hair. This guy seemed to be a quick mover; I'll need to watch my guard if he is going to do the work on the cottage. When Mark had left, Janet said she would go and make the coffee. While she was gone, I opened the envelope to see what

Mark was going to charge for the job I had asked him to do. 'Hmm, I suppose it is not too expensive, but I'll have a word with Janet and see what she thinks as prices down in Surrey would have been twice as much.' I thought walking towards the cottage, Janet was just bringing the coffees outside.

'I'm gagging for a coffee - that was quick.'

'I thought we were ready for a break,' said Janet. 'You need to watch Mark; he's such a charmer.' she continued.

'Tell me about it. I've never known anyone like that; he moves fast, doesn't he?'

'I noticed the envelope exchange with him,' sighed Janet shaking her head.

'Mm, I wasn't expecting that as I hardly know him,' I sighed too and grabbed my cup of coffee.

'Well that's how he works his women, it looks like he's already starting on his next conquest, just be careful, or you will only be another notch on his bedpost,' said Janet casually, but there was a warning hidden behind her words.

'This woman, it's going to be one of them, Janet, I assure you.' I handed Janet the envelope with the prices Mark had given me for doing the job. Janet opened the envelope to look at what he had put for the job.

'Mm, these are pretty good prices Holly, I don't think you'll get a better price from anyone around here,' she said, raising her eyebrows at the parchment.

'This would have been double the price down in Surrey; I wasn't too sure what the prices were like up here.'

'No, that's a good price for sure,' said Janet. 'I'll give him a ring later then, but I'll just have to ignore his charm.' Then, she smirked and said, 'Keep your legs crossed, gal.'

'Too damn right, I'm not going to be a notch on his bedpost, Janet,' I replied.

'He needs a strong woman to put him in his place,' said Janet.

'Oh, I can do that, alright, they just need a punch in the right area,' I laughed at the end.

We spent a couple more hours on the fence line before heading off back for a spot of lunch. I nipped off to the bathroom to wash my hands, while Janet put the kettle on and brought some cakes and pastries out on a plate. I was ready for them; she had brought them back from the bakery last night.

My stomach was rumbling, sitting down, taking the weight off my feet; I switched the TV on to listen to the news and weather. I had turned it on halfway through the new caster reporting about a drug bust in the Surrey area with one officer shot dead and one badly injured. My heart sank as I turned the volume up and stared at the TV. Janet brought through the cakes and coffee and realized that there was something wrong.

'Holly, are you alright? you look as though you've seen a ghost.' Janet sat down, putting the tray on the coffee table, waiting for me to reply.

'Well, it may be nothing, but I might know who they are,' I said subtly. ' I have never told anyone that I was married to a police officer, he was working in the drug squad in Surrey, while the divorce was going through and still was when I moved up here. I was wondering if he was in this raid and got shot.'

'Oh, Holly, I'm so sorry why you don't phone up to find out?' said Janet rubbing my shoulder.

'They won't tell me anything, but I'll try and find out from my friend Debs who still lives down there, her husband's still in the force.' I picked up the phone and dialed Debs's number, but she wasn't picking up. 'Damn, something must be wrong; she normally picks her phone up. I tried the station, but they wouldn't tell me anything. God, who else could I phone? *Oh, I know,* I thought- *Mags*. She'd find out for me. I phoned Mags; I was lucky she was just going on duty.

'Mags, I'm glad I've got a hold of you. I can't get hold of Debs.' I said in a rushed voice.

'No, you won't. Pete's been shot, and he is in the hospital.' Mags dropped the bomb.

'Oh, my God, how serious is it, Mags?'

'He's stable, but he's lost a lot of blood, they had to give him a blood transfusion as the bullet nicked his main artery, but it did help with a doctor being nearby when the shooting started.

'I'll have to go to her and give her some support,' I said, all panicked.

'No, you can't; the police won't let anyone near due to the case and people involved, Holly,' she said.

'Oh shit, that's a bummer. You don't know who died, do you, Mags?'

'No, but it wasn't Mick. If that's who you were going to ask, he had a lucky escape,' said Mags.

'Oh, that's good, not that I have any feeling for him though Mags,' I said with relief.

'Holly, you were married to him for three years, despite what happened between you two you must still have feelings,' Mags went on.

'I suppose I do, but I'm trying Mags.'

‘Anyway, don’t worry, he’s fine. Holly, I am sorry I can’t talk much as I would love to catch up, but I’m just about to go on shift,’ said Mags with a small voice.

‘Yeah yeah. Thanks for letting me know Mags, and I’ll catch up with you soon.’ Janet sat there, listening to my conversation with Mags. I had to tell her the details; she had to know, but to what extent? I argued it within my head and sighed as I faced her.

It was time to share my life with my new friend.

CHAPTER ELEVEN:

After the shock of watching the TV report and finding out who was involved, I was relieved to find a distraction in getting back to the cottage and carrying on with the fence line. Janet had a call from the bakery asking if she could go in, as one of the part-timers had rung in sick. She had stepped in, taking off into the town, which allowed me some breathing space; I thought she might have asked about Mick, and I didn't want to have a conversation about my past today.

I had made good progress cutting back the brambles and weeds winding their way up between the fencing. I had just got down to the bottom, not realizing the time was running short as it was getting dark. As it hit me, I picked up all the tools, and while packing up the stuff, I heard a noise like someone was approaching.

I thought it as Janet, but as I waited, I couldn't see anyone.

“Hmm, strange,’ I thought out loud, ‘I must be getting tired.’ With that thought, I put the tools in the boot of my car, started the engine and set off down to Janet’s cottage. Janet hadn’t got back from the bakery, but she had left the door unlocked for me. I left the tools in the car, knowing I would need them the following day. I was ready for another bath and wasn’t hungry, so taking off my boots, I went straight into the bathroom, deciding to have a shower instead of a bath to relax my tired muscles. After the shower, since I was tired and needed a drink before going to bed, I fixed myself a hot chocolate. I must have slept soundly, not hearing Janet coming in that night.

It was after 8 in the morning when I woke up, only because the sun was shining through a slit through the curtains, with the ray of sunlight caressing my face. Janet was up as I walked through the kitchen.

‘Morning sleepyhead,’ said Janet grinning.

‘Morning Janet, what time did you come back last night?’ I smiled sheepishly.

'I was late, at about ten, I think. A couple of us from the bakery went over to the pub for a pint and a sandwich,' she said

'Oh, I was out for the count. I never heard you come in last night.'

'You must have had a busy afternoon after you went back,' said Janet.

'Yeah, not too bad, got far down to the end, so I'll be going across today.'

'What time did you come back then?' asked Janet.

'I don't know it was starting to get dark. What plans have you today Janet?' I sipped some water from a glass.

'I'm going back to the bakery to cover for Sarah; she has the day off. Why? did you need anything done or fetched from the town Holly?'

'No, I'm hoping to get the fence cut back today, ready to be painted.' I shook my head.

'Have you spoken to Mark yet about the jobs?' Janet asked casually, and it reminded me.

'No, I forgot to phone him last night, but I'll phone him later today.'

Janet went to work while I washed the breakfast pots and packed a few bits to take with me to the cottage; I headed out, locking the door behind. It was nearly the end of May, and I was desperate to get the basics done so I could move into my own home soon. While taking my stuff from the car, I noticed a red pick-up truck pulling up and stopping in front of my cottage; it was Mark.

That's good, saves me phoning him tonight, I thought to myself, pleased.

'Good morning, beautiful,' waved Mark; I rolled my eyes.

'Less of the charm save it for someone else,' I muttered.

'Oh-uh. I like it when you are angry,' he smirked.

'Yeah, well, I'm glad you've called in; it saves me phoning you tonight. You have got the job doing the cottage, but how long will it take? I need to be in by September.'

'Ahan, I should say it will be done by then,' said Mark with a cheeky grin, which I ignored.

'Alright, when can you start?'

'Well, I've got three or four jobs on the go at the moment, but you could make it worth my while,' he replied with a raised eyebrow. 'I've got one I have to finish off as I've got the roof off at the minute so I could start Thursday morning.'

'So, I'll expect to hear from you at 8 am on Thursday, and I'll have coffee waiting.'

'Now that's an offer I can't refuse,' said Mark, and I shrugged.

'And if you behave yourself, I won't put any laxative in it.'

'Better bring my own, then,' laughed Mark.

'Whatever, you'll just have to behave yourself, won't you, Mark?' I said. He went off with a smirk on his face. Well, time would tell.

Once Mark had gone, I took out the tools from the car, ready for another day hacking the hedges and weed on the fence, but coffee must come first before I started. While I was in the makeshift kitchen, I thought I heard some twigs break outside near the door. Taking my coffee, I stepped out to have a look. 'Hello?' I called out to check if anyone was there, but no answer, was I starting to hear things?

I could bet that I had heard someone out there. After finishing the last few mouthfuls of my coffee, I rinsed the mug under the tap and set off to tackle the fence line hoping it was going to be the last day before slapping the paint on. Some of the fence lines weren't too bad; I must have done the worst of it the day before. It looked like good progress, and I felt confident that I'd finish it that day.

Just when I was about to finish, I heard a vehicle pulling up outside the cottage, which I did hear this time. I walked towards the front of the cottage, where a black 4x4 was parked next to the garden fence. A middle-aged man wearing a flat cap, checked shirt and jeans was walking towards me, by the looks of him he had got to be a farmer, by the dressing sense.

'Hello, you must be Holly Benson? I'm James Holland. I sold you the cottage, sorry I didn't meet then, my wife and I were away. We live at the farm down the bottom there,' he said as he pointed his finger towards its direction.

'Oh, it's nice to meet you, at last. I didn't know that someone was living down there until Janet mentioned it.'

'Janet told me that you were staying with her until you get the cottage livable,' he said.

'Yes, it's very nice of her, I'm hoping to move in by September, and I've got Mark starting on Thursday,' I told him in detail.

'Haha, you'll have your hands full with him, just be careful. He has a reputation with the ladies,' James said grimly.

‘I know, I’ve had his life story from Janet, and I’ve threatened him to put laxatives in his coffee if he doesn’t behave,’ I said with a cordial smile.

Well, someone needs to get the better of him; he’s broken a lot of hearts,’ James said as he shook his head.

‘And he won’t be breaking mine. I was just coming up to make a coffee, would you like one James?’

‘I’ll have one another time, thanks. I’ve got to go and get some feed for the chickens my wife looks after, but thanks,’ he smiled sincerely.

‘Well, you are always welcome to drop in anytime for a coffee when you’re passing.’

‘Thanks, I’ll be taking you up on that, Holly,’ he said, and with that, James walked back to his vehicle, setting off down the road towards the main road for the town.

I made coffee and took it outside, where I noticed there was an old garden bench I hadn’t seen before, and I sat down to drink my coffee. It felt good laying back, taking in the scenery and thinking about what I was going to do with the wilderness of the rest of the garden. It took me another couple of hours chopping the brambles and weeds. Luckily, I had the shears as some of the brambles were thick to chop and needed cutting. Once I'd finished, I picked up the rake, dragging them up onto a heap ready for burning once the pile had dried off a bit over a day or so.

My phone rang, and I answered while thinking about who it could be. It was Janet, asking if I wanted some fish and chips. She said she could bring the food back when she left work in half an hour.

'Oh, yes, please, I was hungry.'

'I've nearly finished for the day, so I'll see you in half an hour then,' said Janet.

Once I'd finished, I collected the tools and decided to lock them in the cottage instead of taking them back to Janet's cottage. As I opened my car door, I was surprised to find one red rose with a card on the driving seat. The rose brought back my memory of the time when I had a full bouquet of them delivered to me while I was recuperating at my parents' home. It was a surprise; I picked up the card and opened it; the message wasn't in English, and it read 'Il primo giorno che ti ho visto ti amavo.'

I wondered what it meant. I smelt it; it smelt precisely the same as the others. It must be Liam whoever he was, but then I thought of the New Year's Eve party at the station back home. I must check this out when I got back.

Janet was just arriving as I walked into the cottage. I quickly needed to hide the rose, or she would be asking questions, walking straight into my bedroom. I placed it on the sideboard, thinking I'd sort it later. I rushed back into the kitchen; Janet was there with the fish and chips she had brought.

'I timed that right Janet, I'm starving,' I said as Janet got the plates out while I put the kettle on.

'I thought it would save cooking tonight,' said Janet. 'I've been rushed off my feet in the shop, and you being busy with your cottage, I thought it would be a nice change.'

After we had eaten and cleared the dishes, I nipped into the bathroom for a quick shower. Janet wanted a soak in the bath and would be a while. Drying my hair, I looked at the rose and the message on the card, I had to find out what it meant.

In one of my packed boxes, I managed to find a slim vase to put the rose in. While Janet was having a soak, I took the vase through to the kitchen to fill it with water slipping the rose in and taking it back before Janet saw it.

I had to find out what these words meant, but at least I knew the words were in Italian. I did have an Italian guide book when Mick and I used to go to Italy for long romantic weekends and to taste the wines. I only would have to find a library in the town to translate it.

The following morning the weather had turned, raining off and on, so I couldn't work in the garden. Janet was asked to work in the shop again. I thought I would go into the town to find a library to get these words translated without Janet asking questions. Plus, I was going to source kitchen units and appliances and a bathroom suite.

I parked in the car park nearest to the town centre, thinking that it would be somewhere nearby, but I had to ask someone where it was. I was only a street away, but it didn't open until 10 am. I had an hour to kill; there was a market on in the centre with all different stalls selling their wares, so I had a wander around until then.

It was 10.30 am before I got there, getting carried away with the market stalls finding items I could decorate the cottage with. I would have to come back when I was at that stage. The library was an old building with three-floor levels holding thousands of books. I just wondered if the librarian knew anyone who could translate Italian.

Seeing an older woman behind the counter, sorting some books that needed to go back onto the shelves, I went straight to her and told her what I was looking for.

'Well, can I help you? I'm a retired teacher, and I used to teach a little Italian apart from French and German,' she smiled kindly.

'Wow, err, it's a bit delicate, really,' I said. But I thought she didn't know me, so it was safe to show her the card I got with the rose. She put her specs on and read the card.

'Hmm, it says, "**the first day I saw you, I loved you**." Your man is romantic, is he Italian?' she asked with a gentle smile. I nodded and gulped; I had to come up with something.

'He is always writing notes, and it's the first time he's written it in Italian.'

'No problem! If he sends you more, it would be my pleasure to translate them for you,' she said earnestly.

'Well, thank you,' I said genuinely, and with that, I left and headed to the car. My mind wandered back to Zorro and Count Dracula. Both of them did have a bit of an accent, but I wouldn't have thought it was Italian. I'm sure they were the same guy; they kissed the same. It's got to be someone in the force; firstly, because Zorro wouldn't be able to get into the station if he wasn't connected to the force in some way and secondly, he seemed to know that Mick was up to something.

It had stopped raining, and the sun had come out. I got back to Janet's cottage just after mid-day. Janet wasn't at home, so I made coffee and sandwich, deciding to rest for a while before leaving for my cottage to do some more work in the garden. It took the rest of the afternoon to clear all the brambles and weeds onto a pile ready to burn. On the other side of the fence line was a large grass field, where the sheep were grazing, keeping the grass short next to the outer fence. *James could have put them in the orchard and garden to save me a job*, I thought, *but never mind now, I got the job done.* I needed some paint too; *I'd been into the town I should have gotten some. Never mind, I'll go and get some tomorrow after Mark comes and gets started on the work*, I made a mental note.

My phone rang, it was Janet, saying that she was home making tea and something to eat. I told her that I'd be down straight away. I gathered my tools, locked them in the cottage, and made my way back to Janet's cottage.

'I didn't realize what time it was until you rang me, Janet. I thought you were working through until 7 pm.'

'No, we got caught up, so we all left early,' said Janet. 'I've brought some cakes and pastries home with me so that we can have them for after.' Janet had made a chicken salad, the table was laid with the tea just waiting to be mashed, and I was hungry after working in the garden.

We sat down and ate, and Janet went for a bath after that. I also decided to shower as I stunk of sweat with all the hard work in the garden. After washing and drying my hair, I felt more refreshed as I came out of the bedroom in my dressing gown. Janet was in living with the TV on watching a drama. I asked her if she would like a cup of tea, as I made my way into the kitchen. I hadn't even reached the kitchen when there was a knock on the door.

When I opened the door, I realized I was in my dressing gown. It was Mark, of all the people it had to be him.

'Hello, gorgeous, you're ready for me then?' said Mark undressing me with his eyes.

'Watch it,' I said drily.

'Yeah, I am watching it, alright,' Mark scratched his chin, looking at me up and down.

'Mark, you have an answer for everything, don't you?" I said, annoyed.

'Only to beautiful women in a dressing gown.'

'You are getting a bit, cocky, mate,' Janet appeared from behind. 'Now, what's the occasion for the call?' she asked, neutralizing the conversation.

'I was just passing to say that I'll be starting the day after tomorrow,' said Mark.

'Well, thanks for letting us know, Mark,' said Janet in an unchanging voice.

'I'll see you then,' said Mark in a boyish tone as though he had been told by the teacher. Closing the door, I turned to walk to the kitchen to make the tea. Janet followed.

'You will have to be careful with him Holly; he's so full of himself, he thinks all the women in the area think he's the best looking guy around. He's so arrogant with it'" said Janet getting a bit uptight about.

'He is a bit cocky; I'll have to up my game then Janet. I think I'll have to obtain some liquid laxatives for his coffee.'

'What you're really going to do it? Put it in his coffee?' said Janet, sounding a bit shocked.

'I sure would if he stepped out of the line, would you like a bet on that Janet?'

That will be interesting to see Holly,' laughed Janet.

'Yeah, I suppose it will, time will tell.'

The following day Janet came into the town with me to buy some fence paint, there was a choice of three shades, light, medium, and dark. I decided to get a light colour, buying twenty litres, thinking that even if I didn't use all of it, I would keep for the following year. I also purchased some liquid laxatives.

The weather was warm and sunny the next day; Mark was due to turn up and start working on the cottage. It was gone 9 am when he turned up, his long blonde hair unruly.

'I had a job to finish off before I started here,' he said. He started with measuring up the windows and doors to get them ordered, as it took about three weeks in the making. In the meantime, he would be getting on with the bathroom, but first, he was going to get the heavy out by knocking a couple of walls out for the bathroom and kitchen. The adjoining outbuilding compensated for the extra room for the bathroom and kitchen.

Janet didn't come to the cottage with me, but she did say she would be down later in the afternoon. So I was going to be on my own with him, this was going to interesting.

Mark started to get his gear from his pick-up truck, ready to knock the walls down; I took myself into the rear of the garden with the paint I had purchased the other day. Tipping the paint into a paint bucket, I started to paint the fence; it was a good choice of colour; the other two colours would have been too dark, I thought. The morning seemed to be getting warmer, and after a couple of hours, I decided to have a break and have five minutes on the garden bench. I could hear a lot of banging going on inside the cottage.

There were bits of rumble and dust coming out from the door. Standing near the door, I shouted to Mark,

'I'm going to make coffee, would you like one Mark?' The banging stopped, I let the dust settle, and when I saw Mark, and I was taken aback. He was stripped down to his jeans, showing off his tort body and muscular arms. *Fuck, he is lust!* I thought. But no, I had to get a grip.

'Hello, darling, you've come to see my body?' said Mark in a provocative way.

'Are you sure you just want coffee in your cup and nothing else?' I said sarcastically.

'Okay, I'll shut up; coffee, please,' said Mark toning it down. Luckily, I had the cool box with my coffee and milk in, I picked it up and dusted it out, the kettle needed a good clean it was covered in dust. Mark started to pick up the rumble into a wheelbarrow, emptying it into the back of his pick-up. While I was waiting for the kettle to boil I got the mugs ready, turning around once I'd finished with the mugs, I watched Mark filling the barrow with the rumble, god his body was getting me horny.

I hadn't been with anyone since Mick; no wonder women fancied him with a body like that, but he knew it and was making the most of his body as he knew I was watching him; *Bloody tart*, I thought. The kettle started to boil, just in time, turning around to pour the hot water into the mugs. When I had finished stirring the coffees, Mark had come back with an empty barrow ready to take his coffee. He wiped the back of his hand across his forehead; I pushed passed him before handing him his coffee.

I went to sit on the garden bench in the garden, giving my back a break from painting the fence. Mark followed me out a few seconds later with a cigarette in his mouth, which he hadn't lit up yet but had a lighter in hand to light it.

'You can put that out for a start; I hate cigarettes,' I said. Grabbing hold of the cigarette from his mouth, I threw is to the ground and screwed it into the ground with the heel of my trainer.

'What the fuck have you done that for?' said Mark irritated on the unexpected action I'd taken.

'I don't like cigarettes; they stink, anyway they are bad for your health,' I gave him a smirk.

'Oh, and what else don't you like my queen?' said Mark with a grin.

‘Okay, I give up, you just have sex on the brain, and I don’t think you can have a proper conversation,’ I said. I had started to get slightly annoyed.

‘Alright, alright, what do you what to talk about?’ said Mark, holding his hands up in surrender.

‘I don’t want to talk. I just want to sit here in peace. You’ve got your coffee, and I’m paying you to do a job. Get on with it.’

‘Aren’t we bossy here?’ taunted Mark as he got up off the bench and walked back into the cottage. I was relieved because he was distracting me, and I didn’t want to be reeled in by his banter.

I was sure it was going to be complicated, having him around all the time and not lusting over him. My body had started to act weirdly in his presence, and I had to get a grip on myself. He was bad news. *I should know it better*, I thought. I sighed as I picked up my mug and walked inside the cottage without looking at Mark. I had to avoid him; it was for my good.

CHAPTER TWELVE:

I decided not to take my mug back into the cottage where Mark was working so I wouldn't start another banter with him. I went straight around to the back of the cottage to begin repainting the fence. It was nearly mid-day, and the sun was up really heating up the day. I stripped off to my vest top, exposing more of my skin to the sun and soak some of it. After a short while, I was sweating quite excessively. Beads of sweat were running down my forehead, which I had to wipe with the back of my hand over and over again.

I found a piece of cloth, fished it out, and tore it into strips to make a bandana; *this should sort out the sweating running down my face*, I thought. I then tucked the rest of the cloth on top of my head to protect me from the sun. That helped a lot, so I carried on painting the fence.

I couldn't hear anymore banging going on inside the cottage, and I figured that he must have finished knocking the walls down. But then I heard his pick-up start and pull away. Was he getting rid of the rubble from the cottage? I thought now was the time to go and have another coffee before he was back. Picking my mug up, I walked up to the front of the cottage door, peering in to see how far he had got with the job. The dust had begun to settle, so after cleaning the kettle off again and filling it with water, I switched it on to boil the water.

I had my mug all washed and ready by the time the water had boiled. I wandered around the rooms trying to assess the room sizes now that both walls were down, and smiled with satisfaction; they were going to be a decent size now.

I could hear someone walking on the gravel, reaching the cottage; I went outside to see who it was. I saw Janet as I approached the gate.

'Hey Janet,' I called out to her, 'I was just checking who it was. I am making coffee; would you like a cuppa?'

'Yes, please, I'd love one. Where's Mark, I thought he was starting today?' asked Janet.

'He has, but he's gone off in his truck with some rubble. He's been knocking a couple of walls down inside,' I said. I found the mug Mark had used earlier and washed it under the tap, before flicking the kettle on to boil again. Janet stood at the door, looking at the mess on the floor.

'This has made a big difference, hasn't it?' said Janet in an excited tone.

'Yeah, it's surprising how big it looks now. It will make the space more workable.' We sat on the bench outside with our mugs of coffees in silence, taking in the short-lived peace until we heard a vehicle approaching.

It was Mark returning with the pick-up to take some more rubble away. Reversing back down the drive as near to the door as he could get, he jumped out of his truck and started to barrow more rubble into the back of his truck. He hadn't seen us sitting on the garden bench yet; Janet was watching him wheeling the barrow to and fro, but it wasn't the pushing of the barrow she was watching, I could tell.

Mark hadn't put his tee-shirt on since taking it off while knocking the walls down in the cottage. His muscular body taut with pushing the barrow to and fro was a sight, the sweat giving him a gleam looking like he had been smothered in body lotion. I gave Janet a nudge on the arm to bring her to her senses; she quickly got it together and cleared her throat.

'Oh, I forgot to tell you - Bill's coming home next week for a couple of weeks,' she broke the news to me.

'That will be nice for you, Janet,' I said happily. 'Will you be doing anything special when he comes home?' I said as I thought I would have to make myself scarce, not wanting to be in the way.

'Yes, he's planning on taking me to Paris for a few days,' said Janet with a huge smile playing on her lips.

'How romantic, Janet!' I smiled back and nudged at her arm again.

'Haha, yes! He usually takes me away somewhere every time; he arranges it all. I just make sure my passport is up to date.' Janet shrugged.

Mark had finished loading the rubble in his truck and was off down the road, where he was taking it I had no clue about, as long he wasn't fly-tipping. I asked Janet where he takes his rubble and rubbish from his building work?

'He takes it back to his yard and sorts out what he wants and does not want, like this rubble he will probably use it on another job.'

'Oh, it makes sense. Well, I'll have to get on, Janet - the fence won't paint itself,' I said as I stood up.

'I'll be making tea at about 6 pm unless you're coming back before then,' said Janet, standing up too.

'I probably will. My back's aching, and I could do with a soak in the bath for half an hour,' I said, taking the mug off her and stretched a little. My back did ache badly.

I headed back to the fence, looking at it as I approached. I had painted half of one side. Jesus! This was going to take me nearly all week to finish this off on the inside of the fence, then I will have to do the field side of the fence, and that is going to take me a least another week unless it rained. If it did, it's going to be longer. But at least I'm out of Mark's way that was the main thing.

Mark left just after 4.30 pm, and by then, he had managed to knock the two walls down and clear all the rubble out of the cottage leaving a large area in the cottage. I was glad the worst of the mess had been done. That too, with no more banter from him since I had a go at him, he seemed to have gotten the message, how long for time will tell.

I was back at Janet's cottage before 5 pm just in time to have a soak in the bath before tea. While washing my hair, I felt sore in my shoulders. Drying my hair in the mirror, I noticed that my shoulders were red; I must have caught the sun today. Damn, I had no cream to put on. I would have to ask Janet if she had some. Putting on clean clothes with a vest top to stop anything rubbing on my shoulders, I went through to the kitchen to ask her if she had any sun cream of sorts.

'God, you've caught the sun today, Holly, that looks sore; I go and find you some,' said Janet looking at my shoulders.

'Yes, they do a bit,' I replied, patting my shoulders lightly, feeling the heat coming out to my touch. Janet came back with the sun cream; it was soothing as she applied some to my shoulders.

After tea, we sat in the living room watching the TV when I went on.

'So, Janet, I noticed you were eyeing up Mr. Candy man when he was barrowing that rubble out of the cottage,' I said casually.

'No, I wasn't,' said Janet sharply.

'Yes, you were. I saw your eyes on him; you had him undressed by the time I gave you a nudge,' I smirked at her.

'Mm well a little a bit, I suppose. But it doesn't hurt anyone window shopping as long as you don't buy the goods you don't need,' Janet smirked back.

'Uh well, his goods would be soiled,' I added with a laugh.

'You're sure right on that score, Holly,' said Janet laughing out loud too.

Janet applied some more sun cream on my shoulders before I went to bed, and I had to cover my shoulders, so the cream didn't mess up the sheets on the bed. I had a bit of an uncomfortable night turning over, feeling the soreness on my shoulders. God, I wish I'd covered my shoulders up as I had done with my head.

The next morning my shoulders felt tight, having been burnt by the sun. I needed some more cream; Janet was up making tea and breakfast.

'How did you sleep?' she asked as I walked into the kitchen.

'Oh, Janet, not very well. Can I use some more of that cream? My shoulders are so tight and sore,' I begged.

'Course you can. I'll just go and get it,' she replied. While Janet went to get the cream, I made myself a cup of tea. 'Would you like some toast?' I shouted out to Janet in the other room.

'Yes, if you're making some.'

Janet was working at the bakery until 4 pm after she had to see one of her tenants due to them having a water leak and needed some repairs. Janet could do general stuff, but if it were something more serious as plumbing, then she would have to call someone out. Soon after breakfast, I went down to the cottage, unlocking the door I could hear a vehicle coming up the road. I thought it must be Mark, but it wasn't it was James, the farmer. Seeing me there, he pulled in with his 4x4, stopping the engine and getting out of the vehicle.

'Morning. How are you getting on inside the cottage?' asked James.

'Well, the work only started yesterday, but it's made a difference after knocking the two walls down,' I said, opening the door, and James followed me in.

‘Yes, it does.’ nodded James. We heard another vehicle coming up the road and then stopping outside the cottage.

‘This must be Mark,’ I said to James.

‘Oh, you’ve got your hands full with him, young lady,’ warned James.

‘Yep, I have had the low down on him, and I have told him to behave.’ I shrugged.

‘He won’t give up; he’ll wear you down as he likes a challenge.’ James knew him well; it seemed.

Before I could answer, Mark, walked through the door.

‘Oh, hello, James. What are we up to today?’ waved Mark.

‘I’m just seeing how the cottage is coming on,’ said James casually.

'Oh, we'll soon knock it into good shape, won't we Holly?' laughed Mark.

'Yeah, I'll keep you going with cups of coffee.' Mark didn't say anything in front of James as he would have done with his rude jesters.

James inspected the areas Mark had knocked through, and with a nod of approval, he left. Mark had gone back out to his truck to bring in new piping for the plumbing and a boiler and header tank for the central heating. I had drawn outlining where I wanted the pipes to go, so there would not be any confusion.

The morning was a bit cooler, giving me some rest bit from the sun. I still had half the fence to paint, plus I had the outer fence as well. Getting myself set up with the painting, I made sure I kept my tee-shirt on so as not to expose my shoulders even though the sun wasn't out yet. I started to paint the fence, but my tee shirt was rubbing on my shoulders, I'd have to go back to Janet's cottage and put a loose top on that's not going to chaff. I didn't bother telling Mark where I was going before walking straight to my car.

As I got back to Janet's cottage to change, I went into my bedroom and pulled out one of the packing boxes to find an old loose fitted tee-shirt. On finding one, I noticed the box which I had been given on Christmas I was at my parents' house when I was recuperating from my accident. Opening the lid, I saw the gold necklace studded with rubies and the note underneath with the message. It had been a while since I last thought about who sent it, and then the red rose in my car with that message in Italian. I wondered if this guy knows that I'm divorced and single.

My mind wandered to the Halloween party and the kiss from Count Dracula and the Zorro at the New Year's Eve party. It was the same guy, his beautiful eyes like I'd never seen before. I felt a physical attraction towards him, whoever he was. Putting the lid back on the box, I placed it back in the packing box and slipped my old tee-shirt on. Yes, this did feel better.

When I got back to the cottage, Mark had laid out all the piping ready to fix it together and to the wall leaving gaps for the radiators to go.

'I'm making a coffee. Would you like one?' I asked him.

'Yeah, please, I'm parched,' said Mark, with no rude comment. I wondered what was eating at him as he was not his usual self. He carried on working while I made the coffee.

'Coffee's here,' I said, making him stop what he was doing, handed him a mug of coffee, and stood back a bit from him.

'I've had a call from the window company; your windows will be ready in a couple of days. They had a few cancelations, so they brought your order forward,' Mark informed me.

'Oh good, that will shorten the building time,' I said with enthusiasm.

'Yeah, probably a week or so. When are you getting your kitchen units and bathroom suite?' asked Mark.

'I didn't know you would need them so soon. I suppose I'll have to sort something out.'

'I can get them if you want, I can get a good discount,' offered Mark.

'Yeah, okay then, you'll have to come with me to the builder's merchants,' said Mark.

'No problem. When did you want to go?'

'Monday, if that's okay, I need to order boarding and plaster and get them to deliver it, so I'll pick you up at 7.30 Monday morning,' said Mark.

'Yeah, okay, thanks.' I was happy that at least the work was getting done.

It was getting on for 4 pm, and Mark had just about joined all the pipes together and was fixing them to the wall, leaving early to sort out a water leak for one of Janet's tenants. I took a stroll around the back of the cottage, looking at the pile of brambles and weeds, which had dried off over a few days.

'I think it's ready for burning,' I mumbled to myself, then it hit me that I had no light. Damn! I rushed back to the cottage to see if Mark had gone; he would have a light. I was lucky he was just walking back to his truck to leave.

'Mark, hang on a minute, have you got a light? I need to burn these brambles and weeds,' I shouted from behind.

'Well, I don't know if I should give it to you seeing that you told me not to smoke, so what's it worth, eh?' Said Mark with a raised eyebrow and a smirk.

'Don't start; are you going to lend me your lighter or not your smug arse?'

'Oo touchy, aren't we?' said Mark in a sarcastic voice. He threw over his lighter, saying I could keep it as he had a spare one in his truck. I caught it in one hand and said thank you. I turned around and walked off before he said anything else. I looked at the heap to find the best place to light it. It was a bit slow in starting, but once it got going, it soon started burning the greener bits in a heap. Using a long-handled fork, I kept tidying up the heap, keeping it together, something I use to watch my dad do when he was burning stuff around the farm. The only thing was that I had to stay with it until it had completely burnt out so that there weren't any stray embers drifting, causing more fires elsewhere. It took about an hour to burn. I left to get something to eat, but I was going back to double-check just in case there were any stray embers.

Janet was at home making the tea; 'I see you've been burning.' said Janet as she looked at me.

'Yeah, thought that I'd get rid of it while it was dry. I'm going back after tea just to check that the fire's out completely.'

'Oh, I'll come with you to see the progress on the cottage,' she said.

'Yes, okay, no problem. I was thinking of going for a walk further down the road towards the woods if you fancy that, Janet.'

'Yes, that would make a change.' We made a quick plan.

It was after 7 pm when we started our walk to the cottage to check that the fire was completely out. Everything seemed fine. While we were there, I showed Janet what Mark was up to with the cottage. Janet seemed pleased with the progress.

After locking up, we headed down the road towards the woods. 'So, where does this lead to?' I asked Janet.

'It goes down to the farm where James and his wife live.'

'So does he own all the land around us?'

'Yes, it goes far back to his grandfather, who owned the mansion which is on the other side of the woods. His grandfather bought most of the land in the area and beyond. Over time, he had to sell it to pay death duties to the tax man when his grandfather died. His father took over and tried building it up, buying land and property from within the town. Now that James has taken over, he's finding it hard financially, so he sold the cottages down the lane over the years.'

'What sort of farming does he have?' I was curious.

'He's mainly livestock, as you can see, there's sheep in the field behind us, only because the ground isn't very good for growing crops,' said Janet.

'Yeah, I noticed when I was clearing the garden that the ground was very sandy, it must die off in summer if we have too much dry weather?'

'There have been some years when the ground had been that dry the grass just dies off, and there's no greenery just brown all over,' said Janet.

'I suppose it saves weeding and mowing the lawn.' I nodded.

'Well, you are right on that.' agreed Janet.

We got to the woods where the track split into two tracks. The right took you to the farm, and the left into the woods. The lane was a public path through to the woods, so we weren't trespassing on James' land. In a couple of months, I had been here, I had noticed the trees filling out, you could see through to the other side, but now the trees were full of leaves making the woods dense. There was a track shooting off in different directions where the public walked and biked through seeing the tracks in the mud, which had dried, causing small ruts in the earth. We walked through to the other side where you could see the mansion, Janet had said that James had sold that a couple of years ago due to the place needing a lot of money spending on it, so selling it was the best option. They moved into the farmhouse where one of the tenants had vacated and was in reasonable condition.

'James seems to be having a lot of financial problems over the years,' I said.

'Yeah, the only problem he's going to have is when there's nothing left to sell.' sighed Janet.

'That's true.' The grounds to the mansion were manicured to perfection. The grass had been cut in stripes like a bowling green. Hedges and fruit trees had been cut and pruned back, standing to attention in a regiment waiting to be assessed.

It was starting to get dark, so we headed back; I checked the fire at the cottage one more time before walking back to Janet's cottage. As soon as we were in, I made a beeline to the bathroom to take a shower. I washed the smell of the fire and sweat out of my hair, and I felt fresh with a set of clean clothes to put on.

Janet had made some tea when I had come out of the bathroom.

'Thanks, Janet I need that,' I said, gratefully taking the mug of tea off her. We walked into the living room and sat down, taking the weight off our feet. Our feet had been aching a bit from the walk to the woods. I was getting used to the surroundings, and it had started feeling like home. I was so glad to have found a friend in Janet and a home in the cottage else I would have driven myself nuts after the divorce. I finally knew that I had a life too, something to look forward to and a new beginning.

CHAPTER THIRTEEN:

Before going to bed, Janet rapped lightly on my bedroom door.

'Holly, do you fancy going out tomorrow night into the town?' she asked.

'Oh, I don't know, Janet. I've got so much to do in the cottage,' I said as I twisted my fingers, sounding a little reluctant to go.

'Come on, Holly, you need a break, and I can introduce you to some of my friends and colleagues from work, and we can eat out for a change,' said Janet.

'Um, okay, okay.' I gave in, holding my hands up

'Good, that's settled then.' Grinned Janet.

The following, day I woke up with the sound of the rain beating down on my bedroom window. 'Great, that's just what I needed,' I groaned, turning over to see the time. It was only 6 am; I lay there, hoping that the rain would stop soon. The grass needed cutting now I had finished cutting the brambles back from the fence, luckily, I had burnt the heap yesterday. Turning over, I snuggled down to have another hour's sleep.

It was after 8.30 am when I finally got up, to my utter disappointment, it was still raining. Janet was up filling the washing machine with dirty clothes, which between us had mounted up over a few days.

'You're not going to get them dried?' I asked Janet.

'Yes, I will. The weather is supposed to fair up later,' shrugged Janet.

'Oh, good! I might get the grass mown then; I'll have to do something inside the cottage for now, because Mark isn't working today,' I said.

'No, Mark never works on a Saturday. He will have been getting a notch on his bedpost,' Janet smirked and then winked.

'Oh yes, but how do you know that?' I questioned her with a smirk on my face.

'Don't give me that look! It's common knowledge, as you know. Everyone in the town knows,' Janet said as she tried to suppress her smile.

By 10 am, the rain had completely stopped, but I wouldn't be able to cut the grass yet. I set off in the car down to my cottage to see what I could do inside. The plaster needed to come off; I would save some time by doing it myself. Mark could start re-plastering straight away. Mark had left some tools behind, and picking through them, I found a chisel and a hammer. I set off, taking off the old plaster. It was lime plaster, which came off easy but was also causing a lot of dust. I could have done with a mask but carried on with the job in hand anyway.

It was a tiring job, and I had been at it for over a couple of hours. As a treat, I made myself a mug of coffee and took it outside to give myself a bit of a breather. I sat down on the garden bench, still feeling damp from the morning rain.

My peace was disturbed by an approaching vehicle. I wondered if it was James, but no, it was Mark. I was surprised to see him as he turned into the driveway, stopped the engine, and got out.

'Hey, you, what are you up to on a Saturday? I heard someone say you don't normally work?' I said in a sarcastic voice.

'Ah, very funny,' said Mark sounding a bit pissed off. 'I need something out of my bag. Janet has had an emergency. Anyway, what the hell have you been up to?

You look as though you've been doing demolition, the state, you're in,' said Mark looking at me up and down.

'Yeah, I'm saving you a job. I'm taking the plaster off the walls ready for you to plaster again,' I said, looking proud of myself.

'Well, I hope you're going to clear the mess when you've finished,' joked Mark.

'No, I thought a strong guy would do that for me,' I said in a flirtatious tone.

'I wonder who you have in mind,' said Mark with a smirk.

'I'll find one unless you know anyone?' I smiled in a flirtatious manner and batted my eyelashes. I shouldn't have flirted with him, because that opened the door for him to come on to me. But, I thought I'd play with him and call his buff.

'You look sexy when you're dirty,' said Mark in a suggestive voice.

'You're not so bad yourself in the dirty,' I said, smirking. He stepped closer towards me.

'Well, we could both get down and dirty,' he said, raising his eyebrow suggestively. He was just about to put his hand on my arm, but I quickly turned around and walked back into the cottage.

'Well, the plaster won't jump off the walls on its own. I need to get on,' I said. I walked inside, leaving him standing there. It was his choice now, whether to follow me in or not. He followed me into the cottage, but only to the door to see what progress I had made in the room.

'Hmm, not bad for a city girl,' he praised sarcastically. I didn't bite as I didn't want him to know my past, so I let it go. Mark walked over to his bag of tools to find what he had come for. Once he found it, he walked back to the door and shouted out, 'You're doing a good job, sexy!' before rushing out, smirking as he disappeared through the door.

I thought Mark was not a bluffer, and that he would have gone with it. I'd have to be careful about what I said from now on.

I managed to take off the plaster in the room by 5 pm with another coffee break in between and decided to call it a day. I was filthy from the plaster, so a quick tidy up was the best I could do before leaving for the day. With all the grit and dirt in my hair, I was more than ready for a shower. Janet wasn't in when I got back, so I stripped off and got under the shower, the water changing colors from the grit and dirt I was carrying. My hair felt like straw and needed good conditioning, so I spent nearly half an hour in the shower trying to get clean. I put on some more work clothes as I didn't know when Janet would be back, and then switched the TV on. I sat back, putting my feet up on the sofa, waiting for Janet to come home.

It was 6.30 pm by the time Janet was home. She shook my shoulder, waking me up. I must have nodded off.

'I'm sorry I'm late, Holly. That blasted water pipe turned into more problems further along the pipe, Mark was having problems connecting the pipes as they were different sizes, so he had to renew most of it, and the water had gone everywhere,' Janet was exasperated as she started speaking.

'Oh, Janet, why didn't you phone me? I would have come down to give you a hand with the clearing up.' I felt terrible for her.

'No, you have enough to do Holly, but thanks,' said Janet looking tired.

'Do you want to go out still?' I asked Janet, trying to sound I wasn't bothered about going out.

'Yes, it's just been one of those days, so get yourself ready, girl,' she replied in a sprightly tone.

'Would you like a cuppa before we go?' I asked.

'No thanks, I'm ready for something a bit stronger,' she smiled brightly.

'Okay, I'll go and get changed then.' While Janet had a shower, I slipped on a pair of jeans, a tee-shirt, and a pair of comfy trainers; I didn't feel like dressing up. It wasn't as though we were going clubbing anyway. When Janet had finished in the shower, she walked through to her bedroom to slip on her jeans and a blouse top.

'I'll just need to phone for a taxi,' she called out to me.

'No, there's no need for that, Janet. I can drive! I'm not bothered about drinking.'

'No, you're not, my girl. You are drinking, and you need to relax, so we'll have no more of that,' Janet waved her hand in front of my face.

The taxi arrived at 7.30 pm to take us to town. We were going to the Rose and Crown pub for our meal before moving on to meet Janet's friends and colleagues from work. I insisted on paying for the taxi as we got out of the vehicle, and Janet didn't resist. I let Janet lead the way into the pub; the barmaid behind the bar greeted us.

'Hi Janet, you're ready for your table?' asked the barmaid politely.

'Yes, please, Sarah, but we need a drink first, and I want to introduce you to Holly. She has bought the cottage next to mine and is renovating it at the moment,' said Janet introducing me to the girl.

'It's nice to meet you, Holly,' smiled Sarah. We got our drinks and went to sit at our table near the window. A few people were dining, and some tables were reserved.

'They must get busy here?' I said, looking at the reservations.

'Yes, they are always busy. They're very popular, especially with the tourist, and they let rooms upstairs as well,' Janet told me, pointing towards the upper floor.

We ordered our meal and waited for it to arrive, while Janet asked me how I was getting on. I mentioned that Mark had turned up at the cottage to get something out of his bag. I told her he wasn't in a very good mood until I spoke to him, and then he was back to his usual self.

'Yeah, I had to call him out. That's probably why he wasn't very happy, with it being a Saturday and all. He did mention he had to go to the cottage for his pipe cutter, and that he saw you up to your eyes in plaster dust,' Janet laughed.

'Oh, yes! And what else did he say?' I asked with a grin.

'He's definitely gotten you down for his next conquest, Holly,' said Janet smiling at me as if to say he would get to me.

'No, Janet, it's not going to happen. I won't let it,' I replied dryly.

'We'll see, then,' Janet barked out a laugh and started looking out of the window.

'Yes, we will. Won't we?' I said.

By this time, our meal had arrived. I was starving as I hadn't eaten since breakfast, only coffee during the day. After our meal, I insisted on paying again. As we left the pub, walking towards the town centre, I could hear music coming from a pub called the White Rose. Janet led the way in, the music blaring out, the pub was heaving with people. We pushed our way to the bar, several people saying hello to Janet. The music brought back memories of when I was at home with my parents recuperating and went out with Mags to the station, taking up the dance floor with our routine; it was a good time.

I was on my fourth glass of red wine and had started to relax; when Janet saw some of her colleagues and introduced me. Charlotte was a girl in her early twenties wearing a skirt or a belt as it was that short and a skimpy top, caked in make- up with shoulder-length blond hair. She worked in the shop at the bakery, but she was one of those girls who thought she was better than anyone else. She looked at me as though she had stepped on something unpleasant. *I'll have to watch her*, I thought. She was probably trouble.

Janet had started to let her hair down, singing to the beat of the music, and then was dragged off onto the dance floor. I needed to go to the toilet, so asking where it was, I made my way in that direction. Luckily, I managed to get the last cubicle. I was washing my hands after I had finished the door opened, and in came Charlotte with eyes heavy with eyeliner. She looked at me up and down and went on;

'You better keep your hands off of Mark. He is mine.' Her voice was venomous.

'Wait. What?' I said, unable to believe what I was hearing.

'I know he's got the hots for you bitch, so keep your hands off him,' said Charlotte spraying me with spit.

'I don't know where you've got that idea from, but I can assure you I won't be having anything to do with him, girl,' I raised my voice a bit.

'Well, I'm warning you, you bitch,' said Charlotte with some more spit spraying over me. I walked out before I punched her for slagging me off like that. I was fuming; I needed to go back to the cottage. I shouldn't have come out tonight. Never in my life had I been spoken to like that, I thought to hurry back to find Janet and let her know that I was going back home.

I found her on the dance floor. Pushing my way through and taking her arm, I informed her I was leaving but for her to stay and not to feel obligated to come. She was okay with that, and I left the pub with the music blaring out.

As I walked down the road to find a taxi, I was still fuming. If I hadn't come away, I would have smacked her. She was looking for a fight, accusing me of something I don't know anything about. For a few moments, I felt as though someone was watching me. I turned around, seeing a taxi coming down the road. I hailed it down; it stopped, thank god for that.

'Can you take me to Rose Cottage on Brown Edge Road?' I said in a panicky voice.

'Sure, jump in girl,' said the taxi driver. I was relieved to be back at the cottage. It was only just after 10 pm, and I had had enough of today, so I went off to bed. I didn't hear Janet come in; I must have been tired.

The following morning, I was up early despite the fact it was Sunday. I needed to get my cottage done and move out, I needed my independence back and space; not that I was ungrateful. I did appreciate what Janet had done for me. It was 7 am Janet was still in bed, a least she made it home last night.

As I arrived at the cottage, there was a bag hanging on the door handle. I stared at it, wondering who had dropped it off. Taking the bag off the handle and unlocking the door, I went in and decided to make myself a coffee before starting to take more plaster off the walls. With a mug of coffee in one hand and the bag in the other, I walked over to the garden bench and sat down. On opening the bag, I found a box.

'Hmm, what's this?' I mumbled. It was not big enough to help with the renovation of the cottage. The box was wrapped up in gold paper with a red bow. Unravelling the paper off the box, I opened the box. I was gobsmacked to see a ring lying on the velvet box; it was a gold band with a ruby surrounded by diamonds.

'Who the hell could send me a ring?' I wondered out loud, taking the ring out of the box. I slipped it onto my middle finger, and it fit as though it was meant to be mine.

'God, this looks expensive,' I said, then noticed a folded note underneath the ring holder. Picking it out and unfolding it, I saw it read 'Questo è il mio amore per voi fino a quando ci incontriamo di nuovo. amandoti sempre dai tuoi occhi beautiful, Zorro'.

Oh my god, it was in Italian. I could bet it was from Zorro, what was he saying? I re-read it, with my heart pounding with excitement, and I felt like a teenager in love. This feeling gave me a boost, especially from what had happened last night. I was in love with this guy, and I didn't even know anything about him.

Sipping my coffee slowly, looking at the ring on my finger, I kept thinking about him and why he wasn't showing himself. Now, I was divorced. Or would that go against him if he was in the force? Then I thought of the necklace at Christmas at my parents' home; it was exactly the same type of gold and stone setting. What was this guy trying to tell me? *God, I wish he would show himself.*

Coming back from my thoughts, I took the ring off, putting it back into the holder of the box and placed the box and bag in the pocket of my dungarees. I needed it close to me, probably for comfort knowing that someone was looking out for me in some sort of way.

I started working on the walls chipping at the plaster; some just fell off while some bits needed a bit more hammer.

It must have been around 2 pm when Janet came up. She looked rough, which didn't surprise me as she was ahead of me last night with the drinks before I had left.

'Aw, Holly, have you got the kettle on? I need coffee, and lots of it,' groaned Janet sounding rough.

'I was just finishing off but stopped to make coffee. You're looking a bit rough, Janet. What time did you come in last night?'

'About 2, I think,' said Janet propping the side of the door with her head to one side.

'Sit outside, I'll bring the coffee out,' I said, and with that, she was gone. Janet was on the bench with her head in her hands, leaning over when I brought the coffee.

'Here,' I said, handing over the mug of coffee and sat next to her.

'I'm never going to do that again,' Janet groaned again. 'Anyway, what happened to you?' She looked at me with a wearied expression. I didn't want Janet to know that I had a confrontation with Charlotte, so I lied.

'Oh, I was tired. I did come to see you before I left, but I thought you had enough to drink.'

'Yeah, you're probably right,' Janet sat sipping her coffee in silence; she must be in a bad mood.

'Janet, why don't you go back to bed, and I'll make some tea when I get in?' I attempted to get her to go so I could finish the second room I'd been taking the plaster off .'Well, if you don't mind,' I smiled sheepishly as Janet stood up, putting her mug on the bench, 'I needed to get this finished.' Picking both mugs up, Janet walked slowly down the road, and I continued scrapping the plaster off the walls.

It was just around 4 pm when I'd finished. Mark was going to be busy moving this plaster I'd scrapped off the walls. After locking up and putting the key in my pocket, I felt the box with the ring in my pocket. I just had to have another look at it, the sun made the diamonds sparkle around the ruby. I was excited, and I felt loved as I had an admirer.

I put the ring back into the box and stuffed it back in my pocket and then made my way to the car and drove back to Janet's cottage. As I walked in, it was quiet. She must still be in bed, I thought. I went through to check that she was there in her bedroom; she was fast asleep. I nipped into my bedroom, taking out my secret box, and put it with the necklace. I had time for a shower and a change of clothes before I started preparing the tea.

It was Monday morning. Mark was picking me up at 7.30 am to take me to the builders' merchants to choose kitchen units and a bathroom suite. He was on time; I picked a bag up in case I had to pay for them in advance. I rushed out of the cottage over to his truck, opening the passenger door, he sat there looking dog rough,

'Oh, yeah? Had a rough weekend?' I said sarcastically.

'Something like that,' he mumbled, turning his vehicle around. The builder's merchant was on the other side of the town, which meant we had to go through the middle passing the bakery shop. I thought and hoped that Charlotte wasn't at the shop at that time of the morning, not that I was scared of her. We drove through in silence, and I made the most of it as he would soon be back to his cocky ways and backchat.

Mark went off to the trade count while I disappeared to the showrooms, first looking at the bathroom suites. I just needed something basic and plain; the assistant showed me the most popular selling suite. It was white, but I could choose the tap and fittings at an extra cost.

'Yes, that will do,' I said and asked him if they were a stock item.

'Yes, everything you see is in stock; you can take it away now if you would like to,' said the assistant.

'Oh, okay, I'll just have a word with Mark and see if he can fit it in the back of his truck.' I turned to find Mark.

'So, what kitchen units have you got again? I started asking the assistant walking towards the display of kitchen units in their displays as Mark was still nowhere to be seen. I walked into each one, opening doors and drawers. I wondered what would suit the cottage? Janet had an oak effect, but I thought it would be too outdated, so going for a light color in plain ivory would make the kitchen look larger. The handles were extra with a good section to choose from. I went back to find Mark to ask him if we could get the bathroom suite in the back of his truck. He was still at the counter gossiping to another guy of similar age, but he was of a stocky built, had short hair, and he was wearing baggy shorts and a tee-shirt. The conversation was cut short when I went up to him.

'Have you found what you wanted?' he asked me.

'Yeah, but can you get the bathroom suite in the back of your truck?' I realized the other guy was giving him the eye as though I was Mark's next conquest. I rolled my eyes at the guy.

'Yeah, of course, we can,' said Mark being perkier.

'Good, I'll go and get it sorted then.' I turned around and walked back to the showroom.

Perhaps it was Mark who was giving such an impression to people like I was his next bedpost. He was annoying, and I had to sort it out with him soon.

CHAPTER FOURTEEN:

After 10 minutes, we were loaded up with the bathroom supplies we purchased, heading back towards the town centre.

'What happened to you Saturday night?' asked Mark out of the blue.

'What do you mean?' I frowned, not giving away much.

'You came into the pub with Janet, and within the hour, you were gone,' he said. I couldn't remember seeing him there, which explained that Charlotte was threatening me because he was there.

'Oh, I was tired and decided to call it a night,' I replied drily and then quickly changed the subject to the cottage.

'When do you think you will get the bathroom up and running?'

'I need to plaster all the walls first before fitting the bathroom suite,' said Mark. 'You're a bloody slave driver, aren't you?' he smirked.

'No, I just want everything done soon, that's all.' I shrugged and looked out of the window.

'Getting fed up living with Janet then?' he said, sounding as though I wanted my own space, which he was right about, but I didn't let it on.

'Nah, I just don't like the mess.' We passed the bakery shop, and I avoided looking in as I didn't want to see Charlotte.

As we reached the cottage, Mark reversed into the driveway. I unlocked the cottage walking straight in to make coffee while Mark unloaded the bathroom suite, and he didn't need a hand with the lifting. There was another small outbuilding joining the cottage, it was fairly dry and watertight, so the bathroom suite was put in there temporarily until needed.

As Mark walked inside the cottage for his coffee, he saw the heaps of plaster on the floor and wrinkled his nose.

'You want to see my work out with the wheelbarrow again?' he joked.

'Don't flatter yourself, Mark, just drink your coffee and get on with it,' I said sharply. I didn't want to give him any reason to come onto me again. I just wanted the cottage done and him out of the way so I could get on with my life. I finished my coffee, putting the mug to one side and picking up the hammer and chisel set off into the next room to scrap the plaster off. Mark finished his coffee in silence and then carried on emptying the two rooms I had filled with the plaster from the walls.

There was just enough room to fill the back of the truck after clearing both of the rooms. Mark went off with the truck back to his yard to empty it while I carried on scrapping more plaster off, setting him up to take another load. Between the two of us, we managed to stripe back off all the plaster in the cottage; it was a good day's work.

As Mark finished for the day, taking with him a full load of plaster, I had a sweep around with the brush ready for the next stage, getting closer to my goal. The radiators were being delivered, along with the plasterboard, plaster, and the windows the following day in the morning. Mark was going to be busy, so I thought it would be better if I could help him where I could instead of tidying the garden and orchard as the cottage was the priority.

The following morning, I was up early while Janet was still in bed. Topping up with milk, coffee, and a pack of biscuits, I made my way down to the cottage. It was going to be a hot day; the sun was already out temperatures due to rise to 25c.

I followed a lorry down the lane stopping outside my cottage. It was good that I had decided to come down early. They were delivering the radiators and plaster-boarding. Two guys jumped out of the truck opening the side of the vehicle ready to unload. I went to unlock the cottage, checking to see where the best place was to put the boarding down. I thought the largest room in the middle would be the best place. The guys started offloading while I supervised them, checking that the boards were ok.

I could hear a vehicle coming up the lane. It was Mark pulling up behind the lorry, he jumped out and walked over, checking that what he had ordered had arrived. Once the lorry was unloaded, the guys drove off. Mark started to take off the package from the radiators; he was going to set up the heating and water to ensure that there wouldn't be any leaks before hiding the pipes behind the boarding. *What a day to do this, with temperatures to reach 25c*, I thought. It took a couple of hours setting and testing the heating; we both were sweating as it was scorching. Mark had taken off his t-shirt, exposing his sweaty tort body showing off his muscular arms. I tried to ignore him, but he knew that I was looking at him now and again. I rolled my eyes at how he was making it obvious purposefully flexing his muscular frame, so I exited, deciding to go and do some gardening instead.

It took me a long moment to decide what I was going to do; I needed a lawnmower.

Jumping into my car, I drove down to Janet's cottage to pick my bag up, then I remembered the ring. I needed to go to the library with my mystery note. The first stop was the library, and I was hoping the same librarian was there to translate my note. Spotting a parking space outside the library, I picked up my note and walked in. My stomach was filled with butterflies at the thought of what it may contain. As I arrived at the desk, my heart sank; she wasn't there, a younger woman in her late forties stood behind the counter, sorting out the returned books ready to be put back onto the shelves.

I was just about to ask her where the other lady was when she came out from behind a shelf, and I sighed in relief.

'Hello my dear, it's nice to see you again,' She smiled at me. 'Got anything for me to look at?' asked the librarian who I saw the first day.

'Gosh, you still remember me?' I said in a surprised voice.

‘How can I forget?’ She now smiled broader and put her glasses on. ‘Have you another note for me to look at?’ she asked in a joyful voice.

‘Yes, if you wouldn’t mind translating it.’ We stepped over to a more private area in the library, and I unfolded the note for her to read. She took it and read it on raising an eyebrow and smiling.

‘Did you just get this note?’ she asked.

‘No, there was this ring.’ I hesitantly brought the box out of my bag to show her.

‘Wow, this man must love you very much, and this is an expensive ring. You do know that it has diamonds with a ruby set into it?’ She looked at it closely.

‘I guessed so but wasn’t a hundred percent sure.’ I blushed and shrugged slightly.

'questo è il mio amore per voi fino a quando ci incontriamo di nuovo. amandoti sempre dai tuoi occhi'

'Beautiful,' she murmured as she translated it for me.

'This is my love to you until we meet again. Loving you always. -from your beautiful eyes'.

Oh my God, it was Zorro all this time. I explained how I briefly met him and told him he had beautiful eyes when he was dressed as Zorro at a New Year's Eve party.

'How romantic and you haven't met him since then?' she asked.

'No, only these gifts he leaves me.' I shook my head.

I left the library feeling all love struck like a teenager. I jumped into my car and headed to the gardening suppliers I had seen when I was going to the builder's merchant with Mark. The supplier was trying to sell me a tractor mower, but sticking to my guns, I bought a robust drive mower.

When I got back to the cottage, Mark was still there and gave a hand getting the mower out of the back of my car. He was putting the plaster-boarding up when I walked into the room.

'So you're still here then?' I laughed with sarcasm. 'I went into the town to get a mower, would you mind getting it out of the car for me?'

'Well, that depends, it'll cost you,' he said it with a raised eyebrow and a smirk.

'It's a coffee then,' I said drily and walked off to make it leaving him before he could answer me. Waiting for the kettle to boil, I watched Mark lifting the mower from the back of my car, his muscles tightening with the weight as he placed it on the ground. The handles were folded up for easy transportation. Mark unfolded the clips holding it together. He pushed the mower towards the cottage, leaving it next to the cottage door. I brought the mugs of coffee outside, giving one to Mark.

'What do you think?' I jerked my head towards the mower, asking his opinion on it.

'Hmm, not bad, but you would have been better with a tractor mower to do all this,' said Mark.

'Uh, not you as well, they were trying to sell me one at the garden place,' I said, feeling a bit miffed. Mark was looking at me and smirking again.

'What?' I said sharply.

'Nothing, just looking.' He shrugged.

'Looking at what?'

'You look sexy when you're angry, and when covered in dust and dirt. You look as though you've been dragged through a hedge backward with your hair,' said Mark eying me up.

'You can bloody well stop that.' I gritted my teeth and walked away.

After washing the mugs, I walked into the room where Mark was boarding the ceiling; it was a slow process due to him lifting and balancing the board on a makeshift lift. I had to help him raise the boards while he nailed them into place. I was thinking I ask if he needed my help and block out the banter and trying to seduce me? I wanted to get the job done quicker. *I'll see how he gets on today and assess it in the morning*, I decided.

I went to get the can of petrol from my car for the mower. After filling it up and adjusting the settings, I pulled on the cord to start it. It started on the first pull. It was heavy, as it went over the grass with clumps of grass in various places in the thickest areas, but I persevered for an hour. I had only done a third of it when I needed a break. As I walked back to the cottage, I could hear Mark talking to someone, but there wasn't another vehicle parked outside the cottage. Walking into the room where Mark was working, I spotted Janet standing there looking fresher than the last time I saw her.

'Ah, it is you, Janet. I was wondering who Mark was talking to.' I waved at her.

'I thought I'd come up to see how you're getting on,' said Janet.

'Oh,' Mark sighed heavily. 'I'm going as fast as I can.'

'If you need help, you only got to ask,' I said a little irked.

'Well, I don't want to keep you from your garden,' said Mark in a sarcastic manner.

'I don't mind if it means getting this job finished quickly and you out of my hair sooner.'

'But you can be in my hair anytime, darling,' said Mark laughing.

'Now Mark, Holly's your client, you should speak to her like that,' said Janet bringing the conversation out of the gutter.

'I know Janet, but you know what I'm like.' Mark scratched his head.

'Yes, I do, and that's a problem, Mark.' Janet retorted. I decided to call it a day, Janet waited while I put the mower in the shed, leaving the key for Mark to lock up and drop it off at Janet's on the way home.

I had been up early that morning, so leaving early made up for it. The day had been stifling with the temperature reaching 25c. I was ready for a shower and a change of clothes. While I had a shower, Janet made some tea which was waiting for me as I came through into the living room with my wet hair tied up in a towel, it felt good to get the sweat and dirt off, putting fresh clothes on.

'Bill's coming home this weekend,' said Janet excitedly.

'Wow, that will be nice for you, how long his he home for?' I asked.

'Two weeks, but I did say that he is taking me to Paris for a couple of days,' said Janet.

'Yes, you did, I forgot; I thought wishing I could go with my mystery man.' Janet was back to normal after our night out; well, sort of, seeing that I had gone home early while Janet got leathered and feeling rough the next morning. I was going to have the cottage to myself for a couple of days; I was looking forward to it, having my own space again.

Another early morning, I was up having a bit of breakfast before leaving to go to the cottage, Mark was already there. He hadn't dropped the key off the day before saying that he had forgotten about it, just as well as he would have been waiting for me. When I entered the room he was boarding, he hadn't done much since I'd left him, so I decided to help out and to ignore his remarks. It took us the full day to finish boarding the room out, and what was even more challenging was shutting out his sexual comments. I had survived the day without causing him any damage.

Bill had arrived back from ten weeks on the rigs, he should have been back sooner, but he was asked to stay on to cover for one of his colleagues. It was the first time I had seen him apart of a photograph in Janet's bedroom. He was a couple of inches taller, looked older than Janet having short mousey hair and a stocky build; they must feed them well on the rigs.

'Hello, you must be Holly that Janet has been talking about since forever?' said Bill with a deep throaty voice.

'Hi,' I said, not sure of his personality or if he had a sense of humor. I asked him about his work on the rigs and had a general chit chat that could give me some indication if he had a sense of humor. He was down to earth; I was more relaxed now that he was on leave for a couple of weeks, knowing that I didn't feel l was in the way. Janet hugged him, saying that she had a bag packed ready for Paris. Bill had booked a flight out to Paris, leaving within the next three hours, so with his arrival, they didn't have much time to get to the airport.

It was after 6 pm by the time I had the cottage to myself, what a relief; not that I was ungrateful, but it was so lovely to have my own space back. Seeing that I was in a mess from working with mark at my cottage, I decided to have a shower and a change of clothes, thinking that instead of cooking, I would nip out and buy some fish and chips. Driving into town to the fish and chip shop, I called in at the off-license and purchased a small bottle of Amanti; despite that, I should be buying white to go with fish. By the time I got back to the cottage, it was 7 pm, and it was bliss having the place to myself. Switching the TV on, I settled down with my feet up. With a glass of wine that I had bought with the fish and chips in my hand, I started eating them from the paper they were wrapped in.

Bill and Janet were soon back from their romantic few days in Paris, Janet being all lovey-dovey like a teenager still at school. While Bill was off, he called on his tenants, checking that there wouldn't be any problems before he went back to the rigs. With Janet having a problem when a tenant had phoned her about water pipe bursting, Bill wanted to make sure that everything was ok.

On another early morning, after a quick breakfast, I drove down to my cottage, finding that Mark was already there again, and luckily, I had given him a spare key so that he didn't have to wait in case I was late for any reason. It was another day of sexual comments, but I was fighting through it soldiering on to get my cottage finished.

Over the period for the next two months, I helped Mark with the renovations putting up with his sexual innuendos; I must admit he was persistent. But I could handle it just fine. On the weekends, I worked on the garden as Mark didn't work; this gave me breathing space I needed away from his comments. It was starting to come together, looking brighter and starting to come alive.

The day had finally come when mark had finished his last job. I had been ordering furniture and a bed to be delivered while I picked soft furnishings for each room in the cottage. Mark fitted the curtain poles up for the curtains and plumbed in the washing machine.

It was September by the time I moved into my cottage, Keepers cottage, as it was called. I was excited now that I had my own space. Painting the cottage throughout in white made it easy, and it brought out the size of the rooms, making them look bigger and brighter with a fresh feeling. I used colours in the soft furnishings, tiled the floors in the bathroom and kitchen, had wooden flooring in the hall and living room but a light colour brown carpets in the two bedrooms. Fitted wardrobes were built in both bedrooms using spaces top to bottom with Mark building them from scratch.

We were now in October, and I had moved everything from Janet's cottage to mine, all the boxes and bags that were stored in my bedroom at Janet's now had a place in my fitted wardrobes, having a chest of drawers and a couple of bedside cabinets in each bedroom. Janet had brought a few bits I had left around with a bottle of wine to celebrate my move. Drinking the bottle between us, Janet asked me if I would go with her to a Halloween party at the White Rose. Feeling relaxed with the wine and now that my cottage was complete, I said yes.

Fancy dress was optional; I didn't feel right dressing up, possibly because I wasn't out with Mags. Janet had made an effort dressing up as a witch with loads of makeup. I walked down to Janet's while waiting for the taxi. Janet opened a bottle of wine as she slapped her make up on. The taxi arrived to pick us up at 8 pm, taking us straight to the White Rose pub in the town. We could hear the music blasting out as we approached the pub, pulling up to the door. We paid the taxi driver and waited for the music to blast our eardrums as we opened the pub door. They were playing 'I Hate myself for loving you' by Joan Jett. That brought back bad memories with Mick. It was good that it was ending as we entered the bar.

'Get a grip.' I reminded myself, 'It was in the past.' Pushing through to get to the bar, I bought the first round of drinks. We had drunk a couple of bottles before coming out and were slightly light-headed. Knocking back the drink, we went straight to the dance floor. Janet started dancing doing her thing while I kicked off doing my shuffle dance routine, causing the dance floor to open up and people watching and clapping. When the music finished, I got a round of applause as I walked off for another drink at the bar. People gave me compliments and patted me on the back, asking me where I had learned to dance like that. I was brought drinks by people I didn't know, and I started to get tipsy slowly. People I didn't know were chatting to me, but they seemed to know that I had brought Keepers cottage and had been renovating it with Mark.

Two hours into the party I had to make a move to the loo, this time I had to queue. While I was waiting for some of the girls who had seen me dance asked me that I must work out to keep fit to do it. I shrugged it off, not making it a big deal. I was the last to go in, and by that time, I was bursting.

I was washing my hands and checking my make up when the feeling of Deja ve turned up, only that it was real. There was Charlotte again.

‘You slag you think you are better than anyone, don’t you?’ said Charlotte, slurring her words in venom. I had enough of this woman, seeing that there wasn’t anyone around. I turned, getting hold of her arm twisting it and turning her around, pushing her up to the wall with my hand grabbing her hair tight and pulling it back.

I said in a menacing tone that shocked me, ‘If you don’t know how to keep that fucking gob shut, I will gladly shut it for you. Do you understand you, slag?’ After I spit it out, I pushed her arm higher up her back and pulled her hair tighter, making her groan in pain to surrender.

‘Yeah yeah, sorry, sorry,’ she said in a disgruntled voice.

‘You’re not fucking goby now, you fucking tart,’ I said, speaking to her in the ear in a calm manner, and then I let her go and walked out of the ladies. Fuck that bitch, I thought, I had to nip it in the bud before she took over my life bulling me every time she was around me, so I was glad I’d done it well hopefully.

CHAPTER FIFTEEN:

Janet was enjoying herself dancing and drinking with her friends, while I watched Charlotte coming out of the toilets with a face like she had the wind taken out of her sails. I thought to myself, 'It must have worked, me talking to her.' There was a tap on my left shoulder; I turned around to find a guy dressed in a Dracula costume.

'Hello, sexy,' he whispered in my ear.

'Hello Casanova,' I mumbled, knowing it was Mark.

'Oh, you knew who I was then?' said Mark sounding disappointed.

'I know your voice,' I said with a smirk.

'So, where are your mates?' he asked curiously as he usually had a woman on his arm while ready to put another notch on his bedpost.

'We've just come in; they are at the bar getting the drinks in.' I shrugged casually.

'Could I buy you a drink?' asked Mark grinning at me. I narrowed my eyes, not sure what he was up to?

'Yes, please, I'll have red wine.' He went off to the bar to find his mates and asked them to get a red wine. Within minutes, he brought his pint of beer and a glass of red wine. After handing me the wine, he stood close to me; his mates had gone off into the heart of the pub mingling with other people they knew.

'After all, you have managed to let your hair down tonight sexy?' Mark smiled, looking into my eyes.

'Yeah, I thought I better start showing my face now that the cottage is finished.' I acted nonchalantly.

'Hmm, you know what? I'd like to test that bed of yours,' his voice was a whisper again.

‘Right, I thought you would. The only problem is, I haven’t gotten a wooden bedpost to notch up,’ I replied sarcastically.

‘I’m sure I could make you one just for me, sexy.’ He raised his eyebrow, making direct eye contact, homing me in with his eyes.

‘Yeah, I suppose you would, amongst others,’ I said as if I didn’t care. All of a sudden, there was a hand on Marks's shoulder, and a face of the dreaded Charlotte appeared right behind.

‘Mark, I’ve been waiting for you,’ said Charlotte slurring her words with her black smudged eyeliner melting around her eyes and lipstick wider than her lips. She was hammered, and she was acting as though I wasn’t there with all her attention on Mark. Now, this was my time to exit and find Janet.

As I was making my way through the crowd to find Janet, guys in fancy dress costumes were coming on to me. I knew this was the drink talking; everyone usually acted like that when they've had too much to drink and talk to anyone to get their attention. I found Janet on the dance floor singing with the song; she was going to have a bad head again in the morning. I was lucky enough not to see Mark for the rest of the night, thinking he was probably shagging Charlotte around the back of the pub by now.

It was gone midnight by the time we got home. I got out of the taxi with Janet to make sure she was ok and asked the driver to wait until I got her inside and put her to bed; the driver waited as we were the last fare for the night. I didn't feel too bad as I had started to drink water in between my glasses of wine.

November had arrived, and the weather was getting colder. My cottage felt warm and cozy, so I was pleased with the outcome. Now that I had completed my mission with the cottage, it was time for me to get a job, but first I needed to go and visit Mags, I hadn't seen her since she and Tony had moved to the Scottish borders, with Tony getting his promotion in the traffic department as a sergeant. It had taken him a while and after going on with a number of courses until the job came up.

Mags was pleased to see me; she hugged me hard as we met at the train station. Driving back to her home, I kept looking out of the window. Their area was sparse with houses, and with what was there were spread apart, the scenery was beautiful with hills and woodlands small rivers winding through the countryside. Tony and Mags had bought a small detached cottage in a village just outside the main town; it was quiet as the cottage was down a lane off the main road. The place had an average size garden with three bedrooms, decorated in neutral colours but it felt very cozy like mine. I stayed over a couple of nights as Mags was starting her shift. We had a good catch up, telling about Mark and the cottage and my brief encounter for putting slapper Charlotte in her place, it made Mags laugh. God, I missed having her around. Mags dropped me off at the train station before heading off to start her shift at the station.

'Let us know when you find a job, Holly,' she said before waving me off at the station.

'Yeah, will do,' I shouted back.

November and December flew by. I had gone to my parents for Christmas and promised Janet I would be back for the New Year's Eve party at the white rose. This time the party was compulsory fancy dress, so Janet and I decided to go as two girls from St Trinian's. We managed to put together our outfit with a bit of alteration to the skirt; Janet wore high heeled shoes while I wore over the knee boots. The taxi was due at 8 pm, so I walked to Janet's early with my stuff and got ready there. Janet opened a bottle of wine to start the night as we got ready, and we had polished two bottles off by the time the taxi had arrived.

It was 8.30 pm when we pulled up at the pub. Loud music could be heard as usual as the taxi pulled up. There were people already drunk and worse for wear, thinking that they're not going to see the New Year in.

The pub was heaving, so we pushed our way through to the bar, there were so many fancy dresses costumes with the same dress, but we didn't see anyone dressed as St Trinian's. I noticed that we were getting looks as we pushed our way through to the bar. We were definitely turning heads.

The music changed to The Latest Flame by Elvis Presley; I had to go and dance to this. As I started my routine, the dance floor began to part, giving me some space. Janet came over with the drinks after the music had finished with guys giving me wolf whistles and shouting rude jesters. I knocked the wine back and went back to the bar, all this while being slapped on my backside and the odd grope from the guys a bit stoned out of their heads. I had a couple of drinks bought for me asking me for a dance later. After downing the drinks, I needed to go to the loo. My mind wandered back to the last time I was here. I had Charlotte against the wall in the toilet in a position she had no option but to submit to a defeat. Now the coast was clear so far, so I went in to take a wee and washed my hands with no signs of Charlotte. She must have either gotten the message, or she wasn't there.

As soon as I walked out of the ladies' toilets, a hand caught hold of my wrist, leading me towards the back door; it was a guy dressed in a Zorro costume.

'Mark, stop pissing about,' I yelled and tried to undo his grip, but then he turned to me and said,

'Holly, it's not who you think it is,' My heart missed a beat, and I looked into his eyes at once. I knew he was my Zorro, the one I wanted to meet again. He opened the back door as we moved away from the sound of the music. The cool air hit me as we stepped out, taking hold of me gently; he kissed me on the lips.

He was the first person, since Mick, whom I had kissed. 'Zorro, who are you? I need to know more about you; I was hoping to meet you again.' I murmured. I thought I sounded desperate, looking into his eyes, his beautiful eyes. 'You gave me the red roses, the necklace, and the ring, didn't you?'

He kissed me so passionately I melted; I hung onto him this time feeling him. He had a muscular body underneath his cape; I felt it while he was holding me in his strong muscular arms. I felt safe despite the fact I didn't know anything about him.

'Holly I have to go until my mission is complete,' before he left, he said, 'Manterro al sicuro fino a quando non ci incontreremo di nuovo siamo stati insieme per sempre.'

'God Zorro, I think I am falling in love with you, and I don't even know you, my beautiful eyes.' I shuddered with emotions. With that, he kissed me passionately again, pulling away from me, but I couldn't hold him; he was gone. A tear came to my eye; yes I was falling for this mysterious man not knowing anything about him. I felt safe with him despite what had happened to me with Mick.

He knew Mick; he was at the police station at that party; he had something to do with the force, but what? After wiping my tears, I went back into the party, where the music was starting to slow down, inviting the couples to smooch on the dance floor. As I walked through trying to find Janet amongst the crowd, I was grabbed from behind by Mark. Fuck, I thought.

‘Hello, my sexy girl,’ said Mark making eye contact. I tried avoiding looking into his eyes; he was hugging me so hard, squeezing that tight I couldn’t move. He was trying to kiss me on the lips but missed as I moved my head to the other side.

‘Come on, sexy, give us a new year’s kiss.’ Now that he had eye contact with me, he leaned forward and kissed me; it was hard and wet. I pulled away, but he still had me in a strong embrace, I was stuck. Charlotte came to my rescue, grabbing Mark by the shoulder, despite that she was pissed she had opened up his grip. To my utter surprise, she released me so I could retreat out of his way. There were raised voices, but I didn’t stay to listen. I wanted to getaway. It was midnight, and everyone was welcoming the new year by singing and kissing. I was grabbed by a number of guys giving me a quick kiss and hug. Janet was going around all the guys giving them kisses. God was she trying to get into the Guinness book of records?

After the singing and kissing, the music changed tempo to a slow smooch when a guy in a Batman costume took me by the hand, pulling me to the dance floor and wrapped his arms around my waist. He was one of the guys who had bought me a drink earlier in the evening after I had been dancing. He was the same height as me but with stocky built. I cringed despite having to put my arm loosely around his neck. With his build being stocky, I felt uncomfortable, but apart from that, he was a little worse for wear and was stumbling as we danced. Before the music had finished, I released myself from his clutch and made a quick exit turning to find Janet.

Eventually, I found her slumped in a corner sat with her head in her arms, leaning over the table. I thought she was ready to go; she could hardly stand. Exiting the pub, I managed to find a taxi waiting outside, and after bundling Janet into the taxi, we made our way home.

The next day was dry but chilly with an overnight frost. I walked down to see if Janet was ok from last night. It was after 11 am, and I thought that she should be up by now. Knocking on her door, I turned the door handle to enter, but it was locked, she was not up. I knew she kept a spare key under the mat, so picking it up, I let myself in. As I entered, I could smell the stench of puke; there was a trail of it on the floor in the hallway.

'Bloody hell Janet, what a mess!' I tiptoed into the bedroom where she laid with her hair matted up with vomit; she wasn't looking very good. 'Oh, Janet, let's make plenty of strong coffee and get you sobered up.' Tiptoeing out to the kitchen to fill the kettle ready to make the coffee, I found a mop and bucket. Filling it was bleach, I started to clean up the mess in the hallway. Luckily Janet hadn't been sick on her carpet in the bedroom, but she needed a change of bedding, and Janet needed to get into the shower to sober up and to wash the sick from her hair.

I woke her up, and she started to groan.

'Janet, it is me, Holly. Get this coffee down your system.' There were more groans, but she surrendered to the coffee and eventually got up to take a shower while I stripped the bed and replaced the sheets with clean ones. It took me over an hour to clean the mess up. Janet sat on the sofa, looking fresher and clean, but she was still groaning, saying she wasn't going to drink anymore. It was nearly dark before I left Janet looking more human and her cottage smelling fresher after cleaning her mess of sick the night before.

The next morning, there was a knock at the door. Thinking it was Janet, I opened the door, but there stood a woman with a large bouquet of red roses.

'Hello,' she said with a smile, 'is this Keepers Cottage, and are you, Holly Benson?'

'Err, yes, that's me,' I replied, my eyes glued to the roses.

'Well these are for you,' she said as she handed them over. I took them looking surprised and wondered who had sent them. Before I could ask the woman about the sender, she had already jumped in her van and drove off down the lane. I shut the door taking the bouquet into the kitchen; they smelt lovely as I could smell without being too close to them. There was a card; my heart started to beat fast; could they be from Zorro, my mystery man? I thought, unfolding the card which read; *Manterro al sicuro fino a quando non ci incontreremo di nuovo siamo stati insieme per sempre xx.*

Oh my god, it's from Zorro, but what was he saying? I would have to go to the library again to find out. I had to wait until the following week to find out due to the library being closed for Christmas and New Year.

I had to find a job soon as it was the start of the New Year. But what did I want to do? After breakfast, I took the car down into the town to find a paper advertising vacancy in the local area. I had a walk around the town browsing through shop windows to see if anyone had put a card in the window advertising a vacancy before going back home. Still, no luck, which I suppose I was expecting with Christmas and New Year as things usually are quiet by this time.

It had started to snow by the time I had gotten back home, with an icy wind blowing, causing the snow to drift. Janet had mentioned a while ago that if we had snow blocking us in, James from the farm comes up to clear the lane, which was comforting to know and less to worry about. The cottage was warm and cosy as the snow started to come down heavy. I was glad I had come home when I did. Making a cup of tea and taking it through the living room, I took out the papers from my bag browsing through the job pages in the area. It was not looking very good as there was hardly anything in the job pages, only a couple of jobs for engineers.

I thought I'd give Mags a ring to see how her Christmas and New Year went. Luckily, they had both been off, which had been the first time since they had met five years ago. We had a long chat, and I told her about Mark and that bitch Charlotte, and that I had been job hunting and failing badly at this time of the year. But I had never told her about Zorro. I suppose he was my secret until the time was right to tell.

It was over a week before I went to the library, hoping to find my translator librarian. My heart started to beat faster as I was about to have my note translated.

'Hello, my dear. I take it you have another note for me?' She smiled knowingly.

'Oh yes, please,' I said, opening my bag and pulling the note out, I handed it to her to read.

'Hmm, this is interesting, my dear,' She fixed her glasses.

'Please tell me, tell me,' I was excited like a teenager wanting to know straight away.

'He says, "I will keep you safe until we meet again when we are together forever."'

Oh, my God! I thought, practically squealing inside. He was going to be with me, but when?

'You are very lucky; he loves you very much with what you have told me, sending you these gifts and letters.'

'He must,' I said all gooey-eyed.

January turned to February, and I was still without a job. Bill had been home taking Janet off for a romantic a long weekend to the south of France. I was feeling envious of her having a man in her life, but then I thought of Zorro with his beautiful eyes and his soft touch and kisses. I wondered where he was? What was he doing?

'Oh, Zorro, I need you so badly,' I mumbled.

By the end of February, I had no luck on the job front, I would have to look further afield it was nearly coming up to a year since I had worked, but I hadn't regretted it getting away from the city life and Mick.

I was reading the local paper when my phone rang. It was Mags calling.

'Hi, Mags, nice to hear from you,' I sounded surprised even to myself. 'Are you ok?' I asked if there was anything wrong.

'Holly, just a quick call to let you know that there is a job vacancy up here as a live-in housekeeper for a businessman who spends most of his time abroad on business, he's looking for someone reliable, confidential and trustworthy. You basically will be house sitting. Money is good, and you get a car, plus he has an indoor swimming pool. What do you think, Holly?' asked Mags, sounding excited.

'Yeah, but err, what do I do with the cottage? I liked the offer, but I was a bit hesitant.

'Holly, rent it out. You don't have to sell it,' she suggested.

'Mm, I don't know, Mags.' I was still not sure.

'Holly, the place is ten miles from where we live. Oh come to Holly, we can have some fun again,' said Mags trying her best to convince me.

‘Ok, give me the details, and I’ll apply for the job.’ I gave in.

‘Holly, the job is yours if you want it. All you have to do is come up to meet him and say hello and then arranging a date to move up.’

‘Mags, how did you wangle that? I was surprised again.

‘It’s who you know and what you know, Holly,’ she giggled.

‘God Mags, I don’t know what I’d do without you,’ I sighed. ‘Thanks, Mags.’

‘Well, I have to go, so I’ll let him know, and I’ll send you the details later when he is back in the country.’

‘Ok. Thanks.’ I said, and with that, she ran off. Gosh, that was a bolt out of the blue. A job had been handed to me on a plate. I started to feel excited knowing that I had a job to go to with the bonus of Mags being close by.

If I rented the cottage out, I would have to give them notice if I wanted to come back, but then I thought about using my cottage as a holiday let, which then meant I would have total control of dates been booked. Yes, I would go down that path instead of renting. Excitement kicked in, so I had to tell Janet my news. Fortunately, she had just come in after working four hours in the bakery due to sickness.

'Oh hi, Holly, what are you up to?' asked Janet walking into the kitchen to fill the kettle for a cuppa.

'I've got some great news! I've got a job!' I told her excitedly.

'Really? Wow, that's great news, what's it about?' asked Janet.

'Well, there's a catch - it's a live-in housekeeper, but it's on the Scottish border where my friend Mags lives.'

'Holly, you're not selling up, are you?' asked Janet looking worried.

'No, but I'm going to ask a favor of you.'

'What's that?' asked Janet.

'I've decided to let the cottage out as a holiday let, and I was wondering if you would look after it with the cleaning and upkeep of each letting? Of course, I'd pay you for it, Janet.'

'Don't be daft. I would love to,' said Janet hugging me. Taking our mugs of tea into the living room, we had a good chat and talked about things in general.

Mags had sent through the details for the job. I was to see Graham Wallace, and he would be in the country for three days before flying out to the States for a week. I decided to drive setting off early, hoping to be up there by midday. Mags gave me instructions on how to get there; she had told me that it was a small estate. I pulled into the tarmac driveway winding my way through a wooded area on both sides of the driveway until I saw the house in front of me. As I got a good look at the place, all I could say was, 'Are you bloody kidding me?' to myself. The house was a castle - it was enormous! 'God Mags, you didn't tell me he lived in a bloody castle,' I said as I pulled in.

Pulling up to the door and stopping the engine, I sat there for a few seconds taking this beautiful castle in. As I stepped out of the car, I was greeted by a dark-haired man in his late fifties or early sixty; he was of an average-built wearing casual jeans and a jumper. I held my hand out to shake his hand, but he didn't take it;

instead, he hugged me as though I was in a foreign country.

'Hello, you must be Holly?'

'Yes,' I nodded, a bit shocked.

'Did you have a good journey driving up?' he asked.

'Yes, it wasn't too bad.'

'I'm Graham Wallace, come on in, and we'll make some tea. I have been told all about you.'

'Oh,' I said, looking surprised. This guy didn't somehow feel like an employer, or was I just imagining it? He explained briefly that he had a close connection with the police and asked them if they knew anyone for the post, and your Mags said that I was looking for a job.

'I was looking for someone trustworthy, reliable and confidential. She said that you were in the police force as a special constable a few years ago, so that was good enough for me,' he said while pouring the tea into the mugs. The kitchen was massive, part old and part new with the large wood burner at the end of the room burning brightly throwing the heat out into the large kitchen. We walked through the castle rooms; there were ten bedrooms of equal portion, all having a four-post bed, which reminded me of Mark and his notches on his bedpost, he would have plenty of room on these. Each bedroom had an on-suite bathroom fully tiled with a separate walk-in shower large enough for two people; that brought the memory back when Mick had me in the shower before he raped me that night. The view from every bedroom was spectacular and breath-taking, overlooking the woods and the sea. I didn't realize we were so close to the sea.

'Yes, it's actually twenty miles away; it's very deceiving, isn't it?' said Graham. We walked down the beautiful staircase, with five bedrooms either side of the staircase coming together in the middle in a gradual descent made of dark oak with decorative spindles.

There was a large library, a study, another bathroom, three more reception rooms, with a dining room to seat at least forty people at a solid wooden oak polished table. Next to the kitchen was the laundry and boot room. I was just about to ask him where the swimming pool was when we walked through a door next to the downstairs bathroom, and there it was a full-scale Olympic swimming pool.

I couldn't believe my eyes; this must cost a fortune to heat.

'Do you swim?' asked Graham.

'Well, yes, if I have the time.' It looked as though I was going to be doing a lot of swimming now.

'You can use this anytime you like,' offered Graham.

'Oh, thanks.' I smiled. I'll have to dig my swimming costume out, or I could be daring and swim naked, seeing that I'll have the place to myself. We had spent over a couple of hours looking through the castle inside. I was surprised how warm it was as most castles I have heard people visited were cold. This place must cost a fortune to run on heating; there were many enormous wood burners in the rooms downstairs, which helped with extra heating.

We ventured outside to several outbuildings, one of which was an office for the farm estate. A man in his forties with weasel looking features stood up from his chair as we came in.

'Hello, Mr. Wallace. Is everything ok?' said the weasel man.

'Yes, Alex, I'm just showing Holly around the estate. She will be staying while I'm away on business,' said Graham.

'Oh, I see,' said Alex looking deflated as though he didn't want me around. Hmm, I'll have to keep an eye on him. The estate was mainly grassland covering over 10,000 hectares with 3000 hectares of woodland. Farming beef cattle and sheep with a riding school and livery, the woodland offered some mountain biking, walking, hiking, and numerous holiday lodges, all this was run from the office next to the castle.

Before I left, Graham made some more tea, he seemed so easy to get on with and so laid back, but I thought it was different with Alex as he seemed a little uneasy. It would be another two weeks before he was back, so we made a date for me to start in April. It would have been a year living in my cottage by then.

When I got back to my cottage, I was tired, it was after 8 pm, but I needed my bed as I had a lot to do before leaving and renting the cottage out as a holiday let.

The next morning, I went around to see Janet to fill her in on the job and the castle, but she wasn't in. She must have gone to work, so I cracked on with sorting the cottage out for holiday letting. I had to pack some of my stuff away, not wishing to leave them. Janet had graciously allowed me to store a few pieces that I didn't want to take with me or store at the cottage in her spare bedroom.

I was excited. Life had taken an unexpected turn, and I was ready to embrace the change. Things looked pretty good, and I knew now nothing could go wrong. I had this nice, warm feeling about it.

CHAPTER SIXTEEN:

Two days before I was going, it was a Friday night, and I had just about finished what I needed to do, with news that I had some bookings on the cottage for the next three months. Things were looking good to my relief.

It was 7.30 pm when there was a knock at the door. Thinking it must be Janet, I went to open the door. It was Mark dressed in jeans and a slim fitting black shirt with a bottle of red wine in his hand looking rather handsome.

'Oh, hi. I was expecting Janet,' I said, looking at him up and down. 'So, what you have been up to? I haven't seen you in a while,' I said, thinking back to new year's when he had groped me.

'I've spent a couple of months working in the South of France.' Mark smiled. 'It was an opportunity I couldn't miss. One of my mates who works over there wanted someone pretty quick on a job for a couple of months. Not only that but they were playing well too,' went on Mark.

'I see. When did you get back?' I asked.

'Only a couple of days ago. Hey, are you going to ask me in?' said Mark holding the bottle of red wine up.

'Mm, I suppose so,' As I opened the door, Mark stepped in waiting for me to close the door. He followed me into the kitchen, where I took a couple of glasses out of the cupboard. 'What? Aren't you going to open it?' I asked, holding the glasses up at him. He poured the wine after which we walked through to the living room where we both sat on the sofa. Mark seemed quite human for once with no sarcasm or sexist remarks.

‘I heard that you’re leaving us; going to the Scottish Borders to live in a castle,’ said Mark suddenly.

‘Yeah, came as a bit of a surprise. I’d been looking for a job locally now the cottage is finished, Mags, a friend of mine, phoned me to let me know about the job, so I arranged to go up and hey presto I got the job,’ I filled him in.

‘What are you doing with the cottage? I hope you’re not going to sell?’ asked Mark with a slight plea in his voice.

‘No I’m planning on using the cottage as a holiday let while I’m away, and Janet has offered to help with the cleaning and gardening, so I don’t have to worry about the cottage not been looked after,’ I said with gratitude for Janet in my voice.

‘That’s good of her. If there’s anything that you need help with just say, and I’ll be there for you,’ offered Mark.

‘Gee, thanks! I’ll let Janet know. I’ll be coming home subject to the bookings of course and when I can, but we’ll see how it goes.’ We both had finished the wine; it was the first time I was having a proper conversation with him without feeling awkward with his remarks.

‘Would you like another drink? I’ve got a bottle in the fridge, or are you going out anywhere tonight?’ I asked Mark.

‘No, I was just coming to see you before you go,’ replied Mark with a smile. I went to get the bottle from the fridge, to refresh both our glasses.

‘I thought you would be out clubbing it in town tonight,’ I said it with a bit of sarcasm.

'Nah, I'm done with that,' said Mark with a serious expression.

'Oh, that's not like you.' I looked at him, surprised; God, he looked ravishing.

'Hmm, I know, but I have started to realize while I was in the south of France that I need to leave my past behind and start to take life seriously, and finding the right woman first,' said Mark looking at me with a light smile.

'Well, you are going to leave a lot of broken hearts behind,' I said jokingly gulping down my wine.

'I never thought of it that way, being a bloke at first, but now I've found that woman, and falling for her, I don't think she's interested,' continued Mark, lowering his head and speaking in a lower tone.

All of a sudden, there was a knock on the door. 'That must be Janet!' I said, getting up to answer the door.

Mark rose from the sofa, 'I better get off then,' he said.

'You don't have to,' I said as I walked to open the door. Janet stepped inside and looked at us.

'Ah, you have company. I hope I wasn't disturbing anything.' She smiled eyeing up Mark, who was stood behind me.

'I'm just leaving,' said Mark. Janet went through to the living room while I saw Mark out. He turned around on the doorstep and said, 'Let me know when you're back as I'd like to take you out for dinner.'

Surprised, I said, 'Okay, that'll be nice. I've got your number so I'll give you a ring when I'm down next.' I shrugged. He came forward and put his hands on my arms, pulling me into his chest for a hug and then he kissed me. It felt different from the bear hug and New Year kiss in the white rose pub, but he wasn't as good as my Zorro. He pulled away and said, 'I'll see you later,' and then he was gone. God, I hoped he was ok as he was driving and we had consumed a bottle and a half of wine.

Closing the door, I went into the living room, to find Janet grinning and raising an eyebrow with intrigue wanting to know more.

'Well,' said Janet, 'spill.'

'Nothing happened,' I said, waving my hand in the air 'and no he hasn't got another notch on his bedpost.' I attempted to sound all innocent after sharing a bottle and half of wine with him. 'He has told me that he's giving women up and wants to settle down.'

'I must admit since he has come back from France, he has calmed down a lot,' said Janet on a more serious note.

'Yeah, he was just saying before you came that he had found the right woman to settle down with, but he thinks she is not interested,' I told her.

'Ahan, I bet I know who that is,' said Janet batting her eyelashes.

'How do you know?' I asked her in a surprised tone.

'Holly, he's always talking about you.' Janet rolled her eyes.

'What? Me?' I shouted, 'No, you've got that wrong.'

'No, I can see it in his eyes when he looks at you. I also know when he was doing your cottage, he was watching every move you made. I think deep down he was falling for you then,' said Janet. I must admit I was tempted, but I managed to control it, I didn't want to be another notch.

'But yes, I could easily have fucked him.' I put a hand on my lips. 'Oops sorry Janet, that's the drink talking.'

'Don't worry about that love; I hear it at the bakery every time I go there. Charlotte says she has got a gob on her. She has wanted to fuck Mark for ages, but he doesn't want anything to do with her,' said Janet. My mind wandered back to the New Year's party when mark had me in a bear hug, trying to kiss me. Charlotte had come along and distracted him while I made my escape. God, I must have been so blind, but I did have my defenses up as I was warned about him.

The following mornings I woke up with a slight headache due to sharing another bottle of wine with

Janet after Mark had left. It was 9 am, and I was just about to get up when my phone rang, it was Mags.

'Oh, hi Mags,' I answered in a groggy voice.

'Hello, Holly, what's up?' asked Mags.

'Err nothing, just had a bit too much to drink last night.' I stifled a yawn.

'Hmm, I was calling to see if you wanted to come up today instead of tomorrow. I'm working Sunday night, so I'll be in bed most of Sunday. I thought if you come up today, we could hit the clubs,' she said, sounding excited.

'Oh God, Mags, I've forgotten how to go clubbing as it's been such a long time. I suppose if I have a couple of coffees and a shower I'll feel a bit more human,' I said.

'Yeah, go on then. I'll see you when I see you.' After hanging up, I made for the kitchen thinking first a coffee; then I will decide what to wear for the journey, jeans perhaps. After drinking my coffee, I went for a shower, it was refreshing, and with the coffee, my head was clearing. While making another coffee, I rang Janet to let her know that I would be leaving today instead of tomorrow.

It was nearly midday by the time I had loaded the car with my belongings that I was taking with me. I made myself another coffee before setting off on my new venture when I heard a vehicle pulling up outside the cottage. By the time I had got to the door, there was a knock, I opened it and to my surprise, standing there was Mark dressed in jeans and a slim white shirt; God I would have fucked him last night if Janet hadn't come around. He was holding a bouquet together with a bottle of red wine.

'Holly, I had to come and see you, you have been on my mind, and I have to tell you how I feel about you before you go,' said Mark holding the bouquet and the bottle of red wine out. I had never heard him sound so serious and sincere.

'Mark, I don't know what to say, but thank you.' Opening the door wider to let him into the cottage and taking the wine and bouquet, I walked into the kitchen where I had left my coffee on the side. Putting them aside, Mark held his arms out to hug me but didn't force a kiss. I hugged him back, his strong arms around me and his warm chest radiating heat seemed to be getting warmer, and I could hear his heart beating as I pressed my head to his chest.

'Holly, the day that I met you, I felt something, but I wasn't sure, and as we put the cottage together, I felt I was getting close to you. I know that I say sexist things, but it is just a front I hide behind. You are beautiful even dressed in your scuffs with dust and dirt, smelling of sweat and with your long hair all ruffled I think I'm falling for you.' He pulled me closer and lowered his head to kiss me on the lips; I didn't resist and put my arms around his neck to kiss him back. Coming up for air, I looked into his grey eyes; his blond curly hair had grown since he had been away, hanging like a mop on his head, but it gave him a sexy look.

'Mark, I'm going away today instead of tomorrow, and I was about to leave. If you had come 15 minutes later, you would have missed me,' I told him quietly.

'Holly, do you have to go today?' asked Mark in a disappointed voice.

'Mm, I'm afraid so. I promised Mags that we would go out tonight as she starts working nights on Sunday.'

'I'm going to miss you,' he said, kissing me gently on the lips and running his finger down my neck.

He was switching me on fast, but I had to get going down the road as I had a few hours to drive.

'Mark, I have to leave now,' I said, pushing him slightly back. 'I'll let you know when I'm back down again, and we can make a night of it,' I said, looking him in his moist grey eyes.

'I'll be waiting,' he said, kissing me again; he didn't want to let me go, but I had to go. Breaking apart, I washed my mug and put it away in the cupboard. I picked up the bouquet and red wine and had one last sweep of the cottage before locking the door behind.

'Oh, I forgot,' said Mark. 'I still have the spare key for your cottage,' he said as he took it out of the back pocket of his jeans.

'No, you keep it just in case,' I left the sentence in mid-air. I laid the bouquet and wine on the front seat of the car, and then I was ready to say goodbye to Mark.

He stood close, taking me around the waist and kissing me passionately. He ran his hand down my back until his hand was on my backside; he then pushed me into him where I could feel him hard and ready to take me. God, I could take him now, but I had to resist.

'Mark, I've got to go.' With one last kiss, we fell apart, and I got into my car and started the engine. Winding my window of the car, I took one long last kiss. Before waving off, the last thing I saw was Mark looking lost.

I dropped off the keys to the cottage at the bakery where Janet was working in the shop; it was a brief visit as she was busy. I asked her that I hoped she didn't mind that I was going today instead of tomorrow.

'No problem love, I hope you enjoy your new job up there and don't forget to phone,' said Janet in-between serving customers.

'No, I won't.' I turned around and said my goodbyes and walked out of the shop.

It was tea time by the time I got to Mags' place. We both bear-hugged each other with excitement. Mags put the kettle on while I brought in the bouquet and wine that Mark had given me.

'Hmm, where do the bouquet and wine come from Holly? Come on the spill,' teased Mags. We sat down with our tea, and I reeled off telling Mags all about Mark.

'Fucking hell, Holly! Why didn't you fuck him?' said Mags, all excited.

'Well, as I said, he is supposed to be a ladies man, and I didn't want to be another notch on his bedpost. But now he has realized, so he says that he's fallen for me.' I shrugged.

'Will he be waiting for you when you go home for a break?' said Mags sounding suspicious.

'Well, it sounds like it,' I said, feeling optimistic. 'So, where are we going tonight, Mags?' I changed the topic.

'There is a new club that has recently opened in town, I thought we'd go there,' said Mags animatedly.

'Right, so what time are we going out?'

'Well, Tony will be back at about 8.30 pm so he can take us into the town and we can get a taxi back.' She had everything planned out.

As we walked into the night club, music blared out to 'I Hate Myself for Loving You' by Joan Jett. That reminded me of Mick, but I was over him now, so I grabbed Mags and said: 'Come on, let's dance.' The club was filling up; two floors were playing new and older music. As I looked around, I realized the average

age was in the late twenties to mid-thirties, with the girls singing out to the music slowly getting inebriated. We had downed a couple of bottles of red wine before coming in, which was making us slightly inebriated too.

We joined the dance floor, singing 'I Was Made for Loving you' by Kiss, dancing seductively to each other with wide grins on our faces. Elvis kicked in with 'The Latest Flame' so we both started our shuffle dance routine, spreading the crowd off the dance floor to give us some space. The crowd was drinking us in and loving it, guys wolf-whistling and shouting sexist remarks, but I didn't care anymore I was free and single. When the music finished, we both needed a drink and headed to the bar; the barman asked us what we would like to drink. We asked for two glasses of red wine; he went off to pour them out and brought them back quickly. I was about to hand him a note to pay for the drinks when the barman said that they were already paid for.

'Oh thanks,' I said. 'So, who has bought these for us?' I asked.

'The owner,' said the barman.

'Where can we find him to thank him?' I frowned.

'He's busy at the moment, but I'll let him know,' said the barman walking off to serve another customer.

Even though I was slightly drunk and getting rather pissed, I had noticed a group of men standing in the darkest area of the club. A couple of them seemed to be having a heated discussion, where another guy butted in to calm the situation down. Two of the guys were dressed in suits while the others in casual trousers and shirt, all roughly in their thirties. I was wondering if there was a fight going to start but after the intervention from the other guy they dispersed and left the club.

It was 1 am before we left the club; we were feeling hungry as well as soaking up the drinks. After finding a take away further down the road where we had to queue with other clubbers, we waited for our order. We ate our chips while waiting for a taxi; the taxis were busy constantly driving off with clubber as quickly as possible and coming back for the next fare. We managed to get a taxi but shared with another couple making the journey slightly cheaper as they were heading our way home.

I was sleeping in Mags' spare bedroom, making a change from her one-bed flat. I woke up with a slight hangover and wanting to use the loo. I had to get out of bed. I delayed it as long as I could, but the urge beat me, and I had to go. As I looked at the clock it was 8 am, too early to get up and Mags needed her sleep as she was working a night shift starting at 6 pm. I rolled back into bed, pulling the covers up and closed my eyes drifting off to sleep. I managed to stay in bed until midday; the sun was shining through the gaps in the curtains, the beams of rays moving slowly across the bedroom as the time ticked by. I decided that I must get up and have a quick look around outside before I left to go to my new job. I didn't shower not wanting to disturb Mags' sleep, so as quietly as possible I got up throwing a pair of jeans and a tee-shirt on, I crept downstairs to the kitchen to make coffee before going outside to explore.

It was a beautiful day for April; the sun was quite warm. I soaked the sun while taking myself for a walk through the village where there was a number of small shops running through the main street of the village. The village backed onto woodland and open fields; tracks were leading off the footpath giving access to the public to roam, I turned off taking the opportunity to take in the countryside as the tracks started to fork out in different directions. I must have been gone for a while as when I got back; Mags was up making a meal for us before she went to work.

'Sorry Mags, I didn't realize the time. I was going to start tea before I left. I got carried away, and I slightly lost my bearings in the woods with so many tracks to follow,' I mumbled as I spotted her in the kitchen.

'Yeah, you don't realize how big the area is until you're in it,' said Mags. She had to set off to work by 5.30 pm so we said our goodbyes and promised that we would arrange some more nights out as soon as I was settled in my new job.

It was just after 6.15 pm when I turned off the road to go down the long winding driveway to the castle. The leaves on the trees were just starting to come out catching the sunlight, which was bringing them out in their full glory. While some were still in their bud form sheltered by other trees stopping the sun coming through. The sun had gone with dusk starting to fall; I was just in time to get myself settled in before bedtime.

I pulled up outside the door before cutting the engine. I sat for a few seconds taking in the view of the gardens and landscape; it was beautiful. I marveled at my luck how I had got a job in such a beautiful place. As I opened my car door, a middle-aged woman in a tweed skirt and a thin jumper met me.

'Hello, you must be Holly? I'm Moria. I do the cleaning and cooking when Mr. Wallace entertains.'

'Oh, hello, Moria. I thought I was going to be on my own,' I said, sounding surprised.

'Yes, my dear. You will be most of the time. I only visit twice a week unless Mr. Wallace needs it, so if you need anything, my dear just let me know,' said Moria with a sweet smile. 'Mr. Wallace had asked me to meet you as he had to go off on business, so that's why I'm here to meet you, dear.'

Moria showed me to my room that she had got ready for me; it was enormous with a beautiful four-poster bed. I began thinking about the things I could do with Mark in that bed. She helped me empty my car with the things I had brought, before moving the car to the side of the castle where there was an area for parking vehicles. As I walked back into the castle, I could hear someone talking in the kitchen. I walked through to see, and Moria was making a pot of tea and with her was the weasel of a man Alex I had met on my interview. He looked at me as though he was undressing me with his eyes.

'Well, you've made it then? And we thought you weren't coming,' he sounded rather disappointed. I didn't say much only that I was staying with a friend overnight and I hadn't seen her for a while. Moria poured the tea into the mugs, handing over a mug to me, saying, ‘Help yourself to milk and sugar dear.’

I thought I would make conversation, starting by asking Moria how long had she been working for Mr. Wallace.

‘Oh, it’s been over ten-year lass, he’s very good to work for and very generous when it comes to family. I had a few problems with Angus, well he is my husband. He was having problems with stomach pains, and the doctors were fobbing him off with different tablets. I was telling Mr. Wallace about it, so he took control of the situation and Angus finished up going private with Mr. Wallace paying for the treatment. It was IBS, and now with a change of diet, he is a changed man.’ Moria gave me a detailed answer, smiling. Alex was quiet, looking a bit sheepish all this time. I turned to ask Alex, but he had just taken the last gulp of tea saying that it was time he was off and left; now I was sure that he was hiding something.

'So, Moria, how long has Alex been here?' I asked her.

'Oh, not long dear, about six months. He took over from Campbell who was retiring, but still lives in the cottage on the estate.'

'Wow, that's good of Mr. Wallace,' I said, sounding surprised, 'Mr. Wallace seems very generous.'

'Yes, he is that,' said Moria sounding happy with her work.

It would be a while before I would see Mr. Wallace and was very surprised to see that he had a cleaner and cook part-time as well as employed me to look after the house. But why did he need me when he had Moria? He must have too much money and needed to offload a bit for tax purposes.

Moria gave me a tour around the rooms in the castle despite that I had already been around with Mr. Wallace. Still, I enjoyed another tour with Moria who was telling me stories of the history of the castle and what had happened in some of the rooms. I was sure she was romancing with some of the stories. We arrived at the room where the pool was.

'Do you swim?' she asked.

'Yes, but I haven't in a while, but I can soon start.'

'The only time it gets used is when some of his family come over; you have a job keeping the kids out of it then.'

'So he has a family?' I asked her interested.

'Oh yes, he has a large family; unfortunately, his wife died while giving birth to their third son, she had him late in life, but it took her life and their son's. It was just before I started,' said Moria feeling sad.

'That's so sad,' I said, feeling emotional as he came across as a very nice man and his wife cut so short in life.

Moria left me on my own just before telling me about the heating, and the alarm if I needed to go out and the door keys as there were a few doors you could gain entry through into the castle, but there were only three they used.

It was dead quiet now that Moria had gone, I had my own space again in this beautiful castle, some people wouldn't stand it being on their feeling uneasy with the scale of the building, but I loved it. Being on my own was what I was used to when I lived at home on the farm in the large farmhouse in the middle of nowhere.

I went to put the kettle on to make a pot of tea before doing a root march through the castle checking the doors, making sure they were all locked, I wasn't taking anything for granted. Making the tea, I took it with me while switching the lights off as I climbed the stairs to bed. It was only 10 pm, but I was tired from the late night out with Mags. I still had to sort my things out that I had brought with me, but I'd leave that until the morning.

The bedroom was at the back of the castle overlooking the tops of the tree to the sea; the room was like being in a posh hotel with handmade furniture. I was looking forward to diving into the four-poster bed it looked so comfortable. I sipped my tea as I walked around the room looking and poking about at things in the room. Once I had finished my tea, I rummaged around trying to find my bag with my bathroom stuff in and my light, silky dressing gown, luckily, I didn't have to dig deep as I had put it on top after I had left Mags'. The bathroom was large with a large walk-in shower cubicle; Mark would love this, God, I was missing that man already, and it had only been two days. Pulling the quilt back, I dived onto the bed; it was higher than a normal bed. After switching off the sidelight, I snuggled in pulling the quilt back sinking into the mattress and began to relax into a deep sleep.

It was Monday morning my first day at work, but what do I do? I had no one to tell me, it seemed weird not having a routine to work to, so I would have to make one. I had slept for a solid twelve hours, and I felt good after the shower with the volume of water cascading from the over large shower head revitalizing my whole body. I looked out of the window to see what the weather was doing, debating what to wear. Jeans, tee shirt and a cardigan, I could always change later if need be.

Moria had stocked up with food, the fridge was heaving with all sorts to choose from, and the cupboards were just as bad, it would be a while until I would have to go shopping for groceries. I made myself a bacon sandwich and a pot of tea and took it into the living room. Despite the room being overly large, it still felt cozy. I switched the TV on to watch daytime tv while eating my breakfast, sitting on one of three six-seater sofas with my feet up I felt; yeah, this is the life.

I could not believe my luck, having landed on such a job. The times were changing, and so was my life.

CHAPTER SEVENTEEN:

It was after mid-day before I unlocked the front door; stepping out in bright sunshine, it was just warm enough without wearing a coat. Setting the alarm and locking the door behind me, I thought I'd see if Alex was around and see if I could suss him out. I also wanted to see if my instincts were wrong. As I walked towards the estate office, I spotted a black 4x4 and a pickup truck parked outside the office; they must be the company vehicles. I could say about the pickup for sure as I had seen it when I first come for my interview.

I opened the door to the office and stepped inside to find Alex stood there, talking to a man dressed in a grey suit. The man was in the early forties, about 5ft 10 with short brown hair combed back with fecks of blond highlights, but what did strike me was that he had a scar across his left cheek, around 2 inches long. The conversation stopped dead as if I had interrupted a secret meeting.

'What do you want, Holly?' said Alex abruptly.

'Oh, I'm sorry, I was just finding my way around. I'll go, sorry to disturb you.' I turned around and walked out. I had just left and was heading towards the outbuilding around the back when I heard Alex's voice outside the office; the other guy was leaving. I heard his vehicle setting off and skidding on the stones in the yard revving high going up the gears as though he was annoyed.

I was walking through the empty cattle shed when Alex appeared at the other end of the open shed startling me.

'So, Holly, what are you up to?' he said in a more friendly voice.

‘Nothing special just looking around to get bearings of where things are,’ I replied, trying not to sound as though I had caught him up to something.

‘Would you like me to show you around? I’ve got some spare time.’ Alex offered with his weaselly smile.

‘Yes, if you don’t mind.’ I was thinking about what I saw in the office he will be only showing me the areas he wanted to. I bet he was up to something.

Alex walked with me around the buildings explaining what they were used for after which we jumped into his pickup truck heading out towards the woodlands. I wasn’t sure about this guy as he still had that look about him. I tried to strike up a conversation with him, asking him if he was married, but the conversation was short.

'No,' he had said with a blunt answer with no explanation. Hmm, this guy was a bit touchy, he had got to be hiding something. I changed tact and asked him how long he had been working for Mr. Wallace?

'You're asking too many questions, aren't you?' He sounded frustrated.

'I'm sorry. I'm just making conversation that's all.' I tried to make my voice sound normal. I had only asked him two personal questions, and he was getting rather shirty over them. This guy was trouble, but what was he up to?

We approached the entrance to a lodge cabin set amongst trees but was facing out across the open fields. The cabins were about a hundred meters apart with the majority facing out across the open fields. This was the start of a new venture for the estate with the first bookings coming in the next couple of days. Alex told me that Sarah dealt with the bookings, but she also inspected the cabins before each booking and to supervise the cleaning and any maintenance. We must have travelled thirty miles touring the grounds, but Alex turned around saying that he had to get back. The conversation went stale after explaining the workings of the estate. I was glad in some ways he didn't ask questions about me, so I didn't volunteer.

It was just after 4 pm when we got back to the estate office. I jumped out of the truck muttering 'thanks' and making a quick getaway. I could feel his eyes burning into my back as I walked off towards the castle entrance; 'God, the fucking pervert.' Unlocking the door and switching off the alarm, I made my way to the kitchen for a cup of tea.

I took my mug of tea upstairs as I hadn't sorted my stuff out yet. All the wardrobes and drawers were empty, leaving me with plenty of space for my belongings. While I was sorting through, I came across the ring and the necklace. It took me back to the moments of bliss with Zorro and the messages written in Italian. The thought hit me again that why didn't he show himself if he said he wanted to be with me? I was single now and had been for over a year. Then I started to think of Mark and about missing my chance of intimacy with him before leaving to come up here. But then there were Zorro's beautiful eyes and his kiss, yes, his kiss, how could I forget?

All of a sudden, my phone rang snapping me out of my romantic moment.

'Hello, Mags, this is a surprise. Is everything ok?' I asked in a cautious voice.

'Holly, I had to ring as soon as I found out. It's Mick, he's left the force,' said Mags in a shocked voice.

'What? Are you kidding me?' The news was unbelievable; it was Mick's ambition to get to the top.

'Did you know why? Was he pushed, or was it by choice?' I asked her with disbelief.

'Well, as far as I know, it was by choice, but I don't know where he has gone,' said Mags. After the shock of the news about Mick, I forgot to mention about Alex and the guy he was with.

I continued by sorting all my things with a place for everything; after a couple of hours, I was feeling hungry. I took my empty mug downstairs with me into the kitchen to find something to eat.

'Hmm, let's see what there is?' I mumbled opening the fridge door. The salad looked promising, I took out the greens with various meats and tubs of coleslaw and potato. I finished off with a raspberry trifle and found a small bottle of red wine. Opening the red wine, I brought out a glass from the cupboard,

'Hmm, this is nice,' I looked at the bottle, but the label just said red wine. I must ask Moria where she got it from.

After washing my pots and putting them away, I grabbed the bottle of wine and glass, taking them with me into the living room. I switched the TV on and settled down on the huge sofa for the night flicking through the channels. It was after 11 pm when the film had finished, feeling slightly tired. I decided to call it a night.

I got off the sofa to switch the TV off and started my rounds on checking the locks on the doors even though I had only had unlocked only one this morning. I climbed the stairs to my bedroom, after having a quick wash, I jumped into bed, switching the sidelight off and again relaxed into a deep sleep.

The next morning, I woke up just after 8.15 am, my breasts were aching a little probably because I was due to come on, and the skin on my front felt slightly tight, so I got up and jumped into the shower before dressing to go downstairs. I made myself bacon butty and a pot of tea and ventured outside hoping to see Sarah; it was nearly 9.30 am so she should be in by now.

Walking towards the estate office, I saw a blue car but no pickup truck. Thank God for that as I didn't want to see Alex today, especially after his non-talkative mood yesterday. I opened the office door and walked in, looking around to see if there was anyone in. On the left-hand side of the office sat an average looking woman in her late thirties with short dark hair and a pale blue shirt with the estate logo on, to advertise the log cabins printed in red and black. The shirt looked the part.

'Hello, can I help you?' she said, standing up to reveal a pair of smart well-cut black trousers.

'Hi I'm Holly I'm staying in the castle while Mr. Wallace is away.' I walked over to shake her hand.

'Oh I didn't know that there was anyone staying; he usually just has Moria come in two or three times of the week to tidy up and look after things while he is away,' said Sarah sounding surprised.

'I came up a few weeks ago to see him, I saw Alex, so were you away then?' I asked, trying not to give too much information.

'No, I was on site down by the woodlands where the log cabins are. I was supervising; you know what men are like if you leave them, they like too many tea breaks.' She smiled, saying it with a little sarcasm.

'Yeah builders like their breaks,' I said, thinking about Mark; he wasn't one for tea breaks he just wanted to get on with the job. I wondered what he was up to since I had gone.

'Alex tells me you look after the log cabin side of the business?' I said casually.

'Yes, Alex doesn't have a clue about tourism and marketing, he just deals with the day to day running of the estate and the farm,' said Sarah sounding glad he didn't know that side of the business.

'How long have you been here?' I asked.

'Just over a year, we had to start from scratch with the planning and the size of the cabins, etc.,' Sarah explained. Changing the subject, I asked about Alex.

'So, where is Alex this morning?'

'He got a phone call and had to go out,' said Sarah. I didn't want to ask too many questions about him in case she got suspicious. There was something about her which made me feel that I couldn't confide in her about Alex, so I kept my mouth shut about yesterday. Feeling like a spare part, I asked if she would like help with anything, but she was very abrupt saying that she had everything under control and that she had to get on. That was to say, go away and find someone else to bother. I was taken aback by her abruptness. It wasn't as though I wanted to take over her job, so I turned around said my goodbyes and walked out of the door, leaving her to it. Bloody mardy bitch, I thought.

I walked back to the castle to phone Janet; I went into the kitchen and flicked the kettle on to make tea while I dialed Janet's number. It went to voice mail, damn! Then I tried Mark, I just wanted to hear his voice, but he was on the same voice mail, there was no point of phoning Mags, she would be in bed being on nights.

God, I was bored; was I ready cut out for this job if you called it a job.

I was sat at the kitchen table holding my mug of tea when I heard the door open; it was Moria.

'Good morning, lassie,' she said, sounding cheerful.

'Hi, Moria I forgot about you coming in today.' I smiled.

'Don't worry about me, dear; just pretend I'm not here.' She smiled broader.

'How long are you here for?' I asked her.

'Why do you ask lassie?'

'I was thinking of going into town to have a look around.' I shrugged.

'I'm here till 3,' she said, walking off into the living room. Finishing the last mouthful of tea, I washed my mug up and put it on the side to drain. 'Right! Let's go and hit the shops.' I stood up from the chair and walked towards the stairs as I needed my bag.

It was just after mid-day; I took my time as I wasn't aware of the area and had to follow the signs to the town. I eventually found a parking space. As I got out of the car the weather had turned, the clouds gathering looking like it was about to rain, so I picked up my coat from the back seat of my car before heading off towards the shops. The shops were in the high street but with a pedestrianized shopping area leading up to a large shopping centre.

I must have spent nearly two hours browsing around before I purchased a slim fitted tracksuit bottom, some more tee shirts/vests and two swimming costumes. Yes, I decided that I was going to start running and taking advantage of the full-size swimming pool. I could make this part of my daily routine, keeping fit at the same time. Once, I had exhausted the shops and had bought my work-out gear, I headed back to the car but seeing a café I thought I would have a cup of tea. There was a handful of people in the café, so I managed to find a seat next to the window as I liked to see what's going on outside. It had started to rain hard, so luckily, I was in the café. The café started to fill up due to the rain, and eventually, the place was full with no seating. I had managed to place myself in a corner near the window where there was only one seat, so I was on my own. I sat by the window watching the world go by; the traffic had slowed down due to someone had pressed the pedestrian crossing. A black 4x4 pulled up, waiting for the lights to go green. I was sure it was the guy with the scar on his face in the driving seat, but I couldn't see the person in the passenger seat, whether they were male or female hoping that there would be some movement from the passenger. I had focused on the driver then just before the light changed to green the passenger lent forward-facing the driver, yes that was Alex! But who was this guy he was with?

The traffic moved on as did the vehicle. The weather had now changed to fine rain. I finished my tea and left the café heading for my car.

By the time I got back, it was gone at 5 pm; the traffic was a bit heavy due to commuters leaving work. Moria had left already, so it was good that I had taken the keys with me. As I unlocked the door, the alarm started beeping crazily. I had not thought that she would have put it on, dropping my bags, I ran quickly to the alarm panel to punch in the combination code having only 2 seconds spare without it going off. Gosh, that was a close call!

Collecting my bags, I took them upstairs to my bedroom. Looking at my swimming costumes, I thought

I might test one out tonight, but first I was feeling a little puckish. I put away my joggers and tops, leaving out my swimming costume. I picked up my phone and made my way downstairs; damn, these stairs were grand being the centrepiece of the castle where you could make a grand entrance. I wondered how Graham Wallace could afford such a luxury living in a castle as grand as this. I didn't know anything about him only what Moria had told me about his wife, how sad for him to be so alone.

I Flicked the kettle on to make a pot of tea and looked into the fridge to see what I fancied to eat. I didn't fancy a salad, but there was a trifle for after. I craved something hot, 'yes I'll do some scrambled eggs on toast'. By the time I had finished eating and had cleared up, I thought I would try ringing Janet; she should be in by now as it was after 6 pm. I dialed her number and waited, it rang for a while, and I was about to press to end the call when she answered.

‘Hello?’ said Janet sounding out of breath.

‘Oh, Janet I’m sorry I have disturbed you in middle of doing something.’ I knew I sounded sincere.

‘No, no, I was just getting out of the shower when I heard it ringing. Everything ok, Holly?’ asked Janet.

‘Yeah, I’m a bit bored.’ I sighed. ‘I’ve only seen three people, Moria who does the cleaning which I don’t know what she finds to do as everything is spotless, and there’s Sarah who is too far up her own arse running the log cabins and Alex who’s a weasel running the farm estate.’ I filled Janet in on my latest news at the castle, especially the guy with the scarred face and seeing him with Alex in the town.

‘Have you thought that Alex could be gay and hasn’t come out yet?’ said Janet with a laugh in her voice.

'No, I'm sure he's not. Every time I see him, he looks as though he's undressing me, I sure he's a perv.' I was a bit disgusted.

'You probably imagine it, Holly. Is that castle spooking you out?' added Janet with a laugh.

'Hmm maybe.' Changing the subject, I asked Janet about Mark and if she had seen him since I left. But all she said was that rumor has it he's got the hots for someone, and he hasn't been seen in the pub. I wondered if he was thinking of me, but I wasn't so sure he still carried his reputation with him although I was tempted to fuck him. I couldn't say anything to Janet. We had another five minutes of general chat before finishing the call.

Do I phone Mark or just leave it? I argued to myself. Was he thinking of me, or was he trying his best just to bed me? In the end, I decided that I would leave it as if he'd got someone else I'd be more depressed while I was here.

It was nearly 8 pm so I thought I'd wear my swimming costume and try the pool out. I walked through the door as the heat from the pool hit me. It was so warm in there. I dipped my toe in the pool to test the water it was warm.

I slid in the water; it was like having a bath it was lovely. I started to swim in lengths. The pool was lit up with the lights dimmed above; it was very therapeutic. Having done six lengths, I heard a noise coming from the kitchen; I swam to the end to get out seeing who was there. I wrapped a towel around me and padded off towards the kitchen door. I hadn't locked the front door after I had come back from town and had never thought to lock it before I went for a swim. The kitchen was just the same as I had left it. Was there an unwanted visitor haunting the castle I wasn't aware of? I locked the door then padded back to the pool where I finished another twenty lengths before heading back upstairs to have a shower and to wash my hair.

It was after 9.30 pm when I came down with my hair dried and tied back into a ponytail, heading towards the kitchen to make a pot of tea. As usual, I took my tea into the living room and switched the TV on. I settled on the large sofa putting my feet up feeling relaxed after the swim and the shower. It was only after 10 pm, and I was feeling tired, so switching the TV off and taking my mug to the kitchen I climbed the grand staircase to the bed where once again I sank into the bed and drifted off the sleep.

I was dreaming of Mark, having sex with him feeling him entering me, his hands on my breasts, massaging them and holding onto my nipples, making me aroused with pleasure. He started to suck them nipping and flicking with his tongue, running his tongue down to my clitoris making me rise in pleasure, his fingers entering me as he pressed his thumb on my clitoris rubbing hard making me come. I could feel the heat of his body on me, his hardness rubbing up and down on my belly, his mouth on my neck kissing me hard, he shot his lot over me rubbing his cum between us, and finally, his hands rubbing the reminder over my breasts squeezing and pulling my hard nipples.

I woke up suddenly covered in sweat, breathing heavily as though I had just had sex. I felt wet having been sexually aroused in my dream, but it felt so real. It was 4 am so I nipped to the toilet for a wee. I felt as though I just had sex; I supposed I had it was a dream after all. I managed to drift off to sleep until 8 am waking up as though I had sex and needed a shower.

This was the start of a routine in exercise, firstly I was going to swim every morning then a light breakfast and out for a run to explore the grounds for myself without Alex telling where and where not to go. Putting my second costume on, I headed down to the pool, to plunge into the water to make ripples, and it was still the same temperature. I swam thirty-two lengths which took me half an hour. That was enough; I would increase the lengths gradually. There was no point of a shower as I was going for a run after breakfast and decided to have one when I got back.

Locking up and putting the key in my joggers, I set off heading for the woods. I noticed Alex's pickup truck outside the estate office; Alex was watching me from the window until I noticed him that's when he moved away as though I hadn't seen him. With the key safely in my pocket and the weather being cloudy and cooler, I stepped up my game to warm up running quickly, heading straight towards the woods where the log cabins sat. It must be at least a mile from the castle; the road was tarmac for about half a mile turning into a farm track which looked as though it had been beefed up with a stone base making it solid.

The first cabin I came across was made in dark wood having one side all glass with a veranda facing across over the landscape. I walked around the cabin looking and trying to see inside how it was laid out. The cabin seemed to have everything with mod cons. I jogged on passing half a dozen more cabins of similar size and outside space. Roads were leading off to each cabin. The cabins seemed to be placed in rows having one row in the middle and a row each side of the wood facing the landscape.

I finished walking to the end of the woods, finding a track that didn't seem as though it had been used, catching myself on the hawthorn bushes as I pushed through. It seemed that the woodlands were surrounded by grassland containing sheep. In the distance were fields of crops as far as the eye could see.

Climbing over the fence, I started jogging over the grass field, noticing a large hill across one of the far fields. I thought I'd go for that to get a better view from the top. I took a quick swig of water from my bottle before heading off to the top of the hill.

I had been out for three hours, but it hadn't felt like it. The hill was covered in the scrub, but I managed to tread my way through to the top. It took me a good 15 minutes to get to the top. I was able to get a bird's eye view of the surroundings now. There were more woodland and the sea. I could see that view of the sea through my bedroom window over the woodlands thinking it was the woodland I had come through; 'God, it's going to take a while getting my head around this.' I inhaled heavily.

It was later in the afternoon when I got back to the castle. Unlocking the door and disarming the alarm, I went straight upstairs for a change and a shower. I was going through my drawer to find a shirt to put on, and I came across the ring and necklace, which took me back in time meeting Zorro and his kiss, his messages written in Italian saying we will be together. I sat on the bed holding my treasures and the love of this man I had not seen only his beautiful eyes and his strong arms; Oh, Zorro I wish you would show yourself I want to make love to you so desperately and to be together forever.

My thoughts were interrupted by my phone ringing; it was Mark.

'Whoa, hello, what a surprise.'

'Hello, sexy, I haven't called at a bad time, have I?' asked Mark.

'No, no, I was just done having a shower.'

'Mm, I wish I was there in the shower with you giving you a rub down, sexy,' Mark teased in a sexy voice.

'I was dreaming of you last night having sex with you, and it felt so real, I woke up all aroused, sweating and breathing heavy,' I confessed.

'Ahaan I have that effect on you, sexy?' said Mark.

'You are missing me, aren't you?' I asked.

'Yeah it's those nipples poking through your tee shirt when you're sweating and all untidy that make me hard, and it keeps me wanting to make love to you so desperately,' said Mark his voice sounding sincere.

'Oh Mark, you're starting to turn me on with that talk.' I began to feel flushed.

'When do you think you will be back down so I can make love to you all night?' asked Mark with a plea in his voice.

'I don't know. I will have to wait until Mr. Wallace gets back and see if there are any bookings for my cottage.'

'It doesn't matter about your cottage - you can stay with me, just get the time off if you can.' He pleaded.

'Ok, I'll see what I can do, Casanova,' I told him about the people who worked here and that they are not particularly friendly and I was a bit bored, so I started swimming and jogging to pass the time. We finished talking on a high hoping to get some time off when Graham gets back from his trip.

It was got 5 pm by the time I had finished dressing and talking to Mark. With a spring in my steps, I waltzed into the kitchen, starving for I had burnt off, God knew how many calories. Eggs and bacon, it was followed by rice pudding. I enjoyed the calorie busting meal but would work it off later in the pool.

Watching some TV until 8 pm and drinking water, it was time for a swim. Heading upstairs, I went in to search for my swimming costume. Damn, I had forgotten to hang them up to dry, they both were still damp, and I didn't fancy putting them on. Feeling a bit daring and since there was no one around, I took a towel from the bathroom and headed to the pool but locked the front door before stripping off my towel and jumped into the pool, naked. Despite the length of time I had spent exploring the grounds and the lengths I had done this morning, I managed to achieve another thirty-two lengths.

The feeling of swimming without a costume was exhilarating, feeling the water running over my body and freedom. As I pulled myself out of the pool I heard a noise, it was the same noise as the night before, was the ghost prowling the castle again? Wrapping the towel around myself, I headed out upstairs to have a shower and wash my hair. I slipped my lightweight over the gown and wrapped my hair in a towel. I went downstairs into the living room to switch the TV on and then to the kitchen to make a cup of tea. As I picked up the kettle to fill with water, I could hear the loose scale in the kettle moving about, so I tipped the kettle over emptying the loose scale giving it good swill out. The tea seemed to taste better after I had swilled it out.

I climbed the grand stairs to my bed; it was after 11 pm when I slipped under the quilt sinking into the mattress that molded around me. I had never felt a bed so comfortable as I drifted off to sleep, having gone through the start of my exercise routine.

It must have been the early hours of the morning as I felt a chill on my body. I slowly woke up to the sound of a door closing. I was laid in a starfish position in the bed with the quilt rolled back, exposing all of my naked body, no wonder I was waking up to a chill in the air. Hearing the noise, I got up slipping my silky robe on to investigate; it was still dark apart from the shadows of the moon beaming through the windows of the castle. It was after 4.30 am. I listened hard for any further noise the castle was quiet as a morgue. I must be hearing things, so seeing that I was up, I went off downstairs into the kitchen to make a pot of tea.

Moria was due to come in today, so I thought I would have an early swim now that I found swimming naked was more exhilarating than wearing a swimming costume. Taking my tea, I slipped into the living room, switching the light on; I noticed a cd collection in the far end corner of the room that I had not noticed before. It didn't surprise me that I had missed it with the room being so large. I started pulling out several CDs to see what sort of music Graham was into, and I was very surprised he had a varied collection with old and new.

I pulled one of the CDs out and slipped it into the player switching it on and turning the volume up; it was the Lambada. I turned and starting dancing to the music swaying my hips from side to side with the rhythm and moving around the room, closing my eyes; Mark moving with me so close and in rhythm. As the music stopped, I heard the noise of what sounded like a door closing as I had heard when I was upstairs. Opening my eyes, I tottered across the room towards the door and rushed out into the hallway.

Nothing was there; the castle must have a ghost who I must have woken up with the music being loud. I wasn't spooked, as there was always an explanation with living in a large farmhouse in the middle of nowhere. There was one occasion I had a friend staying overnight; we were only ten years old; we were in bed giggling and messing about when we heard a door creaking. The bedroom door started to open slowly, my friend soon stopped giggling she was scared, it didn't bother me, it finally had stopped and in popped the cat, my friend was relieved. I never believed in ghosts, so I was waiting for the opportunity to meet one.

I played a few more discs dancing to the rhythms before I headed off for my morning swim in the nude. By the time I had swum the lengths I had set myself, it was nearly 7 am. Moria was due in at 9 am so I dried myself and towel-dried my hair slipping on my joggers and a clean tee-shirt before going back down to the kitchen for a light breakfast.

Waiting for Moria to arrive I remembered that I had a rucksack in the wardrobe. This would be ideal for carrying my bottled water, a towel, a few first aid bits and the door key in a zipper compartment and most importantly, my phone. Moria arrived on time, with a quick hello and goodbye I stepped outside in the brilliant sunshine, slipping a bandana around my forehead I set off heading towards the woods behind the castle. Out of the corner of my eye, I noticed Alex watching me from his office window, bloody pervert.

I jogged across the open field towards the woods where the sea was hiding; I had some twenty miles to get there with another twenty to get back. Stopping for a breather on the edge of the woods, I sat down and pulled out my bottled water having a good swig. My bandana was working nicely with the sweat soaking into the stretchy material. I had tied my hair up into a ponytail, wrapping it into a bun and pinning it up, exposing my neck and shoulders.

After ten minutes I climbed over the fence making my way into the woodland, it wasn't as dense as it should be with the greenery not fully formed. It was the beginning of May, but if the weather stayed warm, then the greenery would hurriedly fill in the gaps. There weren't any tracks to follow, making it hard to penetrate through the brash. With tackling hawthorn bushes and hedges, I was scratched many times which made my arms bleed. It must have taken me an hour to push my way through to the other side where I was met by another fence to climb and a grass field dotted with trees and sheep. Gagging for a drink, I climbed over the fence seeing a tree that had blown over. I walked over sitting on the tree to get out my water and some tissues to wipe my arms from the blood, followed by an antiseptic wipe.

'Mm I will have to find a different route back even if it takes me longer,' I told myself.

The sun was rising, and so was the heat; it must be nearly lunchtime when I started feeling puckish. I had a couple of granola bars to fill the gap and swigged my water. I could hear the birds singing, and saw four deer in the field with the sheep grazing, but as soon as the deer saw me, they were off running into the woods. I had just fought my way through.

Ahead of me was another woodland, 'God, I hope it's not as bad as what I had just come through.'

Climbing over the fence, I ventured in, at least this wasn't as thick with brambles and hawthorn. I picked up a track, but it was heading to the right of the woods and not across as I wanted to, but to make it easier I followed it and it eventually took me out onto a dirt track wider enough for a vehicle. By the look of the track, there didn't seem to be many people using the track as the grass from the winter was still tall with new growth poking through.

The track led out into the open fields with land only good enough for sheep grazing, dotted with clumps of trees with a few rogue gorse bushes having a slight slope heading towards the sea. I followed the track as far as it would go. It brought me out onto another well-worn track where I could see a large industrial type building probably used for storage. But seeing the sea ahead of me, I headed off breathing in the sea air as I walked down to the sandy beach. The sea was calm, and in the distance, I could see shipping containers, small as they would be many miles out to sea. There wasn't a soul around the beach; it was deserted like the Mary Celeste.

I kicked off my trainers and socks, pulled up my leg joggers and headed for the sea, the water was freezing but felt refreshing for my feet. I spent a few minutes pacing up and down in the water and walked back up to an area to sit down, drying my feet and taking a drink of water. It was nice breathing in the sea air.

It was starting to get late in the afternoon, and I realized that I should be heading back to the castle. I started walking back, picking up the track I had found when I had come out of the woods. When I got the place where I had come out from the wood, I decided not to enter the woods with it being late in the afternoon, so I followed the track which by the look of it took me close to the castle.

Eventually, the track came out onto a corner showing a well-used track so heading right I jogged on. In the distance I could see a vehicle heading towards me, must be one of the estate workers, I guessed.

Yes, I was right, but I wasn't expecting Alex pulling up in his pickup truck with a purvey smirk on his face and stopping his vehicle.

'So, lassie where have you been?' he asked, sounding concerned.

'Oh just down to the beach,' I said, sounding relaxed as I could.

'There's nothing down there for you to see,' he said, sounding slightly agitated.

'I know, but I had a paddle in the sea,' I said just to make a bit of a conversation.

'Well get in lass, I drive you back to castle.' He motioned to the seat, saying it as a command. I didn't want to be sat next to him, but I didn't want to argue with him either. The journey back to the castle was silent, but I could see him from the eye corner looking at me. I must have been looking a bit of a mess with scratches over my arms and my hair coming undone. Twenty minutes later we were at the castle, with a quick thank you to him I jumped out heading quickly to the castle fumbling with my rucksack for the door key. Entering the castle and turning off the alarm, I went back to the door and locked it. God, he gave me the creeps.

It was gone 6 pm, and I was starting to ache as this was the furthest, I had been, together with the scratches from the thorns and hawthorn. A bath was to soak my aches and pains; I had to give swimming a miss this evening. Climbing the stairs, I headed straight for the bathroom, dumping my rucksack behind the bedroom door.

Stripping off while the water was running, I put my clothes in the wash basket for washing. Easing myself into the water and feeling the warmth soothing my aches and pains, I laid there for a while with the occasional top up with hot water. After half an hour soaking, I got out to wash my hair in the shower after which I felt refreshed and was not aching so much.

By the time I had finished drying my hair, I had slipped on my light robe and went downstairs heading for the kitchen. I was starving; it must be the sea air. Checking the fridge, I noticed that Moria had replenished it with freshly produced taking out items. I started with a salad, followed by a yoghurt and a piece of cake. Making myself a pot of tea, I went into the living room with my tray and switched the TV on putting my feet up on the recliner sofa.

While I was eating my meal, I thought I heard a door close but dismissed this as I was watching a film where it could have been from the TV.

It was 10 pm by the time the film had finished. I had my few pots to wash up, and I needed another cup of tea. Heading back to the kitchen with my tray, I switched the kettle on while I washed my pots. Taking my tea back into the living room to watch the end of the news and the weather for tomorrow, I felt tired. After seeing the weather, I switched off the lights and dumped my mug in the kitchen after which I went upstairs where I sank into the mattress and drifted off to sleep within seconds.

The next morning, I woke up feeling as though I had done six rounds with Mike Tyson. I was sore and ached all over. God, I must have overdone it yesterday. Getting up from my bed, I felt wet below. I was not due to come on yet, the bottom sheet was wet as though I had peed myself, I shuffled off to the toilet to inspect myself, but there was no blood but the smell of sex. God, was I dreaming and having multiple orgasms? I had a quick shower washing away the smell, and with the heat of the shower massaging my body I felt a lot better but gave the pool a miss this morning.

It was after 10 am before I had breakfast. I decided that today I was going to leave the jogging and swimming until tomorrow. Filling the washing machine, I switched on having a full load. I decided to go back into the town to buy some more joggers and tops, so it was after midday I left for town. I noticed that Alex's truck was not outside his office only Sarah's, but I wasn't going to bother with her as she seemed so full of her importance.

CHAPTER EIGHTEEN:

While I was in town, my phone rang. It was Mags.

'Mags I'm glad you've rung,' I said with an excited voice. 'I was going to ask you when you were next off so we could go out clubbing.'

'You must be a mind reader, Holly. I was just about to ask you the same thing,' said Mags, reflecting my excitement.

'Oh, brilliant! When?' I asked her sounding so desperate.

'I was thinking Saturday night,' suggested Mags.

'Yeah, great! What time and where?' I asked.

Finally, the arrangements were made with me booking a taxi to meet Mags outside the new night club called 'The Seventh Heaven.'

After I had finished my call with Mags and our night out was arranged, I needed to buy something new to go out in, so I hit out on all the shops I could find trying to find the right outfit for the night. I was just about to give in until I came across a small shop off the high street; it wasn't the usual modern-day fashion. I picked out a pair of slim-fitting black trousers with a red stripe top straight down on both sides, making them look as though they were part of a soldier's uniform. I matched it with a waistcoat with red trim. I was pleased with my purchases, and celebrated with a coffee at the same café I saw Alex in the 4x4 with Scarface at the traffic lights.

I had to wait two nights before we were going out, and it was killing me. I wanted to dance and get pissed. With my aches and pains decreasing, I was feeling more supple and ready to have a good night out. Over the next couple of days, I went swimming four times a day instead of jogging, not wanting to cause any unwanted accidents, so swimming was the best form of exercise with the luxury of swimming in the nude. I started sieving through Graham's collection of CDs and playing them at full volume. Oh, the joys of not having neighbours.

The evening had arrived, it couldn't have come sooner. After taking a shower and washing my hair, I styled my hair, making my long hair curlier and shinier. I applied my makeup, bringing out the blue in my eyes by applying a thin line of eyeliner and two shades of brown eye shadows, followed by a shiny neutral colour lipstick. Pulling on my new trousers together with the waistcoat and black and red-trimmed heels, I went to look at myself in the full-length mirror to check myself and that everything was in its right place.

'Holly, you are sex on legs,' I smirked talking to myself.

Hearing the taxi pulling up, I quickly picked up my clubbing purse and my black jacket and headed downstairs for the taxi. As we pulled up outside the night club, I could see Mags waiting. After paying the taxi driver, I jumped out with excitement, hugging Mags.

'Whoa, Holly, you look fantastic! Where did you get that outfit from?' exclaimed Mags looking gobsmacked. I explained how I nearly didn't get it and had only come across it by chance.

We walked into the club together, where the music played the Lambada. What a coincidence! I was only playing this the other evening. The dance floor was empty with hardly anyone there with it being early, so we had the dance floor to ourselves. Drinking red wine, we stripped off our jackets as the night was going to get hot and I was going to make the most of it.

With the lights low, the scratches on my arm didn't show, but I had tried to conceal them with a bit of concealer just in case. The music was good, playing a variety of eras and numbers to dance to, dancing as though we were working out, we were sweating with beads of sweat running down our faces.

As the night went on the club started to fill with clubbers with an average age range of about thirty. I felt good, leaving Mags dancing with a guy she knew at work, I went off to the loo being lucky enough there wasn't any queueing. As I was coming out, I was grabbed by the waist by a strong arm and a guy about 6ft tall wearing black leather trousers and a black shirt. He pushed me through a door with a sign saying 'no unauthorized persons beyond this point'. The lighting was dim; I couldn't see his face; he opened another door leading into a room which looked like someone's living room. Not switching the lights on, with only the beams of light coming through from the street light outside, he shut the door locking it behind us; Shit was I in trouble?

He kissed me softly and then I knew it had to be Zorro, his height, his build, his arms. I opened my eyes where I met his in the beam of light coming from the window. His beautiful eyes; he was my Zorro. We didn't speak, we kissed, touching each other on the face. I ran my hand through his thick curly long hair.

Fucking hell, I wanted him inside me. He was making me so wet; I was a bitch in season.

'Zorro, make love to me,' I begged.

'Holly, I have been waiting for you,' he said in a sexy voice. We moved to the sofa where I started to undress him unbuttoning his shirt, and in return, he did the same. My waistcoat soon came off revealing my lacy black bra, and then his thumbs pinched the hooks releasing my breasts. I took off his shirt, revealing his muscular body. As we kissed more passionately, I could feel his hard length on my belly, fuck! I wanted him desperately inside me and to savor it. His hands cupped my breasts; they were soft and gentle. He kissed my neck down to my breasts to my nipples, gently flicking one at a time with his tongue.

'Zorro I need you inside me,' I whispered to him groaning with pleasure. He laid me on a thick rug on the floor, taking off my trousers to reveal my black lacy undies. He started kissing from the waist down gently; he was making me come without even being inside me.

'You're going to make me come.' I was groaning, he slipped off my undies, and I parted my legs, hoping he would enter me. He still had his leather trousers on, but I could see how hard he was underneath. He started kissing me again, working his way down my body; it was bliss. I was wet, so wet I felt as though I was leaking with lust, but it was my love for this man.

He sat there, pulling back my lips, licking my clitoris and drinking my wetness in. I was moaning with pleasure; he kept making me come time after time. Finally, he took off his leather trousers to reveal his manhood and oh boy, didn't he have that 'Italian stallion!' He slowly entered me; I felt his length expanding me. He was gentle pushing slowly back and forwards entering me until he was in full.

'Oh, Zorro I have been waiting for you, for this moment to happen. God, I love you so much even though I know nothing about you.' I moaned.

'Holly, I loved you the first day you came to the station,' he whispered. I don't know how my orgasms I had, but his lovemaking was something I had never experienced. God, I wished I had met him instead of Mick.

We made love three times, during which I climaxed multiple times, and then we laid there with sweat pouring off us. It was getting late, and I had forgotten about Mags, who was on the dance floor.

When we had finished our steamy lovemaking session, although I didn't want it to finish, I asked his name.

'Holly, I cannot tell you at this moment, but it will come to light soon,' he promised.

'When can I see you again then?

'Soon but please be patient I will come for you.'

'But you don't know where I'm living,' I said, looking puzzled.

'Mm I do, you're at the castle,' he said.

'How do you know that?' My voice was filled with surprise.

'Holly, I know where you are, I will be close by,' he said, kissing me passionately once again. 'But there is one thing, and I know you haven't said anything to anyone about our brief meetings in the past, but please keep this moment to ourselves,' he insisted.

'Of course, I will. I love you, Zorro, I can wait.' I assured him.

We dressed, and after tiding myself up I made my way down to the dance floor, but before leaving him, I sucked the life out of his face and stared into his beautiful eyes for long since I didn't know when I would see him next.

I eventually found Mags she was leathered and was with a couple of colleagues from work, so she had been in safe hands, which was a good thing as I didn't have to explain where I had been for the last four hours.

Her colleagues assured me they would get her home safely as I lived in the opposite direction.

It was after 2 am by the time I was dropped off by the taxi; luckily, the place was lit with moonlight as I approached the door fumbling in my purse for the key. The key fell onto the path, as I bent down to pick it up I lost my balance and was about to go flat on my backside when an arm reached around my waist pulling me up, sliding the other hand over my breast, pulling me back towards their body. I felt something hard against me. With the key in my hand, I pushed away, turning to see who it was as I knew it wasn't – Zorro - he didn't have that touch and height. I was surprised to see Alex standing there with a grin on his face.

'Are you alright, lassie?' he asked with a smirk on his face. I felt disgusted.

'Yes, but what are you doing out at this time in the morning?' I frowned.

'The alarm went off in the estate office, so I had to come down to have a look,' he explained. I wasn't convinced that he was telling the truth, but I tried to act normal stepping through the door and headed to switch off the alarm. Alex had also stepped inside and was undressing me with his eyes; I had to get him out.

'Thanks, Alex I'm fine now, and I'm dead beat with dancing tonight.' I went on, trying to usher him out. Once he was out, I locked the door, but I had that feeling that he was still there at the door as I hadn't heard him walk off over the stone driveway to the estate office.

I switched the hall light off before going upstairs to bed. I didn't switch the bedroom light on as the moon shone through into the bedroom. Walking towards the window, I could see Alex still there facing the castle, what the fuck was he doing? And then I realized he was jerking himself off in the driveway. Fuck, I knew he was a perv, it was a little disturbing, but I had to watch him. You could just make out in the moonlight, the enjoyment on his face jerking himself off and the relief when he had shot his lot. Putting his manhood away and zipping up, he turned and headed across to his truck. Crap, that bloke has got it bad I must tell Mags when I see her again.

It was Sunday, and I was waking up to rain beating heavily on my bedroom window, the clock showed it was 10.15 am. I was still feeling that I had been in a dream while making love to Zorro last night. God, I wished he was here to make love to me all over again. But he had told me I had to wait until the timing was right, he must be on something important as this had been going on since the accident.

Moria wasn't due until Tuesday, so having the castle to myself I headed for the pool plunging in naked and spent an hour doing my lengths, even the water flowing between my legs was making me aroused.

It was after midday before I ventured out. The rain had stopped with the sun peeping through. With rucksack in hand, I thought I would take a new direction and head down the long winding driveway to the road. There must be an easier way to access the beach from the road instead of cutting across the fields. Turning right at the end of the driveway, I started off jogging down the road. There were a couple of cars I met on my way, I must have jogged five miles before I came to a tee junction with the signpost showing names of places I had never heard of, but nothing giving directions to the sea coast.

I stopped for a breather and a drink before turning right again, hoping eventually I would come across the beach. The road was no wider than the road I had just jogged down. About a mile down the road was a turning to the right onto a dirt track; it was now starting to get late in the afternoon so turning right again should, in theory, bring me back to the castle. What a mistake I had made, the track started to get muddy with deep ruts in the track. I was sliding all over the place with a couple of times slipping on my side, plastering myself down one side in the mud. There were crops in the fields as I soldiered on, in front of me was an extensive woodland I was hoping this was the woods I first struggled with having no tracks to follow, but there were tracks, so I pushed forward hoping that the tracks didn't deter out.

It was getting on for 5 pm, so I had to move fast as I didn't want to be out lost in the woods at night. Pressing ahead, I eventually came to the end of the woodland, but which way to take further? I looked up shading my eyes with my hand and tried to search for the castle hoping there was a slight glimpse through the trees. Standing there, I managed to pinpoint the location I was on the right tracks having to cut across some scrubland towards the end of the woodland. It brought me to the unused track that led to the beach; I was close but headed back home now I knew where I was going.

I had made it home covered in mud and was feeling a little chilly as the weather was turning to rain and the blowing. It was just before 7 pm when I noticed a light on in the estate office with Alex's pickup truck parked outside. The 4x4 was there as well, and I could see Alex pacing up and down the office in front of the window, with the other guy I should call scar-face looking as though they were arguing. I quickly unlocked the door before Alex could see me, switched the alarm off and locked the door behind me. I had cut it a bit fine as it was getting dark and with me only having a lightweight top and a towel in my rucksack I would have been in serious trouble if I had got lost in the woods.

Taking my trainers off and leaving them at the door, I climbed the stairs taking two steps at a time in a hurry to peel off my muddy clothes for a shower. Now feeling warmer and refreshed having slipped my lightweight robe on I felt hungry, so I headed to the kitchen a fry up was in order and a pot of tea. Taking my tray into the living room, I settled down to eat watching the TV at the same time. I wanted to phone Mags, but she was working nights and would be at work by now, so I thought I'd phone Janet to see how she was doing and how the cottage was with letting it out.

The phone rang and rang; I was just about to end the call when she answered.

'Hello, Holly. Sorry, I took so long answering the phone,' said Janet panting for breath.

'Oh am I disturbing you, Janet?'

'No, no, I have only just come in from seeing one of the tenants. They had a problem with the drainage. It keeps backing up, and the downstairs toilet water in the bowel kept rising, so I had to sort it out,' said Janet sounding despaired.

'Where was Mark? Couldn't he sort it out for you?' I asked her.

'No, he has buggered off to Spain with that mate he was working with for a couple of months,' said Janet sounding a bit pissed off.

'How long is he working there for?' I asked nonchalantly.

'Don't know, nobody seems to know or can get hold of him.' scoffed Janet. Just as well, I wasn't coming back to visit him. I was chatting to Janet about the bookings and how she was getting on with it. I mentioned to her about Alex but not going into many details. I didn't mention him jerking off the other morning in the driveway after I came home having a night out. She asked me when I was coming back for a visit, but I couldn't say at the moment due to Graham not been back from his business trip. After some general chat about the bakery, we ended the call.

Taking my tray back into the kitchen, I made another pot of tea while I washed my pots. It was 10 pm just in time to watch the local news and weather for tomorrow. A dry day and warm sunny spells, great I needed an early start tomorrow. Taking the last mouthful of tea, I took it back to the kitchen to rinse out before heading for my bed, falling into a deep sleep.

The following morning, I was woken by a ray of sunlight shining through the window. I didn't bother closing the curtains seeing that the room was that big and not having neighbours to overlook into your privacy. It was just after 7 am I laid there in my bed aching from top to toe; my breasts felt as though they had been pummeled again with my nipples feeling sore together with my lower parts feeling the same as my breasts as if they had been rubbed down with sandpaper and dried out.

Dragging myself out of bed and slipping on my lightweight robe, I headed off to the pool. The water soothed my body as I cut across the pool, doing the breaststrokes feeling the water skimming over my sore bits.

After a light breakfast with my rucksack packaged with a thick jumper just in case I got stuck and clean joggers and top with my second pair of trainers, I locked up and set off this time heading down farm track where Alex had picked me up the other day. As I passed the estate office, I could only see Sarah's car and no pickup. Alex must be around on the estate somewhere.

Jogging as far as the corner where I had come out of the other day, I stopped having 5 minutes and a drink before setting off down the rough unused farm track. Passing through scrubland, spooking the deer on the way I must be nearly there. A couple more stops and I had come to the end of the rough track. Ahead of me was the beach. I spotted an area to sit down to eat a granola bar and have a drink. I breathed in the sea air, smelling the salt, hoping it would clear my lungs out.

I had a quick paddle, but it was windy, and the sea looked fairly rough with a slight chill in the air. I got back onto the track and headed towards a large building ahead of me. I didn't know if this was part of the estate, but I would find out either way.

The building was massive at least two-hundred-metre-long and thirty meters wide, with a large roller shutter door and a small personnel door set in at the end approaching the building. As I walked around the building, I saw several vents and what looked like attractor fans fixed to the side of the building. Having got to the far end there was a door, I tried the handle to see if it was locked, it was, and I was curious what was inside as the fans were running.

Suddenly, I could hear a vehicle approaching; I didn't want to be seen just in case I shouldn't be here. Climbing over the wall to hide from the vehicle pulled in, I managed to find a peephole in the wall, and the vehicle was a red pickup truck.

Fuck! It was Alex's, I must have been ten metres away from him as he walked towards the side door, unlocking it and went inside. I could hear voices inside which didn't make sense as to why would there be people locked inside a building? Within five minutes, he came out holding a small package, locked the door and walked back to his pickup truck and set off down the track. I needed to speak to Mags to ask her what she would think of this situation.

It was after midday; I gathered my belongings and headed back down the rough track to meet the main one where I met Alex with his truck. I was in a hurry I needed to speak to Mags before she started her shift tonight and stupid me, who had left my phone back at the castle. I had been in such a hurry to set off this morning.

Holy crap! I could see Alex coming up from the castle in his truck. He stopped to ask me where I had been, and I tried to sound casual as I said, 'To the beach.'

'Hmm, did you see anyone up there?' he asked curiously.

'No, it was a bit breezy, but I had a paddle,' I said casually. I didn't want to ask about the building, or he would become suspicious, and god knew what can of worms would come out.

'You better get in; I'll take thee back to castle lass,' said Alex as if I had no choice in the matter. I jumped in the truck he turned the vehicle around setting off towards the castle. There was no conversation, but I noticed from my eye corner his trousers were tightening with arousal. Something wasn't right with his man, avoiding any sort of eye contact I looked out of the truck window wishing the journey would soon end. After 20 minutes we arrived, I jumped out of the truck and gathered up my rucksack with a quick thanks and headed for the castle door. I felt his eyes burning into my backside, yeah I bet he'd love to fuck me, but he's got no chance in a month of Sunday.

It was 4 pm by the time I ran upstairs to find my phone to ring Mags.

'Mags, thank God I've caught you before you've gone to work,' I said, sounding out of breath.

'Holly, what's up?' she asked, sounding concerned.

'There's something not right here,' I explained the night I got back from the club and the large building near the sea.

'What do you think, Mags?' I asked.

'You might have something there, Holly, but just be careful you don't know the situation. I would wait until Mr. Wallace got back,' suggested Mags.

'Yeah, I suppose you are right, Mags.' We chatted a while, and she said she enjoyed the night out we had but didn't say anything about me going missing for four hours that night. We ended our call as Mags had to get ready for work. I had a light tea and salad before going upstairs for a quick shower. I watched an hour of the TV before taking a plunge into the pool.

By 10 pm I had showered, washed my hair and dried before coming downstairs to make a pot of tea. Switching the TV on in the living room I sat with my feet up on the sofa when the local news came on. It was reported that drugs were on an epidemic raise with a big push from the force to nip the main sauce in the bud. This got me thinking, was Alex involved in drugs some way? Especially when he went into that building on the coast and I had heard voices, and he had come back with a package in his hand. Everything seemed bolted uptight, and why were the fans working? Feeling tired, I went to bed, sinking into the mattress into a deep sleep.

Waking up the next morning, I felt I had wet myself; god had I started my period early due to exercising too much? Getting out of bed there was no blood on the bottom sheet; my skin felt tight, smelling my arm it smelt like sex, no it can't be I would have known if he was here last night. I would have woken up, not only that but he had no access to the castle. Having a quick shower, I decided to make my way down to the building to see if I could find any evidence of drugs.

Instead of a morning swim, I packed my rucksack with a few bars and a couple of large bottles of water and not forgetting my phone this time; I headed off to the building. I got there by midday; there wasn't anyone around so I thought I would try the door at the far end where Alex had gone through. I tried the handle and couldn't believe my luck the door was unlocked.

I slipped in; the heat inside was like a sauna, 'God is Alex growing something he shouldn't be growing?' I whispered to myself; the smell was a giveaway. I crept further down the building where the fans were making a whooshing noise, and then I heard voices, but there weren't any vehicles outside to indicate people working in here. The building seemed to be divided up with modules having stairs and a gangway leading off to one area. Suddenly, I heard someone coming my way, my heart starting pumping hard, knowing that I shouldn't be in here. I tried the nearest door handle, it opened, and I slipped in closing it slowly behind me. The heat was stifling. I turned around, and there they were - the plants. He was growing weed; all these modules must have plants having someone on-site looking after them. I had to get out, slightly panicking, I took out my phone and phoned Mags, I was desperate for her to pick up, but it went to voice mail. Fuck!

I left a desperate message saying I was in the building, and my instincts were right that Alex was growing weed in the building and had people looking after it who were living inside. I just hoped she would soon pick up the message.

Slipping my phone into my joggers, I opened the door slightly to see if there were anyone there. It seemed quiet, apart from the fans making a whooshing noise. I slipped out hearing voices from the entrance, panicking and tiptoeing further into the building where it opened up into a storage area on one side filled with pallets of an unknown substance and a long bench with people. They were dividing white powder up into small packages.

It was dead serious I had to get out, but as I turned around to leave, there stood Alex with Scarface. I was shafted; my heart was racing, not knowing what they were going to do with me now that they had me.

'Well, well, well, look who we have here,' said Alex with sarcasm.

'Boss ain't going to like this, Alex,' added Scarface.

'Yeah, I know. He'll be here in a few minutes.' Alex scratched his chin and looked at me.

'Well, we'll see what he has got to say about her snooping,' said Scarface grabbing hold of my arm tightly and pulling me towards him. I had uncovered an enormous drug ring worth billions of pounds which meant I was dead meat.

With a tight hold, he pushed me down to the far end of the building, passing the door I had come in. Just a few yards back from the entrance, Scarface opened a door leading into a small room, with a table and a couple of chairs and a bed. There was also what looked to be a small bathroom containing a toilet and a shower. Alex took hold of my rucksack going through it after which he slung it across the floor.

Looking at me, he started smiling, and as he walked up to me, he started to pat me down to see if I was concealing anything on my person. Scarface told me to part my legs and lift my arms. Alex grinned with pleasure and started to pat me down again, but now he was rubbing his hand over me, squeezing my breasts. I punched him in the face - that he wasn't expecting. Scarface quickly intervened and grabbed my upper arms, pulling them back hard and hooking his leg around one of my legs so if I moved, I would lose my balance.

Alex restrained from hitting me back but carried on, rubbing his hand over my body. Finding my phone, he pulled it out, dropping it on the floor where he stamped hard with the heel of a foot smashing it into pieces. He then looked at me with a smirk, and to my utter horror, his trousers were tight.

He pulled my joggers down, rubbing his rough hands over my thighs and slid one of his hands inside of my undies. He pushed his long fingers inside me twisting his hand and pressing his thumb on my clitoris.

With his other hand, he undid my bra, releasing my breasts and taking hold of them, squeezing and sucking hard on my nipple.

'Alex pack it in, the boss will be here in a minute,' said Scarface as I could feel his length getting hard behind me. Alex took his hand out of my undies and started licking his fingers one by one, savoring the moisture from inside me. He was just about to rip my undies off when we were startled by voices, including a woman's voice. Alex quickly pulled my joggers up, and Scarface pushed me onto one of the wood chairs, I quickly adjusted my clothing before the others came in.

With my head hanging down, it hit me that I recognized two of the voices. Looking up, I couldn't believe who I was looking at. It was Mick and Mia, with an older man old enough to be their father. As soon as Mia spotted me, she pushed her way passed Alex and Scarface, grabbing my hair and pulling my head back.

'So, we meet again, bitch? But this time the boot is on the other foot,' she spat, pulling me tighter. I tried to hang on to her hand, stopping her from pulling harder. 'You fucking bitch, I should have killed you that morning I ran you over.' I couldn't believe what I was hearing, Mick would have known but swept it under the carpet.

'You fucking bastard, Mick! You knew all this time?' I snarled. Mia smirked and went on.

'Guess what bitch? Your Mick and I have a son.' I was in tears. After she had spat her venom on me, she walked off, giving me one last tug releasing my hair and turned to Mick saying, 'Kill her Mick.'

Mick came forward, and I looked at him. He had no expression on his face. He had gone downhill ever since I last saw him, looking thin and gaunt in the face.

He grabbed me by the neck, lifting my face to his eyes, and then he said. 'You bitch, who's got the upper hand now? You have no idea what you put me through with the police and the operation.' He released his grip and was just about to walk away when he swung around and punched me in the face saying, 'I'm returning the favor.'

The force of his punch rocked me back on the chair, then he punched me again, knocking me back, causing me to fall back in the chair. Scarface pulled me and the chair back up as Mick slapped me across my face with the back of his hand, causing my lip to split with the ring he had on his finger. Turning away towards the older man, he shouted over to Alex and Scarface. 'Get rid of her.' I was bleeding heavily from my lip; my eyes were starting to swell up with my tears stinging my face.

I was doomed.

Scarface told Alex to get rid of me as he left. After a few minutes when we were alone, Alex pulled out a gun, waving it in front of me. 'Now, you cock teasing bitch, we are going to have some fun, but this time you are going to be wide awake for this.' He smiled devilishly. 'You wear those tee shirts with your nipples poking through teasing a man's cock.' He told me he had been spiking my water in the kettle and had an extra key cut to gain access into the castle.

Then in great detail, he explained what he had done to me under the influence of the drug, spending most of the nights abusing my body. I felt sick now realizing why some mornings my body felt sore, wet and aching.

He waved the gun at me to move to the bed. 'I'm going to tie you to the bed and fuck you so hard in that nice tasty pussy of yours and bite them cock teasing nipples off and then finish off fucking that nice tasty arse of yours so hard you will be screaming just like Mick had done to you.' I felt I had been punched in the gut, Mick had told them everything that had happened between us, and I gave up.

Alex pushed onto the bed telling me to put each wrist through a looped rope as I was told to, but then I thought, Fuck this! I'm going to die anyway so I might as well die fighting.

My adrenaline started to kick in, Alex was confident this was going to be easy as he relaxed, I quickly stood up pushing his arm up and kneeing him hard between the legs, the gun went off. Alex dropped the gun doubled up in pain, seeing that he was already hard down there. But as I pushed passed him, he managed to grab hold of my ankle, dragging me down hanging onto my joggers, I tried to wriggle out of them, but my trainers were stopping me. He managed to hang on to me; his grip was tight, dragging me towards his gun that he had dropped. I was kicking him with my other foot, hoping he would lose his grip, but it was hopeless.

I was doomed; he had retrieved his gun; I was so close to the door. He punched me in the face; the pain was unbearable. I felt faint when he dragged me back onto the bed.

All of a sudden, the door flew open. Alex turned around to fire the gun. I kicked him from behind; the gunshot missed the other person who I couldn't see properly. With being punched my eyes swelled, there was a struggle, and I could hear fists being punched with force, this went on for a couple of minutes before the gun fired. I felt a sharp pain in my lower side of the stomach; I reflexively put my hand to where the pain was and saw blood. I had been shot. I started to pass out just before the next shot boomed out then everything when quiet, but I could hear shooting in the distance.

I woke up feeling sore after the operation to remove the bullet, still having bruising and a throbbing headache. I felt a soft hand holding mine with a male voice speaking to me in whispers. I could hardly open my eyes with the punches I had received to my face, but I could tell with his voice and touch it was Zorro.

He had come to me, 'Holly, my sweetheart, I thought I was going to lose you again when you got shot.' His voice felt broken. 'We are now going to be together, and I am going to be by your side forever.' He kissed my hand serval times rubbing his cheek across. He sounded so concerned and loving—this man I had brief encounters with, who sent me expensive gifts and red roses. I loved him despite the fact I knew nothing about him. I drifted off back to sleep as I was drugged up for the pain. I could feel his presence near me every time I woke up but could not see very well, only his touch and the outline of his body and his long dark curly hair.

It was nearly two weeks before I could focus on people popping in to see me, but Zorro hadn't been in for a couple of days but had rung twice a day to confirm that I was doing ok, the conversation was minimal with the drugs I were on.

I had lost track of time and days, not being able to see very well and they had patched up where the bullet had gone in. I was lucky the bullet had missed my vital organs and that I was on the mend. My face was slowly going down but still showed heavy bruising. I had been taken down for a shower by the nurse. The staff in the hospital were very friendly, and visitors seemed to come and go as they pleased, which I thought was odd as usually, hospitals had visiting times.

I asked the older nurse about it while I showered, she told me I was in a private hospital.

'Oh, I wonder who sent me here,' I asked the nurse why I wasn't being treated in the NHS hospital but a private hospital?

'You were diverted here from the general hospital by your young man, Gino Rossi.' She informed me. Now, I finally knew that his name was Gino, Italian with those beautiful eyes and the long curly dark hair.

I had a room to myself which explained to me being in a private hospital. After my shower and drying my hair, I was wheeled back to my bed. I had just managed to lift myself onto the bed when the door opened. There stood a tall man with dark curly shoulder-length hair with the most beautiful eyes I had ever seen; he moved towards me holding out his arms to gather me up in a hug kissing me gently trying not to hurt me.

'Gino,' I said, 'why am I in a private hospital?'

'Ah, you found out?' said Gino. 'I only want what is best for you, and I'm going to look after you from now on,' he said gently kissing me on my swollen lips and stroking my cheek with his soft touch.

God, I loved this man so much I would do anything for him.

'Gino,' I said 'will you tell me from the beginning why me? I want to know everything.'

The nurse came in with a tray of tea and biscuits and left it on the side table over my bed, and then when she had gone, Gino started to tell me from the beginning.

'I was born in Italy; my parents own a vineyard and are wine merchants; they also own a truffle farm in the north. One of my uncles on my father's side deals in gold and silver buying and selling, he also owns a smaller vineyard in the far south of Italy. My other uncle on my mum's side is a wine merchant and dabbles in farming and holiday lettings. You already know him as Graham Wallace.' I was about to say something to him, but he stopped me by gently pressing his finger onto my lips. He carried on.

'My mum was from Scotland, and my father is pure Italian and met while my mum was on holiday, you could say a holiday romance, they got married as my mum was pregnant with me. My father worked hard to get where he is today. My mum had another son called Andrea. We were only a year apart, so when we reached the age to start working, my father told us to see the world and make your own mistakes before coming back into the family business. I joined the police force while my brother wasn't sure where he wanted to go and finished up getting caught up with the wrong sort of people. He was dead by the age of twenty; he had been murdered in a drug-related case. My mum took it badly with depression setting in. Eventually, she gave up and died of a broken heart.' My eyes were moist with tears, and one fat tear escaped rolling down my cheek. Gino wiped it away gently with his thumb.

'After that, I vowed that I would get to the people responsible. It took me a few years to get to where I needed to be; you could say it's similar to MI5 but specialized in a large drug cartel. There was an operation going on in Surrey where Mick was based at the station. I was called in to keep undercover and investigate, but things started to get messy, so Mick transferred to Nottingham to the CID, and that is when you met him. We had our suspicions on him, and I followed him.'

'The first day I saw you, it was love at first sight; I was besotted. Mick had got there before me; I couldn't say anything else I would have blown my cover. But I wasn't expecting you both to marry. I was devastated when I heard.' Tears started running from my eyes now knowing that Mick had been using me as a front; Gino passed me his handkerchief to wipe the tears from my eyes. 'Holly, I can stop if you want me to,' he said in a gentle and concerned voice.

'No, please carry on. I need to know,' I said sniffing with tears still running down my face.

'When you both moved back down Surrey with his promotion, he was back on his turf picking up the pieces and tried to get his drug operation back on track. Then that December, when you were run down, I was beside myself hoping that you would pull through. I visited you every day while you were in a reduce comma praying you would pull through. I asked the doctors and nurses how you were doing, but I had to be careful not to blow my cover, so I told them I was a close cousin called Liam.'

'Oh, Gino, please come here.' I extended my arms and said. He came and sat on the bed. I shuffled to the end giving him room to be by my side. I wrapped my arms around him, snuggling up to him. It felt so peaceful resting my head on his chest, his strong arm wrapped around me, holding me tight but gently. God how I loved this man, I had never met anyone like him. I was making his shirt wet with tears as he carried on.

'After I knew you were out of danger, I couldn't be seen with you, by people you knew as my cover would be revealed. Then I found out you were recuperating at your parents' house; I was relieved knowing you would be safe with what Mick was up to. I knew about Mia seeing Mick, she is the daughter of the boss head of this drugs bust you uncovered. We knew they had operations in four areas, one of which was near the castle, but we had been given false information,' he continued.

'I had been desperate to see you to kiss you and to touch you, so that was when I caught you coming out of the toilets that Halloween night and again on New Year's Eve. I couldn't control myself. Yes, I sent you the gifts and red roses with a small note in Italian. I eventually found out that Mick had raped you the night you went home; I could have killed him doing that to you. You kept this a secret to use as leverage for a divorce which he resented and had to give up the house his mother had lived in before she died. Mick was given a promotion because of the knowledge he had with the connection as he was seeing Mia. She had a son by him after the divorce had come through, and yes, I know you were told you couldn't have children when you were in the hospital.' Gino hugged my tightly kissing me on the head.

'We knew that it was Mia who tried to kill you that morning when you caught her with Mick, but we couldn't do anything because of the scale of the operation.' Gino squeezed me.

'Then you moved to Derbyshire in that quaint little cottage you renovated with the builder Mark, who was known for his women, but you handled him fine.' His voice sounded so soothing; my eyelids felt heavier with peace.

'Gino, I nearly gave in to him and was going to go back when Graham got back from his trip, please forgive me, Gino. I need you; I want you to be mine.' I was crying. I had to tell him as I didn't want any secrets.

'Holly, it doesn't matter. You would have found out any way that he is in Spain working but still a womanizer.'

'Oh, Gino, I am so sorry and stupid,' I said, sobbing my heart out to him. Gino held me closer, kissing the top of my head yet again.

'Holly, do you still want me to carry on?' asked Gino a little concerned with all the information I had to process. Gino knew all my movements.

'Yes, Gino I need to know please carry on.'

'My uncle Graham needed someone living in the castle while he was on business. It was to make his staff aware of a presence as Graham wasn't sure about Alex, the new farm manager. Angus had retired, and Alex had come with good references but had only been there six months before you came. Graham was having his doubts about him as he was getting visits from unsavory looking character and was starting to disappear in the day and coming back to the estate office at odd hours during the night. Graham got in touch with the local police asking if they knew anyone. So your friend Mags had put your name forward seeing that you had finished renovating the cottage and was looking for a job. She gave you a glowing reference by the way, and that's how you got the job. I didn't know until it was too late Graham told me after you had met him and a date had been set for you to start. I couldn't do anything to stop you from coming we knew Alex was up to something, but we didn't know what. It was good you confide in Mags about Alex, and that call you made being in the building she replayed the message.'

'We then knew we were watching the wrong building as soon as Mags said it was near the sea. That's when I heard Alex telling you what he had been doing to you while you slept under the influence of drugs; I had to wait to time it right. I could have gone in and blown his brains out knowing what he has done to you, but I didn't know where you were in the room until you rushed him making the gun go off, then I rushed in trying to get the gun off him, and the gun went off again hitting you. I had to kill him and managed with a scuffle and shot him where it would hurt the most. All this pain he has caused you my sweet; it was the least I could do for you.' He ran his fingers on my arm.

'Gino, I love you so much it hurts.' I started to cry again.

'Please, sweetheart, everything is going to be ok; we can spend loads of time together now it's over. We have got the main man,' said Gino.

'Did you get Mick and Mia?' I asked, relieved.

'No, unfortunately not, but at least he led us to the main boss. Mia's father, the boss of drugs cartel and his business which will take billions of pounds worth of drug out of the system.

I was in the hospital for a month, feeling better but not a hundred per cent. Gino came to pick me up from the hospital; my face was nearly back to normal with yellow bruises still showing. My side had healed up nicely with a small scar but was slightly stiff apart from that I was ok.

Gino had brought the Range Rover to pick me up as it would be easier for me to climb in without bending to sit in the front. The journey took half an hour back to the castle. Graham was there waiting for me to arrive greeting me with hugs and kisses. Graham made lunch where we sat out to eat with a table set for two on the large patio at the back of the castle. It was just Gino and I sharing this moment.

Graham made himself scarce, leaving the two of us together, our love for each other showed. We took an evening walk to areas I had never seen around the castle; the flowers were in full blossom, and the fragrance smelled sweet. It was after 8 pm before we came in, I reached up to him looking into his beautiful eyes and said

'Can we have an early night? I want you to make love to me.' With that, he swept me up, climbing the stairs to one of the bedrooms on the other side of the staircase.

'I have something to ask you since the day I first saw you.' He sat me on the bed and pulled out of his back pocket a case and opened it to reveal a gold ring with clusters of rubies and diamonds. My heart began beating with excitement as he bent down on one knee and said.

'Holly Benson, I have been waiting for over three years to ask you this but will you be my wife?' I jumped off the bed despite the fact my side was aching slightly, pushing him to the floor snogging his face off and when I had finished, I said yes. We made love all night, his touch, his kiss. I was savoring every moment we were having together; it was out of this world. Gino Rossi was my Italian Stallion to die for with his beautiful eyes.

ABOUT THE AUTHOR:

Sue Vout, currently living a peaceful secluded life in a village near Gainsborough, Lincolnshire, England started writing as a student but is now a full-time writer. Her love for nature and animals turned her sensitive and nudged her to share her thoughts through her stories. Finding joy in short walks, music, art and nature, Sue has always loved the idea of spreading joy and beauty of the world through her writing. Her philosophy of life is reaching the stars as you still can, as waiting for the right moment is stupid. Every moment is the right moment if you see it closely. In her world, women are strong, brave and are capable of living life as they want, true love still exists, and chivalry is not dead.

Made in the USA
Las Vegas, NV
14 March 2022